ON THE KNIFE EDGE

by

S. Mason Pratt

Deer Run Press
Cushing, Maine

Library of Congress Card Number: 2024930694

ISBN: 978-1-937869-23-6

First Printing, 2024

Published by
Deer Run Press
8 Cushing Road
Cushing, ME 04563

DISCLAIMER

On The Knife Edge portrays characters and events at the fictitious Eastern Maine Maritime Academy in Camden, Maine. All such names and characters are a product of the author's imagination, as are any descriptions of Eastern Maine Maritime Academy and any reference to its graduates.

Some of the details of this fictional story were drawn from the author's personal research into the tragic, real-world account of the container ship, *El Faro*. On October 1, 2015, the *El Faro* sank in a category four hurricane off the Bahamas. All thirty-three members of its crew perished, including five graduates of Maine Maritime Academy. Some of these details were based upon the author's reading of a published transcript of the recordings made on board the *El Faro* in its last hours, as revealed in the ship's "black box," which was found on the ocean floor; however, this work should not be considered an accurate historical representation of that tragic event.

DEDICATION

For the thirty-three brave souls who were lost at sea on the
El Faro.

Acknowledgments

Thanks to my friends in the Saint Simons Island, Georgia, Writers' Group, Harvey Gamble, John Simmons, David Millman, Fred Davis, Carol Dumas, Bonnie Tobias, and others. You made this story better.

To my son, Stephan Pratt, who created the cover art.

To my wife, Mary Lyons-Pratt, for your editing skills and inspiration.

My fictitious character, attorney John Edmonds, is largely based upon my mentor, the late Ralph I. Lancaster, forner President of the Maine Bar Association and the American Academy of Trial Lawyers.

PROLOGUE

CIA headquarters, Langley, Virginia.

Harry Field's desk faced the vast parking lot, but his mind was still focused on his recent meeting with CIA's Director of Operations.

"Get me your best agent," the director had said.

"What's the assignment?" A reasonable question, Harry thought.

"Sorry. Can't tell you now. This is need to know only. If the president signs off on it, of course, you'll need to know."

"Well, to answer your question, I need to know what talents you're looking for. Can you tell me that?"

"Sure. A sharpshooter or sniper. And fearless."

"Okay. I'll have to think about it."

"And Harry, he's got to be loyal. He'll be working with a foreign government with its own agenda, and he'll have to disappear and be out of touch for months. We have to know he won't go rogue on us."

Harry dialed the director's number. "I think I've got your man," he said.

***

A month later, Agent Jack Pierce spotted the General sitting on a bench in the Luxembourg Gardens, bathed in late afternoon shadows. He wore civilian clothes under a tan raincoat, a black beret over dark hair. Jack approached, wary. The General glanced up for a split second, then looked away as if disinterested—long enough for Jack to notice the slight twitch in his cheek. "Look for that," Harry had said. He sat on the bench, and unrolled a newspaper for cover. Nearby, a troupe of actors entertained a smattering of gleeful children, their raucous shrieks punctuating the stillness.

"President Hollande is doing well, no?" The General spoke the code words softly, without looking up.

"Yes, according to the polls," replied Jack, as planned.

"You came."

"Yes."

"Good. My government is thankful for your assistance."

General Dimitri Medved's unshaven, pock-marked face and massive body offset a studied and serious mien. Reputed to be a battle-hardened veteran, the General projected confidence and power.

"Your instructions are in the briefcase."

He glanced at the black briefcase at the General's feet. A hiss escaped between his teeth. "Take it."

"What is my mission? I need to hear it from you."

"The Mayor of Sebastopol is Russia's man. You are CIA. D'accord?"

"Agreed. It's good to be working with you." He stood to leave, but the General motioned for him to sit. Jack did.

"When you have completed your mission," the General said, "I have a personal mission for you—that is, if you are willing. It is not for my government. Can I trust your...how do you say this? Your discretion...in this matter?"

"Of course," Jack said. Where was this going?

"I will pay you well. Are you interested?"

Jack had never been tempted to stray from duty to God and country, not for sex or money, but he was intrigued. The General was a trusted ally in a joint operation. "I will listen. What is this personal mission?"

"You have heard of the Russian oligarchs, yes? Well, we have them, too. You see, I have support from both inside and outside the government."

Jack knew their reputation as astute businessmen with a propensity for brutality. Perhaps these oligarchs were now in control of General Medved. "Tell me about it."

The General stole glances around their periphery. "You

must promise never to tell the CIA. You would be...how do you say this? Going rogue? Yes?"

Yes. Maybe Harry didn't need to know.

"And you understand any misstep would carry with it unfortunate consequences?"

"Certainly."

"After you complete our joint mission with CIA, you travel to Jacksonville, get on a container ship called *El Barco de Oro*, and, once at sea, you blow it up."

Jack finally broke the silence. "Why?"

"We want to go into the shipping business. Like the Greeks, yes? And the price for this shipping business is too high, so, if their ship blows up, poof, the price drops. You see?"

It would be a criminal act, perhaps even treason. "What about the crew of this ship?"

"They are, I think you say, 'collateral damage.'"

"How much would you pay?"

"Two million dollars U.S. in a Cayman Islands bank account. Half now, the other half when you complete the mission."

A cool two million. "The Americans will never know?"

"D'accord."

"How does this work?" he asked.

"After our joint mission, you go to Jacksonville, and you contact me from there."

The General left his briefcase. Jack watched the garden's afternoon light pale and thought about his next mission. "A joint operation," Harry had said, "but it's really the Ukrainians' operation, and we're clean." A bold and daring operation to assassinate the Mayor of Sebastopol in the Crimea. Jack's new alias, Sergey Robichek, a Ukrainian name, but he didn't speak their language. He recalled Harry's last words: "After your mission, stay underground until things cool down. Stay in touch. Call in weekly. The Russians will be furious, and they'll be after you. But you're used to that.”

***

Paris. The fourth floor of an empty warehouse opens onto a small park where a crew erects a stage. A Winchester Magnum sniper rifle, equipped with sound suppressor, rests on a table mounted on a bipod, its muzzle set back inches from a closed window. The telescopic sight zooms in on the stage and a beribboned seat reserved for the guest of honor. At about two hundred yards, an easy shot.

At his feet, a grainy photo of Alexei Korovchenko, short and squat, close-cropped hair, unshaven face, and a politician’s ready smile. Next to the photo, a file summarizes the news account of the Russian takeover in Crimea. Jack smiles—Harry had called it a brilliant move by Russian President Vladimir Putin: “He used Russian troops in civilian garb to invade and then incite the ethnic Russian majority to expel the Ukrainian mayor and install his stooge.”

He touches a flame to a cigarette to calm his nerves. The crowd gathers. On stage, the seats begin to fill. A motorcade arrives. A band plays a Russian song and then *The Marseillaise*. His trigger finger itches. Through the pane of glass, Jack hears the mounting babble. Time to raise the window. In nearby buildings, other windows are opening, making it harder to spot him. He lies prone on the table, watches and waits. Soon, he spots the unmistakable salt-and-pepper hair atop the stocky frame, as the dignitary is ushered up the stairs to the stage and to his seat alongside the resplendent President Hollande. He breathes deeply through the endless introductions. President Hollande finishes his remarks and sits. The mayor approaches the mike. Jack tosses his lit cigarette to the floor.

He inches the rifle forward until its muzzle clears the open window, cradles the rifle in his left palm directly over his left elbow, rests his right finger a hair from the trigger, and lowers his right eye to the lens until a head appears in the crosshairs.

Time to start the ritual—snap the bolt open, insert the high-powered cartridge into the magazine and lock the bolt. Then, with a slow, steady rhythm, breathe in . . . and allow the slow release of air, as his right finger puts a hair of pressure on the trigger and slowly squeeze . . . . . A sudden jolt against his right cheek, and the acrid smell of cigarette smoke and gunpower fills his nostrils.

PART 1

Melanie

Chapter 1

Standing tall on the bridge, Second Mate Melanie Ricker watched the deck crew haul in the ropes. *El Barco de Oro* slipped away from Naval Station Mayport, its docks lined with menacing gray destroyers and cruisers, and a Coast Guard rescue cutter, into the calm, open Atlantic. The lights on shore receded. Exhilarated to be at sea, the air thick with brine, she knew the calm was deceptive.

Her job was to plot their course to San Juan, Puerto Rico against the track of the storm. Hurricane Hilda, like an animal on the prowl, loomed out there with a mind of its own. Still a category two hurricane with winds at 100 miles per hour, Hilda would soon become a category three with winds more than 120 miles per hour, on its way to a category four at 150 miles per hour—the first category four hurricane to hit the Bahamas since 1866. On a map, the expected path of its eye directly intersected the ship's route. If, that is, you were looking at the most up-to-date reports from the National Hurricane Center. And even they didn't really know where Hilda was going.

Forcing herself to focus, Melanie checked the latest reports. "Conditions near Bermuda are worsening by the hour."

On Wednesday, September 30, the Lockheed WP-3D Orion had flown out of MacDill Air Force Base in Tampa. Powered by four turbo-prop engines, it flew at 350 miles per hour on a course straight for the eyewall of Hurricane Hilda, now northeast of the Bahamas. Major Stan Nightingale of the 53rd Weather Recon

Squadron spoke into the radio to his copilot, Lieutenant Jock Babcock. Nightingale's baritone voice pierced the comforting hum of the plane's engines.

"That's quite a sight, Jock!"

"It's a beast, all right, and a beautiful one at that," replied Jock.

"Well, here goes nothing!" yelled Nightingale, gripping the controls tighter.

"Yeah," chimed in navigator Bill Wilson. "Let's do it!"

"Right. Tell our guest to hang on."

The local news reporter from the Miami Herald was about to have the ride of a lifetime. Ned Battle rode along for the experience, unaware he'd have the exclusive story on this impending disaster.

"Gave him an upchuck bag," said Wilson, just as the plane's sides shimmied, buffeted by turbulence and winds more than 100 miles per hour. Sudden low pressure overhead squashed them into their netted seats; then the bottom dropped out as the plane sank, plummeting downward and pushing the contents of Ned's stomach into his mouth and then his bag. Finally, the plane leveled out.

Wilson called out, "Bit more than we expected!"

At this distance, the eyewall seemed a thing of beauty, its clouds piled up and out of sight, while inside churned a cauldron of squalls and circular winds so dark that Stan Nightingale felt his first hint of fear. He'd once heard of a Hercules C-130 Hurricane Hunter out of Guam that got trapped inside one of these monstrous storms. It had lost an engine, lost altitude, and couldn't climb up and over it or fly out of it. Nightingale shuddered as he remembered how they ran out of fuel inside the eye.

The captain's earphones buffered the deafening roar of the plane's engines—their steady drone reassured him. Ahead loomed a towering wall of black clouds. They were about to fly right into the wall, where they would be swallowed whole. As they passed through the eyewall, the plane would radio readings of the storm's wind speed, temperature, humidity, and air pressure directly to the

National Hurricane Center. The navigator would drop tubes into the ocean waves to get more information.

"Ready to drop the tubes, Bill?"

"You bet," Wilson replied.

"Here we go, boys!" shouted Nightingale. "Time for inspiration, Jock."

As the plane's sides rattled and shook, they were enveloped in darkness. Jock's baritone voice boomed his traditional message of inspiration over the radio. "We few, we happy few, we band of brothers; for he today that sheds his blood with me shall be my brother..." Then a sudden drop as the plane hit an air pocket, and only their belts kept them in their seats. Jock hardly missed a beat, raising his voice. "And gentlemen in England now-a-bed shall think themselves accursed they were not here and hold their manhoods cheap whiles any speaks that fought with us upon Saint Crispin's day."

All their voices rang out as one: "Hooah!"

Wilson checked on Ned Battle. He was grimacing but laughing and shaking his head, as if to say, *You guys are nuts*.

Chapter 2

Melanie stood with the helmsman on the navigation bridge in the glow of instruments. She'd arrived early for her midnight shift on watch, wearing sneakers, jeans, and an L. L. Bean chamois shirt.

After several voyages as second mate on *El Barco de Oro*, she'd almost gotten used to this rust bucket of a container ship. Proud to be in command, she was the only female officer. Hell, the only female on board! But she'd had better ships. *Why? Why do I still do this?* she grumbled to herself. Since graduating from Eastern Maine Maritime Academy in Camden, she'd been tested by eight years at sea. Why were promotions so slow in coming? And this old roll-on, roll-off container ship? So top heavy they were calling it "roll on, roll over." They'd scheduled her for boiler repairs. Finally. *Would it be too late?*

Maybe it was time to find a job onshore. A smile cracked her face as she recalled her dad's reaction. "No way," he said. "Stick it out. You'll get a good ship." Dad, the retired navy officer. So predictable.

Cut it out, she thought. *Just do your job.* But she wouldn't disappoint her dad. He'd just bought the small house on the East End near the Promenade, where she could stay when not at sea. After this round-trip to San Juan? *Yeah. I'll fly home to furnish and decorate it. Can't wait.* Well, maybe not—she smiled, recalling how she'd first heard the news just before they departed JAX—Jack Pierce, on board her ship! Incredible. What was he doing here? Her friend Peter, the third mate, had told her about the new cook—called him a "handsome dude"—but she thought nothing of it, because Peter had called him Sergey—a strange name, Sergey Robichek. And then she spotted him on the deck from the bridge. My God, it was Jack! They'd met before she started high school, and he'd saved her from the mean girls—got her to run with him, and she'd become popular—her first love. But she'd never told him.

When her shift ended, she headed for her cabin with thoughts of Jack Pierce. She'd grown fond of him, because of his writing. She felt she knew his heart—so emotionally available, a brilliant man. She'd never had a real lover. Rarely allowed herself pleasure of any kind, not at the academy, not in her life at sea. She'd always been cautious in matters of the heart. Now that she was a free woman, maybe it was time to change all that.

Early the next morning, arriving at the galley, ravenous, she noticed the looks. As the only female on an all-male ship, she was used to the special attention from men living without the fair sex. Some guys seemed starved for anything female. Some were probably waiting for release at the next port of call. She'd learned how to turn it to her advantage, even welcomed it. Just act like you don't notice it. She joined Peter at the end of the breakfast line.

"Well, look at that," Peter said. Melanie could see why the line was held up—ahead, the new head cook was taking special orders for omelets. They'd already got their coffees—the sign at the urn said "Arabica"—and were pleasantly surprised at the taste. Peter ordered an omelet, and Melanie was chatting with him when she noticed the new cook eying her. Peter had gone ahead when she reached the special-order station. The new cook seemed to make it a point to catch her attention. She knew it would be awkward—how to address him? They were calling him Sergey. What to say?

And then he spoke to her. "Hope you had an uneventful night, ma'am. Can I whip up a special omelet made to order?" He said it in a conversational tone, revealing nothing.

"Why, thank you," she said. "They call you Sergey now?" It was on his name tag.

"Why yes, ma'am. And yes, I slept well. What do I call you?"

She smiled and tried not to betray any emotion. "Just call me Melanie."

"I want to see you," he said. He said it in a hushed voice, and she wasn't sure she'd heard him correctly. She was watching him break eggs into the skillet with one hand, her eyes locked on his, waiting for his response. How can he cook while staring at me? It seemed like he was not going to be the first to break the spell until he had to.

She was almost out of earshot when she heard him whisper: "Meet at your cabin?" It was risky for him to say it. She was an officer, and he was not. There was no policy against it, but there would be talk. "Yes, later," she whispered, her right hand covering her mouth. She glanced back, but he was throwing together another omelet. She jotted down a note, folded it, and returned to hand it to him. It read, "I'm off at 0400."

Melanie returned to her cabin for a short nap before her twelve-noon watch. And after that, Jack would come. She marveled at her good fortune at finding him again. She'd let him go once. She owed him so much for what he'd done for her. And over the years, all those emails had tied them together.

Her watch was about to end. Jack would come to her cabin, and they would be together again. Her heart beat wildly with anticipation. She feared he wouldn't come.

Perhaps it was crazy to expect anything from him now. After he'd written that he loved her, hadn't she been unwilling to commit? Even then, she'd never expressed her love for him. Why not? He'd been her counselor and cheerleader. He'd helped her survive, and she let him disappear from her life. Her life had become empty with no one to share it. She could see now how much she'd relied on his writings. Who else did she have? Her mother and father and a few friends, like Peter, but no one to share her deepest hopes and fears. The irony struck her—her loveless private life clashed with her outwardly adventurous life as a pioneer, a woman at sea. She'd let caution rule her private life. She struggled to think of any men in her life who'd kindled that spark of passion.

When she was sixteen, she'd gone out with an older boy, Eddie Eastman. He'd pulled his roadster into a park, and they got into the backseat. She liked making out—he was sweet and smelled nice. But when he groped her breasts, she pushed him away. Funny how he'd seemed relieved, so maybe he was a virgin, too. Then there was her fiancé, Cliff—he'd been a man to satisfy himself, not her, so she ended the brief engagement.

She wondered what sort of life Jack had led. He must have had lots of lovers, even though he'd denied it. She knew so little about him and what he'd done with his life.

At the end of her watch, she returned to her cabin and paced back and forth, waiting.

As soon as she heard the knock, she let him in. She sat on her bunk and, at first, he stood, as there was no place for him to sit. He looked sweaty, his face red—must be the heat of the kitchen and his rush to get here. Should she ask him to sit on the bunk? Would it be too forward? She felt the awkward silence surround them.

"Isn't this amazing," she said, "to see you here. I'm sure you're as surprised as me."

"Yes," he said. He was looking around, surveying her cabin, jittery, intense. He couldn't keep still. She had nothing there to offer him, just herself.

"It was so long ago," she said. "I remember when you left to go into the Marines. I was at the bus station and saw you leave. You looked at me from the back window. It was a July 4 weekend. I guess it must have been 2002, right? It's been thirteen years. Wow." She crossed her legs and tried to sit back, but there was no support except the wall.

Looking down at her, he seemed to relax. "You look the same. You haven't changed at all. Just as I remember you in your freshman year. Remember what I told you then?"

"Yes." How could she forget? It was after she'd slimmed down and become popular, after she'd ditched him, when he waylaid her in the hallway at school with other kids walking past and glancing at her like she was crazy to be with this weird guy. She stood with her back against the lockers—he had pinned her against the lockers, staring into her eyes, leaning into her. "Melanie," he whispered. "You are my first and only love." She knew he was asking her to be with him, and it scared her. She had never been with a boy and didn't know how to respond to him. "I can't," she said, ducking under his arms and walking away. That was how she'd ended it, and she regretted it.

"I still feel that way," he said.

She knew this. He'd told her time and time again in so many ways, and she'd never once expressed her love for him. Now, she thought, it's my chance to show him.

"So, what have you been doing all these years? And why didn't you send me an email to tell me you were on board?" She thought, I'm such an idiot. Just kiss him.

"I wanted to surprise you. I'll tell you some of it, what I've been doing all these years." She peered at his dark face, framed by the light behind him, and there was mystery in his mellow voice. "You knew what I was going through at home, right?"

She nodded, speechless, her mouth dry.

"I flunked out of school and hung out on the streets. After my eighteenth birthday, my dad told me I had to join up with the Marines. I jumped at the chance to get away from him."

"I thought it would be good for you. Was it?" She wanted him to keep talking, to calm her insides.

"Sure. I suppose. If you can call killing good. I mean, I was a sniper. Got sent to Iraq and Afghanistan. It was intense. Stuff I try to forget. But they sent me to school, and I made something of myself. And I learned everything from books. On my own. I began to write. Poems. And stories to you."

Wow, he's being honest. "Jack, I loved everything you wrote to me. So, what are you doing here? A cook?"

"Yeah, sure. It's a great job. I love it, and I'm going to open my own restaurant."

She smiled, pleased that he'd made something of himself, that he'd found a way out. She remembered how she'd once seen his father—the man Jack called the major—and she understood why Jack had feared and hated him. With a father like that, and abandoned by his mother, it was a wonder Jack had done so well. But something still bothered her. "Why did you change your name?"

"I had to," he said. "They made me do it."

"Who?"

"After the Marines, I worked for a federal agency. It's all secret stuff I can't talk about."

"Oh," she said. She wanted him to stop talking. "Come, sit here beside me." She patted the bed next to her, leaving him a little room. When he sat next to her, almost touching, she could feel his heat, his taut physique, and smell the sweat on his body. The physical attraction was overpowering.

"Mel," he said, "I still love you. I always have. You need to know that."

She felt she had to protest, to test him. "How can you say that?" She put her hands on her lap and looked at her nails, couldn't look at him. "You don't even know me. Not now. Not after eleven years."

"I know you."

That was all he had to say. Her heart went out to him—she owed him so much. She reached over and kissed him lightly on the lips, and she could feel his desire. She grabbed his shirt, pulled him down onto the bed, and wrapped her legs around him.

Before he left, they talked about plans—she was headed back to

Norway, Maine—her parents had retired to the llama farm her grandparents had owned. He was vague but promised to see her. Later, she dreamed of him in her bed.

When she awoke, everything was moving. What was happening? While dressing, she almost fell onto her bunk. She struggled to reach the bridge.

Chapter 3

Up on the bridge, she leaned forward to peer through windows pummeled with rain, and the bridge floor seemed to disappear under her. An anchor tattoo on her left bicep attested to her steely character and dedication to the maritime life. But this was something else.

The bridge, in constant motion, bucked and rocked. The bow lunged up, forcing her knees to buckle; then the sudden weightlessness lifted her as the ship pitched down into a bottomless trough.

"Whoa, that's the biggest one yet!" she yelled.

Marvin clung to the ship's wheel to keep her steady. The ship shuddered from another blow.

"She's pitching and rolling. Can you handle this?"

The helmsman's voice stuck in his throat, his eyes wide with fear, as the ship rolled steep to starboard, almost fifteen degrees. *Come on. Come on.* Melanie willed the container ship to pull back up, only to feel it roll past level to port. She held her breath as the ship rolled again to starboard. *Oh, my God. Here we go again.*

Her heart raced. "What's our point of no return?" No response from Marvin, who was straining to hold the wheel. As the ship righted itself, Melanie released her breath. *That was too close.*

Every few seconds, whenever the towering waves threw them off course, an alarm sounded.

"The captain's down below in his stateroom," Melanie said to no one. "How can he sleep through this?" Her face was taut with anger, her mouth straight as a pencil line.

"What did you say?" the helmsman yelled above the din.

"I said," she hollered, "how can the captain sleep through this?"

The helmsman struggled in silence, frozen by fear. Melanie, her confidence slipping, felt the first finger of fear in her belly. Her hand felt for the locket around her neck. *I can't show it*, she thought. The only woman on board, an officer, too, she had a special burden to bear.

It had not always been that way. As a young girl in school, she never studied, and good grades came easily. Her only focus? Finding joy each day. After school, her best friend, Jo, would come to her East End home, and they'd dance with abandon in front of the immense living room mirror, singing along with the Archies, shouting, really, to the blaring music: "Sugar, Sugar, honey, honey." Moving and shaking with abandon like that was an elixir, their secret. When Melanie's dad's car appeared in the driveway, Jo would run home. Melanie would talk with her dad, and he'd want her to share everything as if his life depended on it. She was the center of his world then—in a way, still was.

At the academy, there was the joy of close friends, not just at parties but also sharing their studies and sea trials. Always laughing. They knew the day was coming when, no longer midshipmen, they'd have to face reality. And yet, it all seemed unreal. Consumed with newfound duties, she felt her new career had taken over her life. Where was the joy now?

And yet she welcomed the daily tasks and, especially as an officer at sea, leading others by example, treating them as friends and equals, and getting to know their strengths and quirks. She'd come to love her fellow mates—the rough ones, their language a bit trashy, but when you got to know them, surprisingly sweet. The shy ones who opened up to her over time. She knew they liked her, trusted her, and had begun to share their stories. She'd become one of the boys.

As much as she loved the open sea, its vastness had at times overpowered her, leaving her homesick for Maine. Whenever she had shore leave, she returned there to visit friends and family. But this storm had given rise to an entirely new kind of fear in her gut. She suddenly realized that her search for joy was a silly, shallow diversion, considering her responsibility for her ship and shipmates.

Why had she been so focused on the lack of joy in her life? What did joy have to do with anything? She felt conflicted by her need to survive, surely, but more importantly, the overwhelming need to protect her shipmates from this storm bearing down upon them all.

***

The house phone jarred the captain awake. As Captain David Downs reached for the receiver, his body slammed against the wall. He looked at his watch. The digital display read 1:25 a.m. He had to think. *Was it yesterday we left Jacksonville? No, it was late Tuesday. A day and a half at sea. It's Thursday, October 1.* On his hands and knees, he leaned against the bed to keep his balance as he lifted the phone to his ear. *Everything's moving.* "Yes."

"Captain, it's pounding us pretty bad." His second mate sounded breathless, her voice so loud he had to hold the phone away from his ear. "They're saying it's now a category two, increasing to maybe a cat three, and I think we're headed right for the eyewall. Sir! I recommend we take the Hole in the Wall. It's our last chance to escape, to take a safer course!"

"Yes, I know. It's a cat two. Just run it, Ricker. It's nothing."

She wanted to scream. *You bloody fool. It's right there, the last deep channel passage to the Old Bahama Channel, a buffer from the open Atlantic*!

Instead, she said, "Aye, aye, Captain."

***

Melanie hung up the house phone. "Damn." She brushed wisps of blond hair from her eyes. "Shit. He doesn't get it," she said to the helmsman. Some called him a safety-first captain, but he was a cabin captain, she thought, managing from his stateroom. Hands locked behind her back, chin thrust out, she bounced forward on her toes in precise imitation of her captain and mocked him. "It's nothing, it's nothing! Nothing like I had in Alaska." She held onto the console to avoid pitching to the deck.

"Nothing?" said the helmsman, looking confused and exhausted.

"Yeah. You know the Old Bahama Channel would put us farther away from this monster of a storm, right? But the captain, he says we're going to outrun it. You know what's really going on?" The helmsman shook his head.

"Corporate," she shouted, raising her voice. "That's Pegasus!"

"Who?" he yelled, his mouth an O, as the maelstrom swallowed the word.

She leaned closer to him. "Pegasus Shipping in New Jersey, the ship's owner."

"What about 'em?"

Melanie tried to speak, but she staggered and almost fell into Marvin as the immense swell broke over the bow, throwing her off balance.

"Sorry," he stammered. "Can't let go of the wheel."

She regained her footing. "Jeez. Never done that before. You'd think I was a novice."

He laughed, and it made things better for a moment.

She needed to tell someone what was going on, even if it was Marvin, who would never say a word to anyone. "Pegasus pushed the captain to leave port yesterday." She waited to see if he understood.

"They did?"

"Yes. In the face of a damn hurricane alert! So, the captain, he rolls the dice—you know we're an old, rusted container ship built for diesel fuel and steam, right?"

"Right," he said. "So, we're built for speed?"

"Right. So, our front-loading doors and hatches are susceptible to leaks." She could tell that this wasn't news to Marvin, who nodded, silently mouthing the word *leaks*.

"But by God," she continued, knowing she was scaring him, eager to tell the story. "By God, captain decides we can beat this storm to San Juan. So, he tells them, corporate…Pegasus, that is… he says we'll take the fastest route, the direct route east of the Bahamas. And, Marvin, you heard me tell him to take the Hole in the Wall, right?"

Marvin nodded in agreement.

"But captain says no. He tells them, but he's really asking their permission, right?" He says, 'We'll just outrun it.' And you know what? Pegasus approved it. Of course they did." She shook her head in amazement.

"So…" Marvin, too, seemed amazed.

"So, there's no turning back now, Marvin. Oh no. We can't delay the delivery of essential goods to Puerto Rico. That would cost time and time is money. And corporate would be angry. Captain won't risk that, and I can't blame him."

For a long time, they stayed silent, listening to the howling winds, the waves' thudding blows, and the ship's responding groans and creaks. *Would the ship break apart*? Melanie knew that the voice recorder, the ship's black box, was recording everything said on the bridge. But she didn't care. *Someone needs to hear us.*

Swaying to the rolls, rising to the massive swells, and falling forward in the deep pitches, Melanie listened to the howling winds, cocooned in thoughts of other, safer times. To calm herself, she summoned the sounds and smells of her parents' farm in North Norway, Maine, the smell of bread baking in the oven, the sound of owls hooting across the valley, of coyotes howling at the moon. And she thought of the farm animals she loved.

***

She remembered cold nights in the half-lit barn when the bay horse would greet her with a soft whinny. As a young girl, she would stroke the soft nose, the horse's large, knowing eyes shining out of the darkness; the sweet smell of hay and the pungent horse dung would pucker her nose. She smiled, recalling sunny days when majestic llamas grazed in the field and evenings when frogs croaked amid the pond lilies and weeds. And there were always barn cats and kittens to play with. She still missed her old dogs, now buried at the farm. Butch, the big red retriever, had run with her along country roads, unleashed, responding to her voice commands.

***

The helmsman interrupted her thoughts, shouting something, but she couldn't hear him over the storm. "What did you say?" she yelled back, leaning over to hear him.

"I said, remember how calm it was when we left JAX?"

"So, what are they saying?" asked Marvin.

"National Weather Service can't seem to make up its mind. First, it's a watch, then a hurricane warning, then it's a watch. Go figure."

Marvin let out a whistle and shook his head, perhaps in wonder or disgust. She couldn't tell.

Chapter 4

Hurricane Hilda was still a category two hurricane with winds at 100 miles per hour. But it would soon become a different animal, a category three, with winds more than 120 miles per hour, on its way to a category four at 150 miles per hour—the first category four hurricane to hit the Bahamas since 1866. On a map, the expected path of its eye directly intersected the ship's route. If, that is, you were looking at the most up-to-date reports from the National Hurricane Center. And even they didn't really know where Hilda was going.

On the radio, Melanie hailed a passing ship, one of their own Pegasus container ships on the reverse course out of San Juan for Jacksonville. *Wish I was on it.*

"You see the latest report from National Hurricane Center?" she asked the helmsman.

"We're headed right for the eyewall."

For the second time since they'd left Jacksonville, she felt the finger of fear in her belly. And last night, she'd had a nightmare—the same one that had plagued her childhood ever since her little brother Charlie drowned when he was five and she was six. When she met Jack, the dreams had stopped. Until now.

In the dream, she was swimming underwater in a blue lagoon, and she could breathe without scuba gear. In and around the yellow coral reef, small fish with dazzling colors darted past her. Her flippers propelled her down to the bottom, where the light sparkled off the white sand. Lying on the sand were what looked like round, flat sand dollars. Melanie reached for one and, with her hand, brushed the sand off to reveal a shiny Spanish gold piece. As she struggled to pick it up, the sand under it began to move, making ripples. Something was pushing up from under the coins. As she watched, the sand began to lift and, to her horror, uncovered an opening and a dark chasm below. Before she could react, a gnarled hand shot out of the darkness, reaching for her. Melanie tried to scream, but there was no noise, just bubbles of air rising toward the surface. She tried to follow them up. Something was pulling on her flippers, and she let them go, kicking her feet, pulling with leaden arms, trying to get away. Desperate to breathe, running out of air, she could see the surface, bright, beckoning, too far away. She gulped water. She was going to drown.

Awakened, covered in a cold sweat, she tiptoed into the bathroom and gazed at herself in the mirror. She saw a young woman with strings of blond hair falling over high cheekbones and bleary blue eyes, full of anxiety. But she still had her locket, the one from her mom, holding a photo of her and her little brother Charlie—the only one she had of him, taken just before he was gone. Holding it tight, she steeled herself to banish the fear. Why did she ever go to sea?

***

A loud crash on deck caused her to jerk around to peer out the window, but she could see nothing. "Something's come loose," hollered the helmsman. "What's our wind speed?"

"No idea. The anemometer's broken." Why had no one fixed it? "This ship is a rust bucket." She scanned the radar for another vessel. "We're alone." She read the latest message from the National Hurricane Center. "They say it's a cat three now." She yelled at the storm, "Hello, Hilda! You're just getting bigger, and we're going right through your eye!" Marvin laughed, but his face was white from fear.

The storm was tracking them like a hound on a scent. *Can't change course without calling Captain Downs.* She wasn't going to disturb him again.

At 3:34 a.m., Downs appeared on the bridge. Melanie reported on the hurricane, then retired to her cabin to get a brief rest. She decided to write an email to her mother. What to say? Don't cry. Make it short.

"Hi, Mom. We are heading straight into it, Category 3, last we checked. Winds are super bad. Love to everyone."

She'd never ended an email message that way before.

Suddenly, a green and white wave crashed over the fo'c'sle, battering the ship. With each thundering wave, the ship seemed to wince. "Hold onto your ass!" Melanie shouted.

"Does the captain know what we're facing?" yelled the helmsman.

"He says he checked the BVS," she said.

"How current is it?"

"Not very, but he's in love with it." The Bon Voyage System, with its colorful Google-Maps-like display, was using data almost twenty-four hours old. It was useless to predict where Hilda was and where she was going.

A flash of lightning blazed across the sky, making visible the sheets of rain pelting the window, where two mariners stood helpless at the bridge. Captain Downs appeared stolid and determined. The helmsman's face was taut with fright. Both fought to keep their footing.

"Don't worry," Downs said to comfort the helmsman. "Nothing bad about this, Marvin. It's a typical winter day in Alaska."

The course alarm blared each time the ship veered off course. "Turn the damn thing off," said Downs, who strained to stand straight as the ship listed heavily to starboard. He had to find the cause. "Let's correct the list by allowing the wind and waves to hit her port side." But the helmsman couldn't see where the waves were coming from. "Maybe they can pump ballast water from the starboard tank to the port tank to give her balance," said Downs, calling the engine room.

The chief engineer's voice sounded loud and clear on the speaker. "We're blowing tubes to remove obstructions from the engines, but we got a problem, Captain. You know those intake tubes that suck oil from the tank to keep the engines lubed? Well, we're heeling so far, those tubes are going to lose contact with the oil in the tank. That happens, the engines stop."

When Downs hung up, the chief mate delivered more bad news. "Barometer's still going down, Captain. A hatch has blown open, allowing seawater to cascade into the hold."

"Get out there to check all hatches and pump out that hold." Downs then said to no one, "What the hell?" He turned to the helmsman. "Reports say we're on the backside of the storm. We won't be going through the eye. Just steer that heading right there the best you can."

The helmsman, bent over his console, appeared to be frozen with fear.

"Hang in there," said Downs. "You're doing great. Still got us on course." But the captain seemed confused by the conflicting weather reports. "We can't see," he muttered to himself.

An engineer appeared on the bridge. "I've never seen it like this," he said.

***

Downs tried to remember last night's dream. It had given him comfort. He'd been awakened from it too soon. He'd been standing in a field of white potato blossoms in northern Maine's Aroostook County. Home from the academy to pick potatoes headed for the

French fry factory, heaving them into machines, his life flashed before him. He'd been at a dance at the Grange Hall. The band was playing, and he was getting up the courage to ask a pretty wisp of a girl to dance—his sister had taught him how to jitterbug. Instead, he slinked away, too embarrassed. And then she'd come to his rescue, suddenly standing before him with her long dark hair, tight jeans, and sly smile. "Aren't you going to ask me to dance?" It was love at first sight. Mary, still the love of his life. She'd given him five children. But he'd always listened to the call of the sea. As he woke, he heard Mary's last words: "Don't go."

***

Should he seek permission from corporate to change course, maybe take the route that his second mate had recommended? Maybe he'd been too quick to disagree with her. The Old Bahama Channel would have put them behind the barrier islands in relative safety. But they'd lose time and time was money. And he'd once been cautioned for being too timid. He'd already buckled to the pressure from Pegasus Shipping to leave Jacksonville when all his instincts had told him to stay in port to avoid this damned storm. Anyway, they'd be fine. After all, he'd once been captain of a container ship sailing in wild storms off Alaska. This was nothing. He pulled up the BVS report on his computer screen displaying in deep oranges and reds the whirling circle of the hurricane tracking far off their path. No. Don't give the bastards at Pegasus the satisfaction of hearing any doubt in your voice. You've got to project confidence to your crew—don't let them sense your fears. He'd already been rejected as captain of one of their new container ships—any doubts about his mettle would likely doom his chances for the next opening.

Chapter 5

Shortly after dawn, *El Barco de Oro* pitched into steep swells topped by breaking waves thirty to forty feet high. The sea heaped up, and spray and foam streaked off breaking waves. The helmsman fought to hold her steady and straight into the swells and waves. The list to port exaggerated the rolls to more than fifteen degrees, which threatened to cut off lube-oil pressure—if that happened, they'd lose the main engine and the ship would founder, and then they'd be at the mercy of what was becoming a category four hurricane. Each wave thumped the ship with cascading water, and *El Barco* shimmied and shook stem to stern. Each roll came closer to the point of no return. The barometer was still falling. Wind speed approached 120 m.p.h. with higher gusts, but they didn't know the exact wind speed. The windows in front of the helmsman had spinning circles of glass set like bifocals into the pane to allow those on the bridge to see through the rain, but the rain pelted so hard that the visibility was almost zero. Some in the crew were simply in awe of the storm, while others, like the helmsman, had crossed over to terror.

An hour ago, the captain had ordered his chief mate to heave-to. They were taking a pounding. "Let's bring her into the wind, just keep the engines running enough to hold her on course, north by northeast, straight into the waves, and we'll just ride it out." It had helped, until now. The captain ordered them to "put her on hand." So, they were off the autopilot, off the iron mike.

Melanie stared at the radar screen as it went dark. Minutes passed before it flickered to life. She groaned as another tall wave hit. "There goes the lawn furniture," she said as containers flew off the deck.

Between decks, one bolt stripped its last threads, and this stressed the remaining bolts holding the strap, and one by one, these bolts failed, too, and so one strap flew off the trailer, and this stressed the bolts holding the other straps. As the trailer swiveled, the other straps holding it pulled away. The deck fell forward as the ship slammed down the backside of the wave, and the trailer sailed forward and crashed into another trailer; and they began to cascade back and forth and side to side, ripping other vehicles free from their moorings.

The chief mate called the captain. "It's a mess down there below deck. Some cars and trailers have come loose, and I can't send a man down there. It's suicide!" His voice, shrill and frantic, betrayed him. *He's panicking*, Downs realized. The list was now more than fifteen degrees. "We can deal with it," said the captain, "as long as it doesn't worsen." If the oil could reach the engines.

Chapter 6

Below decks, Chief Engineer Art Duclos ruled over the engine room and its turbines, reduction gears, condensers, and pumps and the fire room and its boilers and pipes. The engineers lived in a world of noise, of clanging engines and raging fires, where the air, scalded and softened with steam from the fire room's furnaces, drove the huge steel shaft that turned the propeller. It was a separate world from above decks. Engineers and oilers worked below, and deck hands and deck officers worked up above. Everyone liked it that way.

Down in the engine room, the crew struggled to keep the boilers going. Art, his hands and coveralls smeared with oil, his dark hair greasy, and his creased brow dripping with sweat, wished the captain would come below decks more often. He loved his job—the burning smell of grinding gears and the feel of hot steam. He found the noise comforting. He trusted Dave Downs. They were at the academy together, back when Downs would go out drinking with him. Now he'd become more distant, more official. But Art understood. That's just how it was. Keep it going, he told himself, refusing to think of the unthinkable. We've got enough fuel. The mechanical systems are old, but they're working. Got to keep getting steam. Without steam, we have no power, no propeller, and the ship would be dead as a log. Got to keep up the steam at all costs. It's the rising water, damn it. The crew was pumping it out as fast as it came in. As long as the pumps kept working, as long as the pumps kept up with the inflowing water, they'd be okay. He wouldn't think about what would happen if they lost steam, because he knew the pumps would fail and they'd lose propulsion and electricity, and then all would be lost. Did the oilers know this? Art watched with admiration as his oilers did battle. He loved these guys.

Jimmy the oiler was a strong kid from the Bronx with a sharp tongue and wicked sense of humor. Art loved Jimmy, and sometimes his sick sense of humor was a blessing. But now it was a curse. Jimmy sweated profusely as he oiled the parts to the pump. He stood to wipe his brow and called out to his chief.

"Hey, Chief," he yelled over the din of engine noise, "What's worse than finding out your wife has cancer?"

The chief engineer braced himself against the nearest wall just to remain standing. He hoped the kid would shut up. "Okay, Jimmy, I give up. What?"

"Finding out there's a cure." Jimmy doubled over with laughter. The chief shook his head. Not funny. Not now. But Jimmy wasn't quitting.

"What do you call a man splattered on a wall?"

"I give up. Enough, Jimmy."

"Art. Get it? Art. Great, huh?"

Suddenly, seawater cascaded into the engine room. "What the hell?" Art called the bridge. "Captain, looks like more hatches have blown! We're taking on water down here. I mean lots of it! I don't think the pumps will be enough."

Down in the engine room, the men gathered in the dark, preferring the comfort of the familiar to the deck, where they'd have to confront their fate. The crew clung to each other in a mass of frightened humanity. The silence unnerved them.

Up on deck, the deck hands struggled to repair the hatches, but the wind threw them back and the towering waves threatened to carry them off. With each thundering crash, the ship shivered, and its decks slanted to the heavens.

On the bridge, Melanie could feel the ship, at the mercy of the sea, lose forward progress. She thought, *this isn't right.* "Captain, we've got to call Art." And suddenly there was Art's voice, on his mike—unmistakable, high-pitched, almost a shriek.

"Captain! I've lost the engines! Lost them!"

"For God's sake, restart them now, or we'll founder!"

Art's voice was almost a whisper. "I'm sorry, Captain, we can't restart…" The mike went dead.

The silence from the engines magnified the howling wind and sea.

"I think we just lost the plant," said the captain. Suddenly, the bow sank beneath the dark green water. "Bow is down! Bow is down!" yelled the captain over the intercom. He searched for Melanie's eyes.

It was 6:59 a.m. The captain made a phone call from the bridge to Mike O'Donnell, safety and operations manager at the New Jersey offices of Pegasus Shipping. There was no answer. The call went to voicemail. "We have a navigational incident," Downs said to the recording device; he mentioned the scuttle and said they were taking in seawater. "I want to talk to you." He meant O'Donnell. Where was he?

He called the shipping company's emergency call center: "This is a marine emergency." The operator kept asking him to repeat everything. He did, almost losing it, even spelled the ship's name. He waited for five minutes. "Oh, God!" Then in a resigned monotone, he said, "I have a marine emergency, and I would like to speak to a Q.I." That's a qualified individual, a designated person on shore. "We had a hull breach—a scuttle blew open during a storm. We have water down in three hold with a heavy list. We've lost the main propulsion unit. The engineers can't get it going."

At last, Mike O'Donnell came on the line. It was just after 7 a.m.

"Hello, Mike," Downs yelled. The line was scratchy. "Mike,

you there?"

"I can hear you, Dave." He sounded so far away, so safe.

"Mike, it's bad news—seas over thirty, maybe forty feet, hatches blown, taking in water. It's probably short-circuited the system because we've lost power and communications..." His voice broke as he struggled to hold back the emotions that threatened to overwhelm him.

"What? Oh, my God, sir! No power? We'll call the Coast Guard..."

"Yeah, sure, Mike, but I don't feel good about this. You know, Mike?" The question hung in the air.

"What, Dave? What?"

"It's been a good life, Mike. No regrets. Tell my wife I love her."

"Jesus, Dave..."

After the call, Downs pushed the button that activated a distress alert by satellite. Almost immediately, the ship sent a security alert signal to the U.S. Coast Guard with the ship's coordinates.

Melanie's eyes met her captain's. It was time to think the unthinkable—when to send the message to abandon ship? With a sagging heart, she realized it would be soon. But wasn't it futile? The lifeboats were open, not like the new enclosed ones, and it was impossible to let them down on a pitching sea. All those bulky survivor suits—what good were they in a hurricane? She pushed it from her mind until the force of it almost doubled her over. Melanie knew what was in store for her captain. He'd be the good captain and go down with the ship. Damn it. It wasn't fair. He deserved to survive. She wanted to survive, too.

The ship's electronic distress alerts were sending out pings, one burst every fifty seconds. Satellites orbited overhead, thirty-three thousand kilometers high, passing them every hundred minutes. The system had to detect three bursts to locate them. If a satellite happened to be overhead at the right time. And then the Coast

Guard had to pick up the distress and dispatch a rescue crew. All this took time.

"Captain," Melanie said, "you've done everything you can do. Let's get out."

He looked at her, his face full of pain and sorrow. "You go, Ricker. You have a life to live, so God's speed. Go. And remember me to my wife and son."

"Captain. Oh, my God!"

"Go. Save yourself."

"You gonna leave me?" cried Marvin the helmsman, sitting on the floor up against one wall, unable to move across the tilted bridge.

"I'm not leaving you," said the captain.

"I'm a goner!" the helmsman screamed.

"No, you're not. Let's go," yelled Downs, who could do nothing for his helmsman—the man was dead weight and fell back to the floor each time Downs tried to lift him.

Melanie struggled against the rising floor to leave the bridge. Got to get out of here.

Back in her cabin, she dialed the number. Her cell phone still worked—amazing. The call to area code 207 cut through the night and the storm; it bounced off a satellite and rang in North Norway, Maine.

"Hello?" The familiar voice, so clear she almost jumped, her throat choked with sudden emotion.

"Mom?"

"Hello. Mel, is that you? Oh my gosh, let me get your dad— "

"Wait, Mom, stay on the line. I don't know how long we'll be connected."

"Sure, sure. Honey, are you okay?" She sounded alarmed—never could hide anything from her, still razor sharp. She could picture it—the yellow farmhouse and red barn, moon shining on mown fields, llamas grazing, owls hooting across the valley.

"It's a pretty wild storm and we're in the middle of it out here." She realized she was shouting, her voice thick with tension. "It's not looking good, Mom." I am going to see you again, damn it. "I just called to tell you I love you. And tell Dad I love him, too."

"Oh, Mel, we love you so much. We'll pray for you."

"I've got to go, Mom. Bye."

The line went dead, and she hung onto the cell phone, listening to the silence, and then removed it slowly from her ear, and then the sound of the hurricane drowned out the ache in her heart, and she put the phone back in her pocket. It's then that she felt it again—that finger of fear in her belly.

Chapter 7

For a moment, Captain Downs stood dazed and bathed in the dim glow from a small overhead bulb. The emergency generator must have kicked on. The engine room must be dark. *God, give me strength*. He needed strength for his last message to the crew. He never dreamed he would ever have to say the words. There was a first for everything. He paused, said a brief prayer for them all, and spoke into his ship-wide mike.

All through the ship's quarters, his urgent voice resounded: "This is the captain. Abandon ship! Abandon ship!" Downs looked at his watch. It was 7:28 a.m. He put the mike down, thinking it might be too late for anyone to abandon this doomed ship. The two lifeboats could carry forty-three each. If they could launch over the side—if the ship rolled any more, they couldn't lower it on one side, and the other side would slap the waves below.

***

They all heard it. The klaxon horn as jarring as fingernails on a blackboard, screeching throughout the ship, blaring into the ears of all thirty-three souls on board and sounding the alarm, the unmistakable sound of danger. Not like a school fire drill spilling excited children onto a playground and promising release. No, it drilled directly into the skull its message of panic and dread—insistent, demanding, not to be ignored, even as some covered their ears.

An able-bodied seaman slept soundly, lost in his dreams of San Juan and the pretty girls he'd meet there. They'd show him the sights and the local bar scene. He swayed in his bunk until he was jerked awake and heard the captain's voice and then the sound of the horn. He knew that his whole life before him was now lost.

The bosun heard it, too. He swore at his fate, then felt strangely calm and wondered, what would it feel like?

When the chief mate heard the captain's voice, he swung into action; he headed toward the deck. On the way, he grabbed the man he needed, the bosun: "Let's go! On the double!"

The bosun abandoned his survival suit and left it on the floor of the passageway—never could put the damned thing on. He hollered to a seaman, who joined them in their race to the heaving deck, now listing to its starboard side, imploring others to join them. The chief mate screamed directions as the dozen or so men tugged on the ropes, finally freeing the lifeboat. They saw the engine room stragglers, eyes panicked, rushing toward the lifeboat.

By now, the clanging had been so long it seemed like hours. They could feel it like a bellows compressed by a mighty blacksmith until it became part of their being, and they thought the clanging would never end, melting into the other sounds, the yells and cries of crewmen as they scrambled out onto the heaving, spumy, wind-whipped deck and the screeching of metal containers smashing together. Out there on the deck, the klaxon was muted like a hand over a trumpet, so that the sound blended into the background where it remained part of their consciousness, a fear that would not go away.

"Hurry," the chief mate yelled.

They tumbled into the lifeboat as it swung out over the abyss below.

***

Melanie sat huddled in a corner of her dark cabin, unable to move. She'd put on a brave face for her captain and her shipmates. She'd retreated to her cabin, gripped by the same fear that underlined her days and nights. Because what lay outside is what had haunted her—the fear of drowning. She held the locket in her fingers—inside, a tiny photo of her and her little brother Charlie, calling her to come home, to survive.

She forced herself to think of the sixty-second drills—she'd thought them a waste of time. Now her actions were automatic. Pull down the bag stowed near her bunk, yank out the orange survival suit, lie down on it, feet into the legs, fasten the straps across the legs, stand up, left arm in, the hood over the head, then the right arm, and zip up—leave it open at the neck. Time to face her fears.

Bouncing along the narrow corridor, hands and feet encased in the bulky suit, she struggled to hold the handrails and to remain standing. Reaching the stairway down to the deck, then pushing with all her might against the door lever, thank God, the door opened onto the deck. Facing the pelting rain and howling winds, she was helpless against the blast to her shocked face—her eyes were sightless from the welling tears, her neck suddenly numb from the cold air that blasted through the opening in her suit. For a time-less moment, she staggered, almost falling back down into the dark hole. Somehow, she found the resolve to act. Without hesitation—not a second to spare—with mittened hands, yank the zipper up over your mouth, launch yourself across the slanted deck, slide to the rail, and pitch over the side.

The suit was buoyant. She hit the water hard and flipped onto her back. Her vision limited, she could not move her head. Within reach, a whistle on a lanyard. An emergency strobe light instantly activated upon contact with the water; this also triggered an emergency radio locator beacon. She had no idea how long she could survive. She was at the mercy of the angry sea. The Coast Guard would be out there, but any rescue would be a while in coming.

The ship, silent and dark, except for a few emergency lights—up on the bridge, in the galley, the engine room, and the cabins, all over the ship. Those who remained behind could hear the wrath outside, and they knew it was coming for them.

The third mate, Peter, stood in the dark, dizzy and disoriented. He felt no anger or resentment, just surprise and regret—maybe he should have spoken up sooner.

The engine crew oilers stood in rising water. They looked up in the darkness at nothing. *El Barco de Oro*, without power, swung sideways, swept up and into an immense and powerful wave.

Slowly, unseen, *El Barco de Oro* slipped under the water and disappeared.

***

Dawn had broken, but darkness cast a pall over the leaden, spumy sky. Up on the surface, Melanie fought for her life. She spat up seawater. Her jacketed body was tossed and buffeted as mountainous waves crashed over her. The water was cold, but her suit kept her warm. Did anyone else make it off the ship? Peter? She struggled to recall when she last saw him. *Oh, God, he went below to get some sleep.* Captain Downs? There was no question—he'd gone down with his ship. Her fellow officers? She was already mourning her lost shipmates.

She thought of her family in Maine. Would she ever see them again? She felt so alone. She'd never wanted to live more than this. *Save me, oh Lord.*

Then, outlined against the darkening clouds and through the pelting rain and whitecaps, she saw a momentary vision of a lifeboat outlined against the crest of a wave before it disappeared out of sight. *Oh, my God, maybe Jack made it.*

Chapter 8

Just before calling a news conference, Roger Amiens, president and CEO of Pegasus Shipping, made the phone call to alert the U. S. Coast Guard to the fact that they'd lost contact with the ship, and it might have gone down. It was the right thing to do. Maybe they could find survivors.

The call followed shortly on the heels of the mayday message from the crew, which had triggered a massive search. The message was passed instantly to the National Safety Transportation Board, the U.S. Air Force, the U.S. Navy, and the National Hurricane Center. The Coast Guard was still getting electronic stress alerts from other sources on the ship. They all knew it was urgent—even in a survival suit, you can survive for, at most, four or five days. If anyone got off the ship before she went down. If you could find them.

Roger stepped to the microphone before a sea of reporters. A hush fell over the room, and the sound of cameras clicking could be heard. He'd called this press conference because he was prepared to make an announcement that was the product of an emergency executive session of the board of directors of Pegasus Shipping and advice, protected by attorney-client privilege, from the company's attorney, Oliver McBride III, Esq. There were no minutes. Every board member was sworn to secrecy. They all understood that the future of Pegasus was at stake. Roger had already reached out to family members of *El Barco's* crew to express his deepest sympathies. There are cynics who say everyone knows that in today's media world, you get the story out there right away with all your dirty linen, and after a few news cycles, people forget—it all goes away. But Roger meant every word. And this story was not going away.

"Thank you for coming," he announced. "Our thoughts and prayers are with the crew." He read from his carefully prepared statement. His face flushed and shiny in the television lights, Roger was not used to being in front of legions of reporters and batteries of cameras. After his very brief statement, he said he would answer questions. All over the crowded room, hands shot up and shouts rang out. Confused, Roger recognized a distinguished-looking gentleman in a tweed jacket and tie in the front row, unaware that this reporter had, almost a week before, flown through the eye of Hilda.

"Ned Battle, *Miami Herald*. So why did they sail into a category four hurricane with a ship that was too old and unsafe?"

Another reporter's voice among the many shouted, "Sir, the captain, wasn't he once fired for being overly cautious? So why did you push him to go to sea with this hurricane out there?"

He heard many more questions, all of which seemed like an attack on his company and him personally. He felt outraged. Those lost at sea were his people, and he was personally devastated. Did these reporters care? He had no choice but to read the prepared statement crafted by his attorney. "David Downs is an experienced captain—"

The mike squealed. He paused to let the sound dissipate. He tapped the mike, a normal mistake, because the bass sound pounded the room, which made him jump back like a damned fool. It took another three seconds for his heartbeat to slow. Steadying, he resumed reading. "If anyone could get through this, Captain Downs could."

He paused to look up—better to make eye contact, more convincing. "He was…" Shit, better not say he's dead yet; just read it.

"He is extremely capable, and he's had extensive training. He had a plan to bypass the hurricane."

Now he was hitting his stride—okay, just stay calm. "The storm was nowhere near what it became, so it was a sound plan before they encountered unexpected engine problems that left the ship adrift."

Reporters started to yell out questions again. Ignore them—just get through the statement. He raised his voice to get their attention. "I have tremendous faith in the captain and crew. But the buck stops with me. They were basically disabled right near the eye." He paused for effect. "Sometimes," he said, beginning to choke up, "the sea just overwhelms you." A tear rolled down one cheek. "If there is any fault, it is mine." And he strode out of the room, followed by his minions.

Outside the room, the company lawyer clapped him on the back and whispered, "Nice job, Rog, well done." Oliver McBride was smiling.

"Fuck off," Roger told him.

***

Shortly after 5:00 a.m. on October 3, Lieutenant Commander Jack Huston and his crew boarded a C-130 Hercules in Clearwater and flew toward the Bahamas. Two hours later, at first light, they were twenty-five hundred feet above sea level, buffeted by Hilda's hurricane winds. Their C-130 almost touched the never-ending swells of twenty to fifty feet as their weary eyes scanned the scudding sea. Now into the third day of the search, the crew had had little rest, and the odds of someone surviving had narrowed.

They were not alone. Coast Guard Cutter Northland sailed from Portsmouth, Virginia, and Resolute sailed from St. Petersburg. They'd scrambled two U.S. Coast Guard HH-60 Jayhawk helicopters from the Bahamas, where they'd been at the ready. A navy P8 jet was in the air from Jacksonville. Three commercial tugs also joined the search.

Huston's voice startled his copilot: "You still awake over there?"

"Hell, yeah," said the copilot, slurping black coffee. "You get any shuteye back home?"

"Nah. I'm okay."

"Can't see a damned thing. And we're searching eleven hundred square miles. Needle in a haystack."

"It's probably the wrong area anyway," said Huston. "By now the sea and wind have pushed any survivors many miles away from where the ship went down." Three days of endless gray skies above and frothy gray seas below were taking their toll. Yet they strained to find any sign of life or even a piece of debris. They saw nothing for days on end and fell silent.

The silence was a cocoon, shielding them from what they might discover.

Finally, something.

"Hey, see that?" yelled Huston. There was something in the water looking like a big box, and pieces of twisted, rust-colored metal, with shards of wood.

"Looks like parts of a container."

"It's clearly debris," he said to the navigator. "Can you mark it?"

"Okay, marking the spot."

When they found other debris—an oil slick and floating cargo containers—they narrowed the search. Then, about seventy miles from the ship's last known location northeast of the Bahamas, they found a life ring and an empty lifeboat.

Then, an orange survival suit, still floating.

The navigator radioed the navy chopper with the coordinates. Minutes later, navy SEAL Mack Dugan was leaning out the chopper's side door, black flippers hanging over the edge, held there only by a cable.

"Swimmer away!" yelled the chopper's pilot.

Blasted by the wash of blades overhead, Dugan's legs pushed his black-suited body out and away, and they lowered him down toward the swirling waves. It was his decision. Don't do anything foolish, he'd been told. Want you out of there as soon as possible. His eyes scanned the churning sea below until he spotted it. Thumbs up, he released himself, fell, and smacked the water.

For a moment, he was swallowed by the sea. His white helmet bobbed up and seemed to come out of the water, then disappeared again. He swam for his life. Hurled about like a stick, waves from everywhere, his eyes fixed on the bright orange object, the survival suit, bobbing like a cork yards away. He couldn't tell—dead or alive? Just like the other one, pulled out by the other chopper. Would they both survive? It would be a miracle. He was almost out of strength, and it was pure adrenaline that allowed him to reach the suit despite the towering waves. He hooked the lifeline onto a ring on the suit, then gave the thumbs up, and they hauled the survival suit up and into the chopper. His heart sank. Maybe this one didn't make it. Dugan didn't know. Dead or alive? Either way, they found someone, and that would bring closure for the family. Okay, now let's get out of here.

For Dugan, trying to tread water and remain in place under the chopper was a joke. He was a strong swimmer, but this storm was having its way with him. Drifting farther and farther from the now distant helicopter…Where is it? No flutter of blades. But he knew it was there. They would not abandon the mission or him. Up there, somewhere, hovering, its blast swallowed by the storm. He'd almost despaired. A last look up. Where is it? And the life ring almost hit him. He grabbed hold of it with arms of steel. He rose out of the water, pulled by the cable, until the crew hauled him in the door. He lay there panting. Mission accomplished, he hoped. Soon he sat huddled on the floor in the wash of chopper blades, wrapped in blankets, his teeth chattering, the crew all smiles, a few thumbs-ups and pats on the back, and words like "well done." The pilot got air, then wheeled around to the northwest, already picking up speed, heading home. It felt good to be alive. This is what it's all about. Why he signed up. Why he'd fought through all the exercises, all the rigors of training, the weightlifting, the endless runs, all of it. Dugan was a religious man. A godly man. God, let this one live.

News announcers hailed them as heroes. The celebration was overwhelmed with sadness, of course, for the rest of *El Barco's* crew, those still lost at sea. The families had not given up hope. Gathered in Jacksonville at the Seafarers' Union Hall, they were heartened to know that two had been found alive. A man and a woman. Officials were holding back their names until their families could be contacted. The world wanted to hear from them. How did they survive? What did it feel like?

Chapter 9

Melanie lay in the ICU at Miami General, her life signs displayed in green and red waves and lines on overhead screens that beeped as nurses flitted in and out. Still unconscious, but alive. Her doctors were guarded as to when and if she would come out of it. Hospital officials could say nothing to the public because of federal privacy laws. Melanie's parents, thrilled and grateful but fearful, were on the way from Maine.

"Do we tell her?" the nurse asked her supervisor.

"Tell her what?"

"About the other survivor?" It was the question on all their minds.

"Do your job, nurse."

Neither one of these two survivors knew of the other or that they were the only two survivors. So far. And time was running out for their shipmates. Most of the nurses thought this, but none of them could, or would, say it out loud. They all knew that their patients were heroes, and they would work overtime to provide whatever care was needed.

Melanie was underwater again, the same familiar struggle to reach the surface, but there was no urgency, and she soon gave up fighting it. She felt at peace, let go, and let the water take her down to the depths, down to the darkness. And that is when she saw them—Captain Dave and Peter and Art, and the others, and they were smiling at her, welcoming her, and they were at peace. She didn't want to leave them, would stay there and rest. But she felt herself rising, fought against it, but couldn't stop being pulled to the surface, toward the light. She looked away from the light, down into the comforting darkness, wanting to return to her mates. But she couldn't stay underwater.

Melanie opened her eyes, alone in a world of empty whiteness. Slowly, she felt for her hands, fingers, legs, knees, toes, then reached for her face and the top of her head. Miraculous. Everything seemed to be okay. But numb all over. Probably the painkillers. Her right hand reached for the red button, and she pressed it repeatedly.

"Hello, there," said a nurse. "How do you feel?"

"I don't know. Where am I?"

"Miami General Hospital. You were rescued at sea. Do you remember anything?"

"Yes, I'm afraid so. What day is it?"

"Monday, October 5."

Four days since she pitched into the sea. *Maybe Jack made it.*

***

She dreamed of him—it was the summer she turned fifteen when she first met him … Summer in Maine when you're young, each day a precious gift, fall never far away. She dreamed of those halcyon days of August, when she would lay on the sand at Portland's East End Beach, watching white sails tack across the harbor under cotton clouds. When school days loomed like a squall in the outer harbor, winter a distant memory to be pushed away—like the "mean girls" at school, that dope-smoking gang of sycophants, always lying in wait on her way home.

She could still feel the shame: how she'd cringed at the sight of them. She'd barely survived middle school when, plagued by dreams of drowning, she'd lost sleep, gained weight, and suffered from depression. She had no friends, but it was better to be left alone. That was how screwed up she'd been. Until Jack. She smiled to think of the first time she'd seen him.

"Hey, you'll get sunburned like that." She jerked around, now awake—must have dozed off—heard a boy's voice. She was blinded by the sun and shaded her eyes to see him. He was thin, not tall, and stood out with his ripped arms and military crewcut. He wore a blue T-shirt with "Portland High Track" in front. He was too nice-looking for her, so she thought, *forget about him.*

"Guess I fell asleep."

"Easy to do that here." He had an easy smile, and, to her surprise, he wasn't going away.

"Guess I should thank you." Feeling self-conscious, wondering if her bathing suit made her look too heavy, she wanted to brush off the sand that covered her, but didn't.

He sat down beside her. She thought of standing to leave but was stuck.

"I've never met you. Are you new here?"

Why was he asking this? "No. I'm going to be a freshman at Portland High this fall. You run track?" She'd never done sports—a foreign land, another form of embarrassment.

"Yeah, just finished my freshman year. Don't know how. I never study, so they'll kick me out this year. You live on the prom?"

"Quebec Street. You?"

"Down in the projects. Dad's a retired Marine. Mom's abandoned us."

"Wow," she said, not knowing how to respond to this strange come-on, if it was one. Maybe he was a loner like her.

"You want me to put some suntan lotion on your back?" He grabbed the lotion, and before she could say no, he was squeezing it onto his hands, rubbing them together. And then she felt his hands on her back. She'd been too surprised to act. At first, she felt physically threatened, her personal space violated, and she pulled away from him. As she thought about it now after all these years, if he'd done anything else, everything would have been different. "Oh!" he said, jerking away, jumping to his feet, and standing over her, mouth open, looking like a little boy caught doing some silly prank. "I'm so sorry," he said. His face looked so sad at that very moment that she assured him it was okay, and she settled back onto the sand, a secret smile forming on her lips, waiting until he knelt beside her. Until, now cautious and tentative, he began to move his hands, sliding them slowly, gently, as softly as a caress, over her shoulders and then her neck and down her arms.

It was sensual. She'd never had a boy do this to her, for her, and she was wild with excitement and worry, wanting to be with him forever but at the same time wanting to escape to her safe self.

He finished rubbing the lotion on her, and she wanted him to put it on her legs, too, but he was too coy and handed her the bottle. "I've got to go. Got to report to the major or I'll be in the brig." He leapt up. "What's your name, Miss Charming?"

When she said "Melanie," he saluted her.

"Well, Miss Melanie, shall we meet here again? I'm Jack Pierce." And he dashed off, barefoot. She watched the muscles ripple in his legs and back, his arms pumping as he disappeared up the hill.

***

The lights and sounds of her hospital room intruded, until she dozed off, and Jack's voice came to her again: "Meet me at 6 a.m. down here at the beach in running shorts and sneakers."

That first morning was a slow jog and it almost killed her. He taught her how to stretch, to roll her calves, to wrap her legs with Ace bandages. She could tolerate pain, wanting more of him. She loved the early mornings on the prom with the mist on the harbor and coffee after the morning run.

When school started, they would run a mile on the track at Hadlock Field. Soon, she could make it without stopping. He told her to go out for the track team and she did. Running was still all about pain, but she noticed the changes—the loss of weight, toning of muscles, and self-confidence, a sense of purpose in her life, how boys noticed her and girls liked her. She missed her runs with Jack. No one had seen him at school. One day after class, she walked down to the projects and found his home, a small apartment, trash in the front yard, a big dog barking inside. She knocked on the door. No answer. She found him sitting on the ground against a wire fence littered with papers and bottles, disheveled, clothes torn, disconsolate and spaced out on drugs. She hugged him. "I'm sorry, Mel," he said. Her heart ached for him, wanting him, and she thought of seducing him but didn't dare.

All the years since high school, Melanie hadn't seen him. Her last sight of him: his forlorn face pressed to the rear window of the Greyhound bus as it pulled out of the station onto St. John Street. She'd arrived just in time to see him disappear, off to join the Marines, and it had torn her to pieces. She'd never told him she loved him before he'd been swallowed by a strange new world.

She'd never forgotten him. For years, they'd corresponded. He had begun writing to her soon after he joined the Marines. She always responded, revealing little of herself. She never encouraged him. How had he become so eloquent? She knew he read books. And he wrote poems, and they thrilled her, and she learned something of his life. Said he hated it, hated the things he had to do. She knew not what, but discerned hints, things of a violent nature, but she thought he was not really like that. She knew he was still interested in her, had intimated it in his emails, and sometimes in ways not so subtle. Recently, he'd expressed his love for her. Like his last email. It still resonated with her. She pulled it out and read it again:

Melanie,

You are the woman of whom the poet Walt Whitman wrote these words: "Whoever you are, now I place my hand upon you, that you be my poem, I whisper with my lips close to your ear, I have loved many women and men, but I love none better than you."

But, of course, I have never loved another woman. Only you. You remain close to my heart, even as we remain apart over the years and over the waters. One day, we shall meet again. I know this. Until then, keep me close.

Jack

Maybe she'd been too guarded—never could tell him how much she loved to hear from him, how he'd become her silent lover from far away. And then she'd seen him on *El Barco*. With those same piercing blue eyes and good looks. Just as he'd predicted. It had to be fate…

She dreamed of her dad. The winter after she'd met Jack, her dad had helped her build a tiny sailboat in the cellar—a turnabout dinghy less than ten feet long, five feet in the beam. They had made her tight with oakum between the planks in the hull.

The next spring, they'd put her on a trailer and drove her down to the East End boat ramp, where they put the mast up with the attached sail, threaded ropes through the pulleys, and inserted the centerboard. When they launched the turnabout, Melanie held her breath, then screamed with delight as her boat floated light on the water, not a single leak. Life was simpler then. Her dad had served in the navy and then returned to teach at Maine Technical College, where he taught sailing. He taught her how to tack against the wind, how to let out sail, and later how to navigate by the stars. At first, her dad watched her from the shore, barking out commands. Before long, he let her go off alone to flit around the inner harbor. She fell in love with the sea then—how the brine clung to her skin and hair, how she felt free and in control. One pull on the ropes to change course and go where the breeze takes you. "Got to respect the sea," her dad said. "It can be cruel."

PART 2

Jack Pierce

Chapter 10

Down the hall, in another ICU room, the other survivor was conscious. All his life signs were positive. But he had not spoken. Perhaps his speech was impaired—too early to tell. They would give him time.

Jack's mind spun. Disoriented, his vision fuzzy, he saw flashes of light flickering across shadows on the ceiling. Images passed before him in a haze. Suddenly, a memory…

Cast out of the lifeboat into raging water, he'd been tossed and whacked by monster waves—then utter darkness, under water, bouncing up and sucking in air, struggling to swim with the survival suit. He'd grabbed it and somehow got into it, was pushed overboard, then hauled himself back into the boat. He lost track of time and slipped in and out of consciousness. His last memory was being hauled up and out of the water and pulled into a helicopter, loud voices all around him.

How did I get off that ship? He recalled hearing the captain's voice and then a loud horn—they were abandoning ship. He searched for Melanie, headed for her cabin, and then threw himself against her door, crashing inside onto the deck. Everything was blackness. Everything moved. He groped his way, felt all over her bunk. She was gone, and he had to find her. Out in the passageway, he joined a group headed for the deck. Stumbling, reeling, he almost fell over the survival suit.

Other memories flooded back. Tears slid down his cheeks as,

silently, he grieved for Melanie. *If she survived, would she under- stand? Could she ever forgive him? And what would he tell Harry, his handler at the CIA?* He struggled to put the facts together. *How had it started? How had he got onto that ship?* A memory seeped through his tears; a room full of men…

***

"Seafarer's Hall, Jacksonville" read the sign over the door. Jack pulled out his wallet and inspected his shipping card. His photo smiled back at him, blue eyes and blond hair over his new alias. He thumped his body against the door, and it burst open. Inside, a board with the names of ships in port listed *El Barco de Oro*. A dozen men sat on rows of wooden benches. Their eyes, sullen and bored, met his steady gaze, then looked away. He sauntered up to the counter. The frosted window was shut. As he waited, he turned to stare down the looks. When the window opened, a clerk's face appeared.

"How do I get a ship?" he asked the clerk.

"You got a shipping card?"

"Yes," he replied. "What else?"

"You got to join the union and have the qualifications for the position that's posted." Jack's last memory was leaving the clerk's window and thinking he could do it…

***

The sound of voices outside his room…nurses hovering nearby. He tried to assess his situation. In a hospital bed, an IV in his arm, hooked to a bag, probably hydrating him, maybe nutrition—he'd been days and nights without food and water. He struggled to remember, using his heightened powers of concentration: What name had he used? *Sergey. Sergey Robichek.* His life depended on knowing his identity like a new skin—natural, reflexive, and

50

unthinking. Repetition had always worked—well, usually worked—to dispel the confusion of his many lives.

What did they know about him? Did they know who he was and what he'd done? In vain, he reached for pockets, searching for his wallet, his papers, his I.D., his phone. Wearing a hospital gown. His clothes gone. He tamped down the urge to panic. It came to him that he'd worn his clothes under the survival suit. Could he have tossed his papers to hide his identity? He sensed there were others hovering near, people with questions, maybe reporters, even police; so far, the nurses had kept them out. The nurses were his allies, leaving him alone, protecting him, except that tough one, *Nurse Ratched*. So long as they knew nothing, he was safe. He let them think he couldn't speak, until he fell into a deep sleep and the dreams came…a leafy garden, shadows, the laughter of children…a bench…and the Ukrainian general…

Chapter 11

In his room, a nurse had reappeared, chattering away. Jack considered his options—sneak out of the hospital? But no clothes and no money. Nothing. Try to grab what he needed for his escape? Then he'd be on the lam. He would need time. And if he tried to run, they'd be suspicious. He imagined how investigators would eventually dust for fingerprints—he'd touched things, like a water glass— had he ever been fingerprinted? Better to play it straight. He'd be Sergey for now.

He doubted others survived. Only one lifeboat over the side, and he'd been the fittest and strongest in that one. As the sole survivor, he was free to tell his own story, to be his own hero. But there were dangers there, too—being in the spotlight. They would ask more questions, dig deeper. His identity, so carefully crafted, was a lie; if they dug deeper, they would find out his real name. Better to tread carefully.

A plan began to form. If he could get his clothes, and if the key was still there, then he could just walk out and disappear. He could find a way to withdraw from the scene. Got to get that key.

He needed help. Someone who could learn to like him, to trust him and help him. He decided to start with the pretty young nurse with red hair.

Once he was free, he'd call Harry to explain. It would be a long story. How he'd completed his mission, and then how he'd helped our allies, the Ukrainians.

He'd start with how he was able to get on board El Barco. He replayed it in his mind.

***

Jack had walked out of the union hall. He'd driven his rental car north on I-295, crossed the bridge overlooking Blount Island, and exited onto Heckscher Drive. He drove along the river until he spotted the Creekside Fish Camp, where he pulled in and parked in the lot. When he pushed open the rear screen door, it squeaked, then slammed shut. In his hand, he held the classified ad for a kitchen aide, "No experience required." He got the job and was soon assisting the cook.

When the newspaper listed the arrival of *El Barco de Oro*, Jack found it docked and taking on cargo at Blount Island. It took several nights, but his patience paid off. A man fitting the cook's description—so stupid, the man's photo was right there on the union's website—strolled down the gangway onto the pier. The cook pulled a hoodie over his head, then wandered, slouched over, to a waiting taxi. Jack followed in his rental car. The man entered the Buccaneers' Treasure Chest, the kind of bar he'd seen in other ports, blazing neon beer signs fronting a dark cavern. Jack forced himself to stay awake, waiting, watching, for hours. In the small hours of the morning, the cook emerged drunk and staggered into the alley, where he took a leak. When he reappeared, Jack offered him a ride back to his ship—he'd earlier told the waiting cabbie to leave. Then, Jack drove him miles from town, leaving the cook on a dark country road without his cell phone—Jack had taken it from him—where the man wandered into the night. Jack knew that the ship would call for a new cook, because this cook would not show up on time for its scheduled departure, and he would take his place.

Next morning, he turned in the key to his room in the trailer park, returned his rental car, and took a taxi to the union hall. There were no postings for a cook's position, but he knew there would be. He sat and waited with several other men, all nervous. He listened to the chatter—how few jobs remained. Most ships sailed under foreign flags, like Liberia or Russia. Next to him, a man with a grizzled face and white beard sat hunched over and staring at the floor. The grizzled man couldn't seem to shut up.

"I got a good card," the grizzled man said, "but I don't know." Jack stared at the board.

Grizzly droned on. "I thought I had a job once up in Savannah, but this other guy come in at the end and he beat me by one minute. One fucking minute." Open-mouthed, Grizzly gawked at Jack as if he wanted approval or some sign of recognition.

"One minute more in seniority," the man repeated in disgust.

The silence lay heavy between them. To Jack's relief, the grizzled man said nothing more as the hours ticked by.

By evening, several seamen had given up and left, but Jack and Grizzly remained. When the cook's position was finally posted on the board, seven men rushed to the window. Jack joined the line, a step ahead of the grizzled man. When Jack reached the window, he put down his card and he got the job.

Just as Grizzly stepped up, the window slammed shut.

Outside the union hall, Jack hailed a cab for the short ride to Blount Island.

He tossed and turned. It had not gone well on board that ship…

After eight that evening, Jack boarded *El Barco de Oro*. The chief mate greeted him. "You the new cook?" he asked.

"Yes, sir, reporting for duty." He had a sea bag slung over his shoulder and he wore a backpack. Inside it were his new passport, his loaded Glock—he knew weapons were banned on the ship, but he'd take the chance—a new untraceable pre-paid cell phone, and a device that he needed to keep hidden. The sharp edges of the contents of his sea bag dug into his back, but he was immune to pain.

"You're fast. Must have been there in the union hall when they posted it."

"Yes, sir, I was."

"Got your papers?"

"Yes, sir."

"Report to the third mate. He's up on the bridge."

"Yes, sir." He went up to the bridge and waited until the third mate saw him, then handed his papers to him. It was a cursory review. Jack knew they needed him.

"Okay. Sergey, eh?" The third mate peered at Jack with eyebrows raised. "You Russian or something?"

"No, sir."

"Well, all right, Sergey, this seaman will escort you to the galley so you can check it out and then to your cabin. You'll need to get cracking. We've got some hungry seamen on board here…and one woman," he added.

"This way, follow me," said the seaman, who led Jack down to the galley. He took it all in—his first time in a ship's galley. He slid his hands over the gleaming stainless-steel counters and pulled open drawers, like a dog marking his territory. The seaman then led him to his cabin.

He entered his cabin and closed the door, noting that there was no lock on it. He then carefully stowed his sea bag and backpack under his bed. Inside his sea bag was the device he'd use later. After changing into kitchen whites, he headed back to the galley and, once there, gathered his crew together—his assistant cooks and the steward—ready to take command of the next meal's preparations.

"Okay, that will be all," Jack announced. "See you at… What time do you report in the morning?"

"0500," they said in unison.

"Make it 04:30 hours. We'll need more time to set up for special orders."

"Yes, sir," they responded.

He returned to his cabin, where he set his alarm and fell into a deep sleep. He dreamed of Melanie, dancing, her long, slim legs on tiptoes, her long blond hair awash in the moonlight, and, on her face, a come-hither grin meant only for him.

Chapter 12

He'd been cooking omelets to order when he spotted Melanie in the line. What was she doing on this ship? He was amazed at his luck, that he'd found her again. When a seaman offered his plate, Jack served him and asked, "Who's the woman back there?" nodding in her direction.

The seaman glanced at the line behind him, "That's the second mate. She's cool. Everyone likes her, even the captain. She's like one of the guys. Name's Melanie."

After she'd given him the note to meet at her cabin after her watch, he helped clean the kitchen, planned the noon meal, and retired to his cabin to think.

This changed everything. Now he couldn't blow up this ship. How would he explain this to the Ukrainian oligarchs? They could be dangerous. He decided to call Harry. Perhaps Harry could help get him out of this mess. But what to tell Harry? After the Paris mission, he'd failed to report in. The CIA must think he'd gone rogue. He struggled to form a clear story. He'd have to come up with one soon. Memories of past missions haunted him—his years as a Marine sniper in Iraq and Afghanistan. Then the CIA recruited him and made him an agent with license to kill. He still remembered each kill—they haunted him at night. Therapy sessions at Langley with Dr. Treslow had helped, until he could no longer trust him. He couldn't wait to put aside this crazy sideshow about bombing the ship and focus on Melanie. He dialed Harry's number and got the message machine. He tried to sound normal.

"Hey, Harry. It's me, Jack Pierce. Sorry I've been off the grid. We need to talk. I can explain everything. I'll call later. Bye."

What if he just canceled the mission? Or postponed it? It was time to quit. Jack would think about the assignment later and try to get his head clear. His mind returned to Melanie. She had rejected him long ago, after he'd helped her. Now it would be different. She would come around. He had never lost his love for Melanie. There had never been other women. After they'd formed that bond in school—she even came to see him off to the Marines—he'd saved himself for her. He recalled how he'd told her everything about himself all through the years in his emails to her, and she'd shared with him, too. She was his first and only love. He would tell her again, and this time she would show her love for him. He knew some would say it was an obsession, but it was a good obsession, wasn't it? It was like all the romance stories he'd ever read or seen—the guy pursues the girl, and, eventually, if he persists, she comes around.

Jack was about to return to the galley to prepare lunch—this cook's job was becoming a hassle—and as he opened the door to his cabin, a figure in whites darted down the corridor and out of sight. What the hell! Male. Big guy. Had to be the steward. *Why is he here*? Jack slipped a telltale piece of string into the door jamb and carefully secured it shut with the almost invisible string in place. In the galley, he noticed when the steward took his break and made the decision not to follow him. But when the steward returned, he glanced at Jack, and Jack could see that his face looked flushed.

He waited until the steward left the galley and then headed for his cabin to check his door. No sign of the steward, but the string was gone. Jack checked his sea bag and backpack—nothing seemed disturbed. But the steward had been in his cabin. He must have seen everything. He would report it. And then they'd inspect his cabin, and he'd be caught. He had to stop the steward from getting to anyone. He started for the elevator, then stopped. Too late. The steward must have reached the elevator by now and was already headed to the bridge.

His breathing slowed as he sorted through his options. He could explain the weapon—against the rules, it would merit a slap on the wrist—he'd bet other seamen carried and took the risk. But the device? No way.

It was either hide it or seize the opportunity to install it as planned. He wouldn't arm it, not now. Just get it out of here fast. He grabbed his backpack, removed his Glock and inserted it into his shoulder holster, and pocketed his cell phone. Carefully, he placed the device in his backpack, shouldered it, and headed for the galley to pick up a box of coffee. He headed down to the boiler room with the coffee. If anyone questioned him, he was giving out coffee to the engine and boiler room crews.

He heaved open the metal door to the engine room. A wall of humid heat assaulted his lungs, and the noise, a cacophony of engine sounds, assailed his ears and drowned out human voices. He made his way past turning screws, turbines, and pipes. His photographic mind, trained to pick up minute details, searched for hiding places. Not yet. Get to the boilers. Jack put on an engaging smile and casually asked, "Which way to the boiler room?"

The heat was even more intense in the boiler room. Before what looked like a control panel, a man sat at a desk reading a magazine. Jack could see no one else around. He offered the man coffee and asked for a quick tour, and the boiler man thankfully obliged. Time was running out. He saw what he needed to see and cut the tour short. "Got to get back to the galley," he said. On the way back, he left the device in a small storage area opposite one of the boilers, hiding it behind boxes. It looked to remain undetected, at least for a day or two. He quickly retraced his steps to the exit door, then climbed the stairs to the galley, entering without notice.

It was mid-afternoon when he tried to make the call to the

General on his cell phone, but there was no reception, so he sneaked out onto the top deck to try the reception there. He was buffeted by the howling wind. It was crazy out there. *What's with this weather?* He locked his arms around a ladder rung, whipped out his cell phone, and saw that he had a signal. He left a short message: "Mission's canceled. Will call you later."

PART 3

Living with Survival

Chapter 13

John Edmonds had never tried a case like this. He stood at his desk—he'd always liked a standing desk. Edmonds' Portland office was spare, almost spartan; a handful of family photos lined his bookcase, together with a black-and-white photo of a young and serious law clerk standing next to a smiling robed judge. In a white shirt with his trademark bow tie, he bent his lanky frame to stare out the window.

Below him lay a picturesque Maine tableau—lobster boats at a pier piled high with metal traps and strewn with ropes and gear. Above them, dozens of white seagulls blanketed the black roof, where they perched, heads aligned on parade, awaiting an approaching fishing boat. As it entered the slip, they peeled off like fighter planes, wheeling in the air with raucous cries, then swooping down for an easy meal.

John Edmonds thought of the Downs family. Mary Downs had pleaded for him to take the case. The search for survivors had been called off. Now these families were angry, and they wanted answers. What happened to *El Barco de Oro* and why? Why had this ship sailed into the teeth of a category-four hurricane? They wanted money but also the truth. John Edmonds would get them justice. After a distinguished career, he still had a fire in his belly like all great trial lawyers. He knew that it would not be an easy meal.

Edmonds knew that admiralty or maritime law was a specialty

that few understood and fewer undertook. There were federal statutes, and there were probably other laws, state and federal, and maybe even common law, that presented landmines for seamen and their families.

The first key issue in every plaintiff's case? How soon do you have to sue before you are time-barred? Edmonds figured he knew what he didn't know and was not afraid to admit it. It was just one of his strengths. And so, he looked for an admiralty lawyer. There were a couple in Maine, but he guessed that this case would have to be brought in the Florida courts. He was not admitted to the Florida bar, but any lawyer could associate with local counsel and seek admission *pro hac vice,* for that case only. He made inquiries and then called Tobias Chesterfield in Miami.

They'd met at an American Bar function. Edmonds remembered Tobias, who wore his long white hair tied back into a ponytail. Juries loved him. He'd won big jury verdicts. They would make a wonderful contrast—Edmonds, the Maine Yankee, dressed impeccably, his voice so quiet you strained to hear every word, and the wild, bombastic Tobias, who was now telling him the bad news first, just as Edmonds would have done.

"Pegasus will file an action in federal court in Jacksonville to bar all these lawsuits. Take my word for it, they'll do it soon, so we'll have a short deadline for filing suit and a bunch of hurdles to overcome. This federal law is no friend of the seaman. We'll need to get around it to get them what they deserve. Pegasus will claim all they get is the value of the ship."

So, tell me the good news. Edmonds, impatient, jumped in. "Are there ways around it?" he asked.

"Sure. We'll find a way. For one thing, if we can show Pegasus was negligent, we can get around those limitations. I think we should file tomorrow in federal court." Edmonds liked Tobias already.

"You know, John, we'll basically be defending Captain

Downs."

"I know," said Edmonds. "Pegasus will try to cast all the blame on him."

"So, let's nail the bastards."

Next day, they filed suit and began discovery. Edmonds put his own seasoned investigator, Paul Appleby, on the case. Now Appleby sat stiffly on a hard wooden Harvard chair; he pulled out his pen and yellow pad and waited for his instructions. He knew better than to interrupt Edmonds, who seemed to be reading a memorandum at his standing desk. Appleby chuckled to himself. Some junior associate was going to be horrified to learn that Edmonds' red pen was scratching comments all over the draft. Soon, Edmonds put down his pen, sat opposite Appleby, and looked up, seeming to expect answers from the investigator.

"What would you like me to do?" asked Appleby.

"You know there are two survivors?"

Appleby nodded in the affirmative. He already knew he was assigned to the El Barco case.

"They could be key witnesses."

"What are we wanting from them?" Appleby knew that witnesses could be coached, within certain ethical bounds, but that Edmonds would be all over him if he went too far.

"They're likely to know what caused the ship to go down. Hopefully, whatever the cause, it was something that made the ship unseaworthy, and we'll try to show that Pegasus knew about it. Kind of important, Paul."

Edmonds laid it out. Melanie Ricker's parents were reportedly Maine residents and could be easily found. They would know how to contact their daughter, who might be persuaded to help those families who'd lost their loved ones, especially the widow of her lost captain. However, this Sergey Robichek, the cook, was another story; seems like no one knew his whereabouts. He'd gone missing. "Very strange," said Edmonds.

The discussion ended with a clear message to Appleby. "I'm counting on you," Edmonds said.

Chapter 14

Red-haired Nurse Lizzie checked on her patient. His blue eyes followed her everywhere. She was hardened to her patients and to their pain and bodily functions. She focused on their charts and the orders; she followed procedure, and she got through her shift. But this one made it difficult for her to concentrate. Lots of male patients flirted with her, but this one, with the chiseled physique of a male model and a wry smile and those piercing blue eyes, he was dashing. And she liked how he flattered her, asked about her life, like was she married? No, she replied with a twinkle in her eye. She wondered how he was able to get information from her before she knew it. She'd never hooked up with a former patient, but this one? Yeah.

***

Jack knew that Nurse Lizzie liked him. He pleaded with her and told her how he hated publicity and all those cameras. Being shy, he wanted no credit and felt guilty to have survived. Convincing and charming, he told her not to get in trouble. She got him his clothes and his valuables—his I.D., some cash, and the key. Not his gun— they'd confiscated it. That's okay. He'd replace it later.

He walked the corridors with casual ease, and no one noticed him. Off the elevator, he noticed the cameras and didn't care. Soon, he'd be long gone. Then the easy walk to a bus stop and the trip to

Jacksonville. The bus stopped at Jacksonville airport, where he used the key to open the locker. Inside, the key to the safe deposit box. Thank God, he remembered after all these months. There were times when he'd forgotten who he was and how to get back to Langley. He took the bus downtown to the bank. With steady nerves and steely eyes, he signed his name, Jack Pierce, showed his I.D., and the bank official escorted him inside the thick safety deposit door. They used their keys, his and hers, to open the lockbox. She left him alone in a tiny windowless room. Inside the box, he found a new passport with his photo over the name "Jacob Pierce," a gun and bullets, a concealed weapon permit, and ten thousand dollars in cash inside a money belt. Back in the nondescript motel, he went about changing his looks. He shaved his beard, clipped and colored his hair, and set out his new clothes. Naked, he looked in the mirror and didn't recognize himself. The Ukrainian oligarchs would never find him.

He got out of the shower, shaved, and dressed as the television blared in the background. He strapped on this money belt to the mellow voice of Lester Holt, who was questioning an attractive young blond woman.

"So, tell us how you managed to survive," said Holt's admiring voice.

Jack slid his sidearm into the holster at his side, covering it with his shirt. Intrigued by Holt's question, he stepped closer to see the television screen through the bathroom door, and there was her unmistakable face. "Holy shit!" Looking perky and recovered from her ordeal, Melanie brushed the hair from her eyes and smiled.

"I don't know. It was a miracle. One minute I was being tossed about by a hurricane, and next thing I knew, I was hoisted onto a navy helicopter and woke up in a hospital. The navy crews, the doctors and nurses, everyone, they were all amazing. I owe them all my life."

Her eyes, looking directly into the camera, bore into him as if she were in the room. That beautiful face he knew so well. That perfect hair, that iconic smile, that beauty—he was stunned. He'd thought no one else had survived. Memories rushed in, how he'd fallen for her. He laughed, delighted. He must seek her out. They'd share their experiences and resume their lives together. As he watched her, fascinated, he remembered what the steward, Bobby Irish, had spilled. He thought she might know things and might have questions. Because the steward might have told her what he'd discovered about his cook. That's okay, he thought. I can explain everything.

"So, what's next for you?" Holt was asking Melanie.

"Oh, I'm going back to Maine. While I was recovering, I missed some of the memorial services for my shipmates from Maine. But there is a service for our captain, Captain Downs, and I want to be there for that, because he's one of the real heroes in this tragedy."

"Of course. And then what?"

"I'll spend some time with my parents."

"Well, good luck to you, Melanie. And we wish you well in your recovery."

Chapter 15

The next morning, he boarded a Greyhound bus to Portland, Maine. He looked like any other tourist on vacation: torn jeans, bulky sweatshirt, leather jacket, and a Red Sox baseball cap over dark glasses. In his backpack, a loaded Glock, extra bullets, and his concealed weapon permit. He took a seat toward the rear of the bus. Behind his shades, his eyes darted about for danger signs. After arriving at the Portland bus station, he walked across Congress Street to a small, nondescript inn, registered under a false name, and paid cash in advance for the night. He rose early and took a taxi, driven by a Somali who spoke little English, to a used car lot, where he purchased a black Ford pickup truck, again using a false name; he paid extra to keep the plates and the registration under the name of the prior owner, who would tell any inquirer that he had his permission to use it. He then returned to his hotel and used the computer in the hotel's business office before checking out.

All the Maine newspapers told stories about *El Barco*, the grieving families, and the miracle of Melanie's survival. He could find no mention of another survivor. He read a story about Melanie's parents in the *Norway Advertiser*. Norway, a small town in the Oxford Hills of western Maine, a town with friendly, unsuspecting town officials who would have tax records open to the public on Monday morning.

Before leaving town, he decided to call his contact, Harry Field. He knew Harry would be disappointed. He'd failed to report in and

70

had gone missing. He'd explain. Harry would understand. And then Harry would pay him the money they owed him. He placed the call on a pay phone at the Greyhound bus station. No answer. Just a message machine. He expected this. The machine beeped and he had to say something.

"Hey, Harry, it's Jack Pierce. I want to talk with you. Pick up." He was ready to hang up when he heard the familiar, husky voice.

"Hello, is it you, Jack?" Jack could hear Harry's heavy breathing on the line.

"Yes, I picked up my real identity as Jack Pierce. I know I've been out of touch. Harry—"

"Well, you've been out of touch for weeks. You've got to come in. We're worried about you. Just come in and we'll help you."

***

Harry Field sat, breathless, in his office at Langley. He couldn't believe his luck. Jack Pierce, missing and now number one on the CIA's wanted list, had finally called in. Harry had a long history as Jack's handler. He listened closely to Pierce's voice on the recording, and then, in the silence, he heard background noise, an announcement of some kind. An airport?

"Jack, where are you?"

"I survived it, Harry, the hurricane." The voice sounded off somehow, high-pitched, breathy. "My God, it was crazy. The ship went down. The hurricane. I got caught up in it. You understand? I'm sorry, Harry. I didn't do anything to cause it, honest. They wanted me to. But it was the hurricane. That's what I need to discuss with you. It was a plot to blow up the ship, what I was working on, but I couldn't do it, and I didn't, and I couldn't tell you."

Harry couldn't believe what he was hearing. He hadn't dared to interrupt Pierce's voice—breathless, agitated, everything pouring out like an unstoppable stream, to Harry's growing sense that something seemed terribly wrong with his agent.

"The second mate, Melanie, she survived, too," said the familiar voice on the phone, unusually chatty. The Jack Pierce he knew had never been so excited. "Don't worry," continued the voice. "It may take a few days, but I promise you, I'll find her and find out what she knows. Soon. You can rely on me."

The phone went dead. Harry Field stared out his office window. One thing he knew—this Melanie was in danger.

Inside CIA headquarters at Langley, Harry Field called the IT Department. "Trace that call," he ordered. They knew which one—the call he'd just received from his former agent, Jack Pierce, a.k.a Sergey. NSA tracks some ordinary phone calls but not all. But a call to CIA headquarters presents no legal problems, and it's a simple trace. Harry knew he'd have the caller's whereabouts in an hour.

Harry was energized. He'd trained Pierce and taught him all his skills, until Pierce had become their best field agent for dirty work. Then, to Harry's surprise, Pierce had gone rogue. Now, Pierce was on the CIA's wanted list, and it was Harry Field's personal mission to bring him in, or otherwise. Well, Harry thought, I'd rather not face the alternatives; let's see if we can bring him in first. That was the plan, but all the leads had run cold. Until now. Harry Field would move heaven and earth to find his rogue agent, because now, finally, he'd made a mistake: he'd made contact. Harry Field was known to be dogged and patient. An hour later, his phone rang. It was from IT. Harry smiled.

"Gotcha."

They'd traced the call to the pay phone. Field dispatched Agent Alan Black to check the videotapes of all incoming passengers at the Greyhound station, a thankless task, but after watching for hours, Agent Black spotted a man with features that could not be completely masked by the bulky clothes, the baseball cap, and other efforts to conceal his appearance. The man looked up, right at the camera, with complete confidence and contempt.

"Name's Jack Pierce," Black reported to Field. "He arrived at Portland, Maine from Jacksonville three days ago."

"Good work."

"Want me to track him down?"

"Yes, find him. And Alan?"

"Yeah, what?"

"Don't make contact, and be careful. We don't know what he's up to. He's very dangerous. And I think he's delusional."

"How good is he?"

"Better than you," said Harry.

Before dispatching Alan Black to find Jack Pierce, Harry had done his homework and covered his bases within the CIA. First, he'd met with his boss, Daniel Robinson, director of Covert Operations. Robinson was a new appointee, a friend of the president. Harry had come to Robinson's office. Harry needed cover.

"So, you lost Jack Pierce," said Robinson.

"Yes. It happens sometimes," Harry said. "But now we've found him." It was always best to 'fess up, to admit your mistakes.

"We invest in all that training…," Robinson was saying.

Yes, Harry was thinking, we train them how to kill.

Robinson continued, "and they go off on their own, free from ties? What the hell?"

Yeah, it's called going rogue. His boss had stopped talking, and now Harry must explain the reasons for this. "It could mean several things," Harry said. "Sometimes the power goes to their head, and they get to thinking they're super-human and no longer need our direction or control, and they'd rather pick their own assignments."

"Unacceptable," said Robinson.

"Oh, yes, sir. I agree. Those agents are dangerous, and we must…" Harry hesitated. How should he put this?

"You take them out," Robinson said.

"Exactly. It's the last option. We don't like to, but—"

"So, what other reasons—"

"Well, sometimes they get fed up with their assignments, and they're no longer willing to kill, sort of like burnout. They're paid so well they can afford to cut loose and drop out."

"Go on," Robinson said.

"In those cases, we never find them, and it's just as well. I mean, they're not good to us any longer, so good luck to them. You see?"

"Yes, of course. I quite agree. I mean, it's our loss, but what can you do?"

"Precisely."

"So, what about this one? What do you call him now?"

"He was using an alias, Sergey, but now he's Jack Pierce again. Some of them get screwed up in the head, lost to themselves and us."

"So, what do you do then?"

"We try to do everything possible to get them back and to help them. I mean, we feel responsible for them. It's the right thing to do."

"Yes, of course, the right thing to do. So, your Sergey, or Jack Pierce, what's his situation, exactly?"

"We're not sure, exactly."

"So, what do we do with him?"

The ticking clock magnified the silence. Amused, Harry stood to take his leave. "I'm afraid, sir, we just have to wait until something happens. Maybe he comes in, maybe there's an incident, and then we assess and decide what to do."

"You know," said Robinson, freezing Harry at the door, "he's been a valuable agent ever since we…what exactly did we do to train him to be an assassin?"

"Oh, that. Yes, sir. It was a program we had back then. Been deep-sixed for years now. Forget about it, sir. Old history. Long forgotten."

"Right. Let sleeping dogs lie, as they say?"

"Yes, sir, let the dogs lie."

"Our boys and girls up on the Hill, you know, the Congress, they've never looked into it, right?"

"No, sir."

"Good. Just as well. Forget I asked about it."

"Asked about what, sir?"

"Ah. Very good, Harry, very good."

Chapter 16

Harry thought the meeting with Robinson had gone well. But he needed to know if his agent, Jack Pierce, was salvageable. Harry left his office and negotiated several corridors within the Langley labyrinth before entering the office of William Treslow, M.D.

Dr. Treslow's office had a couch, but he never used it. CIA's in-house psychiatrist, he was not there to treat CIA officials, though he did this on occasion. He was more like a consultant. Harry Field thought it was like the TV show *Criminal Minds*, where an FBI shrink would try to psychoanalyze the latest serial killer to help the team identify who they were looking for. But Harry knew the person he was looking for—an agent gone rogue—so he was doubtful Doc Treslow could help. There were photos behind the doctor's desk, showing him with various CIA directors all the way back to Bill Casey, and a black-and-white shot of him with Nixon. Harry couldn't help but think that maybe if Doc Treslow had treated Tricky Dick, things would have turned out differently.

White-haired, Doc Treslow was getting long in the tooth and looked weary of hearing more than any normal human could bear, but Harry figured Doc Treslow had access to drugs. As Harry told the story, Treslow leaned forward in his chair, flipping a pencil in his hands, his large brow furrowed, eyes narrowing. "Fascinating, fascinating," he repeated like a mantra. Finally, Harry fell silent, having unburdened himself, which was a kind of therapy, and he waited anxiously for the diagnosis, for some clue of what to do from this noble head. Harry's gut churned. Doc Treslow took his time, enjoying the day's sole distraction, pinched the bridge of his nose, and stared out at the immense parking lot. After a long sigh, he said: "I remember him. We had a few therapy sessions but that was long ago, so I can't give you a definitive diagnosis."

He's looking for a safe out, Harry thought. "I understand that you've got to qualify it but give me your opinion. Let's have it."

"It could be a split personality. I recall that he was in that top-secret conditioning program. Some of them were hypnotized, subjected to all kinds of stress. As a result, some developed multiple personality disorder. All that's banned now, thank God. But it's sounding like classic schizophrenia. Some of the symptoms are right out of the DSM." Harry knew of the *Diagnostic and Statistical Manual*, now in its fourth edition, a compendium of leading psychiatrists, the Bible on mental illness.

"Like what?"

"The most significant are the delusions, like he's been on some other assignment. And that fits the diagnosis—for example, thinking he's been assigned some other mission when it's just false, and then taking actions, apparently dangerous, even criminal, based upon these so-called assignments. And his anxiety. He admits he didn't do it, whatever it was he was assigned to do, and is feeling anxious that he failed to carry out his assignment. And apparently thinking this young woman, this survivor, is a threat to him, and that he intends to take care of it, or her. It all fits. Or perhaps he's obsessed with her. You recall he was abandoned and neglected as a child, so he's probably got some sort of attachment disorder, and that often leads to obsessive behavior, like a sexual fixation, perhaps with this woman he's talking about.

"All these things are as real to him as the things we know are true. He is, or was, an agent, and he knows you, his handler; and it appears he was able to find the safety deposit box and get his new papers, money, new name, and so forth. Am I making sense? Are these symptoms you've noticed?"

"So far, so good," said Harry.

"This is preliminary," said Doc Treslow, "because we don't know if there are other symptoms, for example, if his affect is flat, if he is hallucinating, if his speech is altered, and so forth. And we don't know if he's developed other personalities or how they might be triggered." His voice trailed off, and he waited for Harry to react and respond.

"So, what can I do to find him? And if I do find him, how do I bring him in? And if I do bring him in, can we treat him in-house, find out what he's done and help him? Would a polygraph do any good if he's out of touch with reality? Can we make him better? Is this treatable?"

"Whoa, whoa, too many questions. I got no crystal ball, Harry. My advice is, find him fast, bring him in. Then we'll see. We can try to help him. If not, maybe we cut him loose, turn him over to the authorities, after some deprogramming."

"How dangerous is he?"

"Scale of one to ten? He's a thirty."

"Shit," said Harry.

Harry knew he ought to warn her. He'd read the papers, seen her on Today. Melanie Ricker was now a national hero and celebrity. If they revealed who Jack Pierce is, everything could come out, all his covert missions. He could see it—Melanie would panic, and she or the cops would go public, resulting in disgrace to the agency, not to mention a ruined career for him. No. Not a good idea.

What was clear was he had a new top priority: finding Jack Pierce.

"Doc, not a word of this to the chain of command. Understood? That's an order."

Doc Treslow drew a line across his mouth. "Mum's the word. What else is new?"

<h1 style="text-align:center">Chapter 17</h1>

On a Saturday morning in early October, under a deep blue sky backlit by crimson and gold foliage, the memorial service for David Downs took place near Rockland on a promontory surrounded by a blue-green sea. Soft waves licked the shore and, receding over pebbles, sounded a low moan against the tinkling bells of offshore buoys. It was a celebration, but October days in Maine could break your heart.

Melanie reached out to Downs's widow, Mary Downs. Melanie's heart was breaking for Mary and her teenage boy, Jamie, about whom Melanie knew a great deal. Dave had shared with her his struggles to help Jamie with his autism or Asperger's; he was somewhere on the spectrum. Back at the reception at their home, she went to him. Jamie wandered around the dining room, its table overburdened with offerings from neighbors, a testament to their hometown hero. She couldn't help thinking, *he's so different from other kids*, and then felt bad for thinking this. Jamie traced his fingers over the table. He seemed to be lost in thought, oblivious to the adults surrounding him.

"Hey, Jamie," she whispered. She froze when his eyes locked on her. "I knew your dad, and he talked a lot about you. Did you know that? He thought you were terrific."

At first, Jamie remained silent, apparently buried in his own thoughts, and his face betrayed no emotion. And then his eyes focused, fixated on her. She could see this—he was attracted to her for some reason she did not understand, like he was reaching out to her, wanting to make the connection. It was not often that Jamie smiled, but he did now, and he didn't take his eyes off her. It was as if he yearned to hear more but couldn't ask for it. She understood and forged ahead.

"He loved you very much, Jamie. He was so proud of you. He said you were brilliant. He talked about everything you read."

"He did?" His words sounded of wonder, of missing his dad, and how this woman could help find him.

"Yes, he did. You were his favorite topic."

Jamie clung to her. When she spoke to Mary, there was Jamie at her side. It was amazing to Melanie because she knew from her late-night talks with Dave up on the bridge that Jamie was unable to make that kind of connection with anyone, and she could tell that he liked her. So, he had feelings after all. She took it as a sign, and she pledged to herself to get to know this boy who was on the spectrum, as they now called it. It was the least she could do for Mary and for Dave. And when it came time for Melanie to leave, Jamie followed her out the door until Mary had to pull him away.

"I'm going to come back to see you and Jamie," she told Mary. "Would that be all right?"

"Oh, yes, I would like that," Mary said.

Jamie's big eyes followed Melanie to her car.

***

It came as a shock to the families. The federal court in Jacksonville ruled on Pegasus's defense, barring all other lawsuits against it and limiting the total amount of damages that they, as a group, could collect. That limit was, said the court, the value of El Banco de Oro, which was now next to nothing. The only way around that draconian limit was if the plaintiffs could prove that Pegasus was negligent. As expected, Pegasus was blaming Captain

David Downs, and so were some of the victims' families.

Meanwhile, the navy found *El Barco de Oro*. She was sitting on the ocean floor, fifteen thousand feet below the surface, her first two decks having sheared off and her black box voyage recorder nowhere to be found.

Everyone eagerly awaited the findings of the National Transportation Safety Board, but no one expected them anytime soon. The NTSB said it could take eighteen months. A Coast Guard Board of Inquiry began interviews, dispatching an official to Maine to interview Melanie Ricker. The investigator couldn't understand these Maine Yankees. They looked with suspicion on all outsiders. No one was talking. The investigator found Melanie's parents, who claimed not to know where she'd gone. Very strange. In Portland, where Melanie had a home overlooking the water, no one had seen or heard from her since the captain's memorial service. The Portland attorney representing the Downs estate would not answer the investigator's calls.

Chapter 18

They sat by a picture window looking out at the lawn in front of the small one-story home at the edge of the sea.

"How do you do it?" Melanie asked Mary Downs.

"Well, you do it because you have to," said Mary. "There's no choice."

"Sorry, I wasn't much help with all my good intentions." Melanie had thought she could find herself in helping Jamie. "You must feel helpless at times."

"It takes a clear mind and resolve. It's a matter of intent. Sometimes nothing seems to work."

Melanie thought that this was true, that she herself was just like Jamie—nothing seemed to work for her either, now that she was done with her life at sea, now that she had no life. She'd fought the hurricane, and, to her surprise, she'd won, but she'd lost all her shipmates. And now there was nothing to fight for.

"I see what you mean. So, you can't have any expectations, right? That was my mistake, thinking I could swoop in with all my good intentions and sympathy, and he would just melt and suddenly change."

"Right. Like he could become normal, just like that. I mean, he is so far from normal, and sometimes I despair at the idea he will ever be normal. And at times, he is so loveable, and I chastise myself for ever thinking—"

"I know. He's worth it, Mary, and I don't know if I can help, but

I will try, even if it's just to be here with you and to share the experience."

So, they formed a bond. And Melanie read up on it, but she needed to talk with someone.

She called a local child psychiatrist she found online and made the appointment. Up a flight of stairs, she noted the name on the opaque glass door, Susan Deering, M.D. Feeling sheepish, she opened the door to a small, vacant waiting room with the usual magazines and uncomfortable straight chairs. She sat to wait, feeling conspicuous, hoping to see no one she knew. A door opened. The doctor appeared and ushered out a young woman who looked flustered, teary, and somewhat familiar. It seemed Dr. Deering saw adults, too. Dr. Deering asked Melanie to enter her office. First impression: middle-aged, curly hair with a touch of gray, a bit heavy, she must enjoy life; and a winning smile that crinkled her tanned face. Melanie was reminded of her mother. And there was the couch, of course. Would she have to lie on it? The office was comfortable but stylish. A picture window behind a desk offered a view of the harbor filled with expensive yachts. Dr. Deering motioned her to sit in the chair in front of her desk. Thank goodness, not the couch.

"So," said Dr. Deering. "Do you want to tell me about yourself."

"Oh! I didn't come here for myself. You see—"

"So, you're here to seek help for someone else, not for yourself?"

This made Melanie think. Why had she come? Had she been lying to herself? She needed help for…what? Jamie, yes. But for the first time, Melanie realized that it was she, herself, who needed help. And here was someone who just maybe could… No. Preposterous. She'd been foolish to come here, and she stood to leave.

"I'm…I'm not sure. You see, I've been trying to find myself, and I stupidly thought that maybe I could help this young boy. He's the son of the captain of my ship, the one that sank in the hurricane, and he has what is, I think, Asperger's, and…"

"Of course," said Dr. Deering. "I read about that tragedy. I'm so sorry for your loss. It's a terrible burden to be the survivor when everyone else perished. How do you handle it?"

It was a question that no one had asked her, and it opened all that had lain hidden in her all these months when she'd been alone in the world. It's the question she'd never asked herself. She was, after all, the survivor, and she was supposed to act the part, the hero, alone to atone for them all. Is it possible that this woman understood?

"I can't." It just slipped out, but it was true, she now realized.

Dr. Deering came to her and sat beside her. "It's safe here, Melanie. You don't need to bear it alone. It's going to be okay."

Melanie told her the story, as much as she could recall, of how she somehow survived. As she talked, the memories came flooding back.

"Have you had dreams about it?"

"Oh yes, all the time."

"Tell me about them."

She told her about the underwater dreams that had kept waking her since she was a little girl and how they returned when she was at sea.

Dr. Deering gently probed until Melanie had to tell her. "I was very young when he died."

"Your brother?"

How did she know? "Yes. Charlie was a year younger than me."

"I know it's hard for you. Can you talk about it now?"

She could not. She needed time.

"That is perfectly all right," said Dr. Deering. "You let me know when you can come back to see me again, and I will be here for you."

Out on the narrow streets full of tourists and shops, Melanie realized she'd never talked about Jamie's problems and how to help him. She'd talked about herself the whole hour, about her feelings.

Melanie checked her purse for the card—another appointment with Dr. Deering. She recalled Dr. Deering's parting words: "Remember, you've got to be whole before you can help others. And I will help you get there." It was the permission she needed.

The morning fog lifted over the harbor.

She drove up to see her parents at the farm in North Norway. It was hard to go back. They'd moved from the city to the farm while she was at the academy, after her grandparents were gone.

Chapter 19

Investigator Paul Appleby sat on a sofa admiring the bucolic scene outside—a small, reedy pond surrounded by a mown field in which five majestic llamas grazed alongside two horses, their heads covered with protective mesh to keep off bugs, and in the background, a sea of dark green firs and pines. He removed a yellow legal pad from his briefcase with his list of points to cover for Melanie's deposition, scheduled for early Monday at his Portland office. She'd agreed to meet him at her parents' farm in North Norway on a Sunday morning.

Paul Appleby was not alone. With him, a bright green and yellow parrot in a cage listened intently to every sound. Melanie entered briskly, offering him a cup of tea. She took a seat directly across from him. His first thought upon seeing her: she doesn't act like a hero, like a survivor against all odds. He would not have bet on her, this nervous, sweet-looking young girl, among all the able-bodied seamen, to be one of only two survivors. He knew looks could be deceiving. She must be of stronger mettle than first appeared. He balanced the teacup in his lap and warmed to his subject—the lawsuit and their need for her assistance to help the families of those who'd perished. He got right to the point—better not to ask for her help, just assume it. "Why did *El Barco* go down, and why did you let her sail into a hurricane?"

It was difficult for her at first, and the memories kept intruding, but as she talked, her voice steadied, and she began to tell the story matter-of-factly, just as a jury would want to hear it, and Paul knew she would be great. She talked about the pressure her captain had to endure from corporate, her suggested change in route, rejected by her captain and corporate, then the shocking change in Hilda's direction and intensity when it was too late. That's all okay, Paul was thinking, no one wants to blame the gallant captain who went down with his ship, or this sweet-looking young woman. But the ship's condition, the boilers scheduled for overhaul, the deck top-heavy with stacked containers, the ship's taking on water and listing, and the smashing of vehicles below decks all contributed. And, symbolizing how old and outdated this ship was: the lifeboats were open-sided, not unlike the ones on the *Titanic*.

The picture that emerged was of an old ship that should have been scrapped before it unexpectedly met Hilda. It added up to a compelling story, and Melanie would put a human face on it—her crew members, all heroes, now lost, except for her and one other. Her survival story would captivate the jury. As they talked, he understood there was a mettle there, a strength, a willpower in this girl. Underneath the long blond hair and sweet smile, there was grit. A farm girl from western Maine, she was not one to quit. Now that he knew her, he understood.

When he brought up the other survivor, he noticed subtle changes. She became more hesitant, nervous, and fidgety.

"What do you know of him, this Sergey Robichek, and his whereabouts?"

"Nothing. Nothing. I haven't heard from him."

Interesting. Didn't ask that.

"Did you know him onboard ship? He was new with this trip, as I understand it."

"Yes, well…" she started. "Of course, he was the cook, so I saw him in the galley. That's all." Something about her, the way she suddenly stopped speaking, suggested to Paul that there was more to it. Or maybe he was imagining it. He waited for her to continue, but she said nothing more.

"Did the two of you see each other in the hospital?"

"Oh no. I was not even aware he survived, that he was there in the same hospital, until, when I was about to leave, one of the nurses told me he'd walked out. And I thought that was weird, but maybe he wanted to avoid all the publicity that I've had to face."

"Well, if he contacts you, would you let us know?"

"Sure."

He said goodbye to Melanie, her mother, and the parrot, who stared but said not a word to him.

Chapter 20

She should have told the investigator. After he left, Melanie thought about the phone call from Jack.

The night she'd arrived at her parents' farm, she couldn't sleep. She was looking out the window and drinking up the scene—a harvest moon—when she felt a chill. She had turned on the light in the room and realized she could be seen by someone outside. Silly, she thought, it's a field and a forest. Who could be there?

Next morning, she was having coffee in the kitchen and soaking in the morning sun when the phone rang; it was the house phone, so she almost let it go to voicemail but decided to answer.

"Good morning, Melanie." The voice sounded familiar. "I'd like to come by and talk with you." She almost leaped out of her chair. The distinctive, familiar voice.

"Is this…Jack? Oh, my God! I heard you made it, too! And then you took off…"

"Yes. It's good to hear your voice. Please don't tell anyone I called. I don't want all those media people on me. You know what I mean?"

"Yes. Where are you? And how did you…?" She felt an alarm inside. Something was off. Why was he calling, and why here?

"Yes, I tracked you down, and I saw you last night…and we need to talk."

"What? You saw me?" She remembered the chill last night. He must have been out there. Oh, my God!

"Yes, with your parents."

"But how…?"

"You're famous, a celebrity. And you said you were going there. Not difficult. So…"

"Jack, I can't see you here."

"Why not? It's your parents' place, right?" How did he know that? She did not want to see him there at her parents' farm.

"It's complicated." She was thinking, where can we meet? A public place, where it's safe? "I can meet you at the Park and Ride at the Gray Turnpike exit. I've got a blue Mazda Miata, one of those sporty roadsters. And you?"

"Ford pickup truck, black, Maine plates."

I'm not getting in his car, she thought, and he's not getting in mine. "Okay, meet there tomorrow morning at ten, and we'll drive to the Dunkin' Donuts and talk inside."

"You might not recognize me."

"What, camouflage?"

"Sort of."

Melanie was alarmed. Before the ship went down, she'd learned some things about Jack. She remembered asking him why he called himself Sergey. In hindsight, his explanation now sounded suspect. Then there was Peter's call from the bridge. Poor Peter, her good friend and third mate, now gone. She'd returned to her cabin to rest before she took the twelve-to-four watch. Peter had called her about the missing steward. "I'll see if he's in his bunk," she told him. But when she checked his bunk, he wasn't there. She called Peter back.

"Want me to do a full search?" she asked.

"No," he replied, "too much going on…" Then he added, "Hey, Mel, I remember now that I talked with the steward before he disappeared. He said he'd searched the cook's cabin and claimed he saw a handgun and a strange device in a sack under his bed. When I checked the steward's cabin, there was nothing there. And Irish didn't like the cook, right? So, I thought his story was bogus. But now that Irish has disappeared, God, I don't know. The cook, this Sergey, maybe he found out the steward was ratting him out. You think I'm nuts?"

"Yeah, completely," she told Peter. "Forget about it." Jack had just been in her cabin, sweaty and flushed because he'd come from the steaming hot kitchen. And she'd seduced him. Kill the steward and then make love to her? Nobody's that callous. Ridiculous. She thought she knew Jack. Back in their high school days, he'd been sweet on her. He'd saved her. And he'd written to her and waited for her. The thought of his soft caresses, his body smooth all over to her touch. Clearly, he'd not been in a fight. Or had he?

No. Impossible. It was after she'd heard Peter's broadcast: "Attention, all hands. The steward is missing. Not seen in the galley. If you locate him, please report to the bridge." Then she'd bumped into the chief mate, who told her he'd sent the steward out on deck with a few other deck hands to tie down loose containers. "I had no business doing that," the chief had said. "Poor guy. He got swept into the sea with the others."

Chapter 21

Saturday morning, the pickup pulled in beside her little sports car at the Park and Ride. She drove to the Dunkin' Donuts shop and entered. He must have followed her.

At first, she didn't recognize him. The man who came toward her booth was about her age, nice-looking, clean-shaven, wearing jeans, a red-and-white checkered shirt, dark glasses, and a Red Sox cap, which he removed to reveal a crew-cut. His athleticism, stealth, and the sidelong glances gave him away. Most local Mainers looked nothing like that—they slouched into their seats or booths with their flabby pouches and long hair. Or the young boys, so innocent, loud, and obnoxious, but cute, too, jabbering about their games, telling jokes, stealing looks at girls. Jack slipped into the booth, eyes alert.

"You look so different, Jack," she said. "How come?" He was jittery, on edge. So was she.

"Look." he said, coming closer, lowering his voice to a whisper, "Now that we're together, we need to talk."

"What do you mean? We're not together. We had sex once, that's all."

"Sure, sure, I know, but we love each other." She tried to interrupt him, but he continued to spill out his words in a rush.

"Mel, Mel. I just came here to make sure you understand what we're dealing with. I mean, there are some bad people I worked for, but they're not the problem, because they think I'm dead, that I drowned. The problem is the CIA—I used to work for them—but you can't just up and leave them. They're probably looking for me right now." His eyes searched the room for danger before returning his gaze to her.

She tried to follow his explanation, but everything he said made the story more confusing. She had to ask him: "Jack, you came to my room right after the steward disappeared." His eyes, no longer roaming the room, remained riveted on her, and it made her nervous, but she was safe in a public place, wasn't she? "I need to know if you were involved, Jack, because I never got to ask you, and then the ship went down."

"What do you mean 'involved?'"

"I mean, did you make him disappear?"

"Why would I do that?" He sounded hostile, and it scared her.

"Because he told the third mate that the steward had been in your room, and he found a gun and maybe a bomb there, and when the mate inspected your room, they were gone." Now she'd said it, and it made time stop. She watched him as he sat there, unmoving, thinking fast.

"So, there's nothing to prove I did anything." It was a statement, not a question. "Look," he said, bending closer to her, "I'm glad that you asked me about this, because I wanted to explain—so many of those deck hands got washed overboard, and I heard that he was one of them, but I don't know why he was out there. I mean, he was a steward, for God's sake. Mel, I really don't know what happened to him, but I didn't make him disappear. You've got to believe me."

She wanted to believe him. And he'd given her the same story she'd heard from the chief mate. So, the steward got washed overboard.

"Okay," she said, "I understand. But why are you in disguise and running away from the CIA?"

"Because I've had enough of it. I need to get away from them."

"So, are we both in danger?"

"We're safe, Melanie. It's going to be okay." He sat back in his seat.

She tried to relax, but she wanted to leave. "I'm not sure we can see each other anymore."

"What do you mean?" he whispered, a new urgency in his voice.

"I mean, you're in danger, and I need some time to think about all this. So, for now, I'd rather not see you. Do you understand?"

"No. No. I need to see you, Mel. You're why I came here. I told you I still love you."

"But it's not real, Jack. I don't know if I love you. I mean, I've always felt sorry for you, but—"

"Sorry for me? Why? What do you mean? When we were together on the ship, it was wonderful, wasn't it?"

"Well, yes, it was, I agree. It was nice. But I'm not ready to be with you."

She had to get out of there. She left him sitting in the booth, his head in his hands.

Chapter 22

Driving back to the farm, something nagged her, like a sore tooth that won't go away. She kept replaying their conversation in her mind, and she tried to make it fit her reality. New questions kept popping up. Think. Jack shows up after the cook disappears. Did he kill the former cook? Jack Pierce, the CIA spy, licensed to kill. Trained to kill by the Marines. What bothered Melanie was the common thread that ran through his entire life, or what she knew of it—a life of violence. From childhood, probably beaten by his Marine father, and a life on the streets. How do you trust a spy? Or the CIA? Why would someone want to blow up the ship? There were so many questions. Was he really CIA? And why would they want to kill him? And what was he doing here, tracking her down? Was he really in love with her? It seemed like an obsession. Would he follow her?

She had taken him to bed because she thought she knew him. And, because of that, he'd followed her to Maine. I don't know him at all, she thought. There's danger all around him. Nothing but danger.

What had she done?

She called Paul Appleby and told him about Jack's contacting her and her meeting with him. And it was so bizarre—he'd changed his name to Sergey and now he was Jack Pierce again. Appleby agreed to meet her earlier than planned on Monday.

Driving down Route 26 past Poland Springs on a crisp fall

morning, she spotted what looked like a black Ford pickup in her rear-view mirror. Spooked, she let it pass and was relieved—a woman behind the wheel. On the turnpike, there were so many pickups it was hard to tell. She parked on the pier off Commercial Street, took the elevator to the fifth floor, and sat in the reception area graced by paintings by Maine artists, this morning's *Portland Press Herald*, and a few classy magazines.

"Well, hello again," boomed a cheery Paul Appleby, in white shirt and tie, looking more businesslike than when he'd visited the farm. Inside the glassed-in conference room, they sat around a table. She liked the modernist touch to the old, restored brick walls. A young woman, whom Paul introduced as Allison Collins, with short brown hair, quietly pretty and confident, joined them with yellow pad and pen at the ready.

"Mr. Edmonds is tied up," said Paul. "He'll join us in a moment for your deposition. While we have a few minutes, why don't you tell me again what you told me on the phone, about this Sergey or Jack Pierce, his call, and your meeting with him. Sounded a bit strange."

She went through it again, how she'd met Jack as a teenager and then on the ship and they'd made love and then the ship sank in the hurricane and they both survived. And now he'd followed her to Maine. She told him some of what Jack said at Dunkin', but not all of it because it sounded so absurd they wouldn't believe her and because she worried what would happen if Jack found out.

"This is the first time you've heard from him since the rescue at sea?"

"Yes."

"Why do you think he contacted you in this way?"

"He says he loves me, but it's like a fixation or an obsession."

"That sounds very strange. Do you think you're in any danger?"

"Yes. He says he's CIA. I know it sounds unbelievable."

"Really. Let us do some digging. Is there anywhere you can go to get away for a while?"

"No. Not really. Any suggestions?"

"I have one," offered Ms. Collins. "I'll talk with you about it right after the deposition."

At the deposition, Melanie sat next to John Edmonds in the glassed-in conference room, surrounded by lawyers she didn't know.

"Good morning, Miss Ricker. I'm the attorney for Pegasus Shipping."

He seemed nice. Well dressed, expensive suit and tie. She remembered John Edmonds' admonition: "They are here to destroy you. He's not your friend."

They badgered her and it was relentless, and it lasted all day. It was her first deposition, and she thought she'd been prepared for it, but nothing can prepare you to be savaged like that. The worst part, she recalled afterward, was when they tried to force her to admit that Captain Downs had slept through the last hours of the crisis.

"Ms. Ricker," said the attorney, "you've said you were on the bridge with the chief mate on the morning of Thursday, October 1, from about 1:30 a.m. to about 2:30 a.m. Where was the captain during that time when your ship was in the throes of the hurricane?"

"He was in his cabin, sir."

"Sleeping?"

"I don't know." It was true, thanks be to God. She added, "He was available to us at all times," then recalled, too late, Edmond's advice—never feel the need to add anything.

"He was, was he? And did you ever try to reach him?"

"I don't recall."

"You don't recall because he'd instructed you not to call him?"

"No, sir, that's not true!"

Afterward, sitting in Edmonds' office, she felt like roadkill and hated all lawyers. Except John Edmonds. Anyway, it was over, thank God. Edmonds told her, "You were wonderful, Melanie, and you took full responsibility for the decision to try to outrun the hurricane, and there's no question about it—the ship sank because of what no one could have anticipated, the loss of power. Maybe they'll blame Pegasus for that, but they won't blame Captain Downs, because the jury will love you. You can feel proud. They didn't lay a hand on you. Go get some rest. Have a drink. And forget about this case. I understand Allison has some place for you to go to get away for a while."

Relief washed over her. She felt like crying. But it wasn't about her. It was about Captain Downs, and she thought of Mary and Jamie. Now it was time to get out of town. Allison had just the place, Greenville. God, such a long drive. Already afternoon. She brightened at the prospect of something new and a way out.

Chapter 23

Melanie pulled off the road in front of the small shop and slumped against the steering wheel of Allison Collins' Toyota Corolla. Late afternoon, she was alone in this little town on a lake on the edge of the wilderness. She looked up at the sign over the shop door: Maine Guide Fly Shop, North Woods Tours.

To get here, she'd driven three hours—up the Maine Turnpike, then north on Route 15 through tiny towns. In Monson, hikers passed through, about to enter upon the Appalachian Trail's most difficult last leg, the "Hundred Mile Wilderness," a punishment for those who'd made it from Georgia to Maine. The trail ended on top of Mount Katahdin. The foliage almost past peak, the hardwoods protested with red, yellow, and orange. Fishing season long over, northern Maine was hunkering down. Winter's chill, already in the works, threatened below zero temps. Howling winds would soon descend from Canada. Up here in the north woods, no tourist buses paraded past full of leaf peepers—they'd wisely confined themselves to parts farther south; instead, Subarus and pickups sported rifles in their rear windows. Bird hunters parked their cars on side roads; occasionally, one strutted along the highway in blaze orange, shotgun cracked open.

At the top of a rise, she'd noticed the Indian Hill Motel and, down below, the deep blue waters of Moosehead Lake stretching into the distance beyond the town of Greenville. She wondered again what she was doing on the edge of the Maine north woods.

What was she thinking? She'd signed up for a late-fall canoe trip after recovering from warmer, wilder waters. It was because of Allison, so enthusiastic about Greenville and this Maine Guide.

And Paul agreed that a week in the north woods would be the perfect escape. "Give us time to discover more about Jack Pierce," he said, "or whoever he is."

At this moment, she wanted nothing more than a hot shower and a night's sleep in a warm bed. Her escape and evasion tactics must have worked. They'd switched cars, Allison driving off with Melanie's Miata—her hooded head would be mistaken for that of Melanie, who'd waited inside to make her departure. At the Gray Turnpike exit, Melanie's parents had passed her a duffel with clothes and accessories. She could buy whatever else she might need for the wilderness.

Here goes nothing, she thought, as she pushed open the door. A bell tinkled. Inside, glass-covered cases displayed dry flies and streamers—a sign said they were hand-tied—and in a corner, a television screen showed an underwater video of trout in a stream, sure to make a fly fisherman eager to buy the tasty lures on display.

"Hello," she called out. No response. A logbook with signatures and comments from visitors lay open on the counter, and she was engrossed in it when she was startled by a woman's husky voice behind her.

"Can I help you?"

Melanie turned to see a rather tall and wiry young woman, hands on hips, wavy black hair, standing in tight-fitting Levi's and L. L. Bean boots. With a wry, inquisitive grin, she radiated a certain indescribable warmth and charm. The badge on her breast read, "Registered Maine Guide."

"Why, yes. I'm Melanie Ricker. I signed up for this trip, and I've just arrived, and…"

"Dina MacKenzie." She held out her hand and Melanie noticed the firmness—this other woman was sizing her up, holding her gaze like they'd known each other forever, two young women who knew how to find their place in a world of men. Well, Melanie thought, once I did.

"I've reserved a room for you at the Greenville Inn and hope you'll join me for dinner at the Lost Woods Bar & Grill. There's a gang of us, and you'll enjoy it."

Melanie recalled John Edmond's advice. "Remember, you're going there to stay out of sight, to get lost, so keep a low profile." She'd told him, "It's the Maine north woods. No one's going to find me." Anyway, she remembered thinking, I'm going to live my own life, and I'll take my chances. Better safe than sorry. "Did Allison Collins tell you why I'm up here?" she asked.

"No. You on the lam or something?"

"No, it's not like that, but I'm trying to get away from a guy."

"I get it," said Dina. "We can protect you."

Good. I'll be okay.

Chapter 24

It was crowded and loud, the barflies hovering, clamoring for drinks. Melanie struggled to remember the names. Sam Morse, Dina's husband, handsome in his Maine warden uniform with sidearm, was not drinking. There was a New Yorker, now a local reporter—Jud something. She'd try to get his name. He was disarming, with a Brooklyn accent; he stood out here. She met the owners, the Whites—June and her husband. Melanie didn't exactly fit in— she was too dressy. The women were wearing snowmobile outfits and Goodwill hand-me-downs. One, a dyed blond, had a fur coat on. After a bourbon, neat, Melanie began to feel she could fit in. The small group was going out of the way to include her. She was able to sit back and watch them. They didn't seem to care about outward appearances. It was a melting pot, some rich, most hand to mouth, no outsiders—they called them flatlanders—these people were locals, northern Mainers. And survivors, like her.

Through a picture window, the sunset's red blaze spread over Moosehead and, like a dying ember, slowly sank into its depths.

They got around to it, as she knew they would.

"So," whispered Warden Sam Morse, "you're one of the two survivors. We're so proud of you. And don't worry, Dynamite told me to keep your story confidential."

Who's Dynamite? Melanie wondered. "Actually," she said, "I'm feeling guilty. They were all amazing mariners. I don't know why it's me who survived."

102

"There's a reason," he said.

What did he say? He's so self-assured. Must be nice to have that faith. She couldn't think of any reason why she was the one…or one of two.

Dina hadn't forgotten her. "What do you think? Quite a place, eh?"

"Yeah." Melanie had to yell over the noise. "Tell me about the reporter guy. What's his name, and what's he doing in Greenville?"

"Name's Jud Jenkins. The short story is Jud was a reality show writer in Manhattan and came up with an idea for a show about the Maine Warden Service. So, he calls his old college bud, that's Sam, and Jud comes up here, starts traveling with Sam, and he's got Sam on constant video feed. And they hit pay dirt—they arrest the key suspect in a murder case, and they're witnesses, Sam for the prosecution and Jud for the defense. Don't ask. Anyway, the guy gets off. And Jud decides he loves Greenville, and there's this reporter's job for the taking, a great fit, at the *Greenville Times*. Meanwhile, Jud's idea for a reality show becomes a reality. It's called *North Woods Cops*. You've seen it on TV?"

"No. I'd like to. So now he's a local reporter?"

"Yeah. So, we've got this talented newspaperman right here in town. Let me get him."

"Wait. Have you told him that I don't want to be found here?"

"I'll speak with him. I've already told Sam. Don't you worry. I'll bring him over." She disappeared, then returned with a man on her arm. "Jud, may I present to you the hero of *El Barco de Oro*, one of two survivors of Hurricane Hilda on the high seas, Ms. Melanie Ricker. But you've got to promise you'll keep this completely secret. You got it?"

"Right. Off the record. Is this an exclusive?" He was teasing, of course. He slid in beside her, a wolfish grin on his face. Curly black hair. Black shirt with a gold medallion at his neck, unusual for here. Bit of a paunch. She'd seen a lot of male types, but Jud seemed unique. Like most New Yorkers, brash and loud, nothing held back. He oozed confidence. A duck out of water up here. Yet the locals seemed to love the guy, as they came by their table and gave him a quick "How's it going," "Hey dude," or a slap on the shoulder.

She asked Jud, "What's the story about your two friends, childhood sweethearts?"

"Sam and Dynamite? God, no. Sam was investigating the murder of a young girl—happened to be the seventeen-year-old daughter of the owners of this bar. You met June White. Her daughter's name was Hannah. Beautiful girl. You never knew if she was an innocent or a flirt. Anyway, Dynamite was this female Paul Bunyan, a logger, for God's sake, from way up in Aroostook County. She and Hannah got to know one another through this environmental group."

"Wait," Melanie said, "they call her Dynamite?"

"Yeah. It's what everyone's called her ever since she joined Save the Forest. They were doing some bad stuff, eco-sabotage. How Dynamite got her name, blowing up stuff."

Melanie could see it, and it cast a new light on Dina, called Dynamite. They were both pathfinders. Melanie had been the lone woman on a container ship on the high seas. And here was this Dynamite, a female logger and environmental activist. Melanie was fascinated by Jud Jenkins, who continued his story.

"Anyway, they find Hannah's body up at Lily Bay State Park, just north of Greenville, and it's where Hannah used to take Danny Tracy, a brain-injured young man, to read to him. When the police focus on Danny, he takes off. Sam finds Danny hiding out at Lobster Lake, north of Moosehead, but he thinks Danny's innocent. It's quite a story, how Sam and Dynamite find each other, fall in love, and save Danny, who, of course, was on trial for Hannah's murder."

Melanie looked over at Dina, this Dynamite, just as Dynamite threw Sam a knowing smile that made Melanie feel like an intruder.

Suddenly, Melanie was in awe of Dynamite, this fearless adventurer who dared to break the mold, whose very name revealed her explosive character, who'd found love, when Melanie had not. Melanie surmised what was missing in her life, what Dynamite and Sam had. She felt drawn to Dynamite, to her inner strength, thinking she could help her find answers to her own questions. Melanie realized the irony—admired as a national hero, she felt it was a sham, unmerited—she had done nothing more than throw herself into the sea, trusting in its mercy. Feeling guilty and alone, she reached out to these hardy Mainers who were somehow able to survive in the north Maine woods because they had each other. She admired and envied their close friendship, and she liked Jud without knowing why. Brash and abrasive, he was easy to be with. He grew on you. He loved people and had close friends—something Melanie lacked. And what surprised her was, he made her laugh.

She realized she needed that. She found herself talking about her ordeal, things she'd told no one. His eyes wide open, his features a blank page, Jud zeroed in on her—she was his bullseye, and his dark eyes drank her in. She felt it was a rare thing. She let it spill out, what it was like when everyone knew the ship was going down, and she caught herself thinking, he's probably like this with anyone with a story, already editing it for the next edition.

"You're not making mental notes for a story, right?"

"God, no. I wouldn't do that. It's a small town. We don't stiff our friends."

Nice, she thought, I'm a friend. That's all she wanted for now.

Later, as Dynamite drove up the hill to the Greenville Inn, Melanie turned to her. "Thanks. That was fun. I haven't had much of that."

"I'll bet." Dynamite glanced at Melanie, who was staring straight ahead into the night.

"It's a good group here. I like the people."

"Knew you would," Dynamite said.

"Can I ask you something?"

"Of course."

"Would it be okay if we didn't do the canoe trip? If I just stayed around town? I don't know if I'm up to an expedition right now."

"Girl, you've earned a rest. Whatever you want is fine with me."

After leaving Melanie at the Greenville Inn, Dynamite headed back through town and out to Beaver Cove. Sam would already be there unless he'd been called out on assignment. She couldn't wait to talk with him, and later they would talk with Jud, as they always did when something new came up. This time the something new was this girl Melanie, and why she was here, way up in the Maine north woods.

Chapter 25

John Edmonds was trying to confirm Melanie Ricker's story that the other survivor, Sergey Robichek, whom she knew as Jack Pierce, now missing, was CIA. Edmonds had connections at the highest levels in the nation's capital. He'd once served as independent counsel to investigate the head of a federal government agency.

Edmonds made numerous calls to his connections in Washington, D.C., but he hit a brick wall. No one, it seemed, knew anything about a CIA agent named Jack Pierce or Sergey, or they weren't admitting to it.

John Edmonds' inquiries made a stir at Langley, and they filtered down to Harry Field. Harry was summoned to the office of the Director of Covert Operations, Daniel Robinson. Harry gave him a full report, nothing held back. Full disclosure could only help him at this point. His career was on the line, and his need now was to get buy-in from the top, so that everyone there would be "all in." He was pleased to find Robinson surprisingly calm.

Robinson mused aloud, summing up: "So, you're telling me that this agent has gone rogue, is delusional, hears voices, thinks he was told to blow up a ship, but he didn't, because it went down in Hurricane Hilda, and now we think he's in Maine trying to wipe out a national hero, the only other survivor."

It was a rhetorical question. A statement of fact. "Is there anything else I need to know? Tell me we've found him and we're bringing him in."

"Well, no, sir. Not exactly." Harry was thinking that Robinson was good at summing things up.

"So, you're now saying, in addition, you've heard nothing from the agent you dispatched to Maine to track down this Sergey or Jack Pierce, or whatever name he now has. And you've heard nothing more from Jack Pierce. So, it's possible that he has eliminated this other agent. What's his name?"

"Alan Black."

"Alan Black, who has not reported back, and may be dead."

"Yes, sir."

"Not good news, Harry, not good news."

"No, sir."

Robinson was unflappable. They would stay hunkered down and maintain deep cover, for now. The official response was we know nothing. Harry's orders were to stop Jack Pierce, who had already killed one of their own. Maybe more. He was dangerous and had to be stopped. It was no longer about how to bring him in.

"Who have you got for this one?" asked Robinson.

"Our best man, the Watchman," Harry replied.

"Just make sure Watchman knows he has full authority."

"Sir, you know that this is outside our authority. I mean, it's on U.S. soil—"

"Just do it!"

"Yes, sir. I'll dispatch him to Maine right away."

"Do we have a fix on Pierce's location?"

"No, sir, he's too smart for that. Ditched his cell phone. No tracers on him. But Watchman will find him."

"One more thing, Harry."

"Sir?"

"I'm going to have to brief the chair of the Senate Select Committee on Intelligence, Senator James Law. Don't worry, Harry, this will remain under deep cover."

Harry wasn't so sure.

Chapter 26

He knew where Melanie was staying. He'd been at the Lost Woods Bar & Grille, but no one recognized him. He was there to watch Melanie Ricker. He'd followed her to Greenville in his loaner black Ford pickup truck. Her evasion tactics in Portland were amusing and served to heighten his desire for her—now she knew he was after her, and she was on the run from him. Let the games begin. He loved the chase, and the riskier, the better.

Sitting at the Lost Woods Bar, he fit right in, one more Maine woodsman, silent, drinking his beer. He could afford to take his time. He'd been taught well how to hide in plain sight.

Now in his room at the Indian Hill Motel overlooking Greenville, Jack Pierce enjoyed the view—the lights of the town and behind them the vast empty darkness that is Moosehead Lake.

***

For two days now, he had followed her, mostly around Greenville, keeping a safe distance. This afternoon, Melanie was with a small group of day hikers climbing Moose Mountain. Pierce was thinking it was time to make a move, to challenge her and find out what she knew. He worried that she'd tell others about him. Maybe she already had. But he'd been careful—she had no idea he was here in Greenville. Still, it was getting too complicated. That other agent had been a challenge, but Pierce, fearing he'd been targeted by the Russians' GRU, the successor to the Soviets' KGB, he'd circled around and caught him unawares. When he searched through his things, he'd been shocked to see his federal I.D. Must be CIA. Why? he wondered. Were they spying on him? Was he a marked man? Did Harry Field know this? Would they send someone else, someone better, to take him out?

At least the Ukrainians seemed unaware that he'd survived. He'd come close to calling the General to tell him he'd accomplished his mission. He could lie and tell the General he was the one who sank the ship.

But the General would ask questions, like "How'd you do it? No explosion?" How could he answer that? That he blew off the hatches, flooding the ship? So that's why the hurricane sank her? True, there was no one to dispute this. So, he could demand payment to his Cayman account.

No. Better to disappear, and the General and his friends would forget about him. Because the ship sank, they got what they wanted. Even though he didn't do it. But he'd have to keep a low profile.

These thoughts swirled in his head as he sat in his truck in the parking lot at the base of the mountain, just below the resort, his eyes focused on the trails. Jack tried to focus on his mission. What was it? He was trained to improvise, but he needed to get his head straight first. He watched and waited and considered his options. He needed to find her alone, away from this group, from this other woman who seemed to be a Maine Guide. Eventually, he spotted the hikers. They appeared jubilant from their hike, and they stood around the base of the mountain chatting excitedly. He grew tired of the wait. When they finally went inside the resort, he kept watch. They would leave soon, perhaps after a drink.

Time passed, and the sun disappeared over the back of the mountain, and, as dark descended, the cold air worked its way into his bones. Perhaps they stayed for dinner. Bored, he settled in for a long wait. He'd just decided to turn on the engine to get some heat and was feeling the relief that he'd soon be warm when lights flooded him from behind. Startled, he opened the door, exited his vehicle, and turned to stare into headlights.

"Maine Warden Service!" said a loud voice behind the lights. "You okay, sir?"

Disoriented, his mind reeled. Were they onto him? In a flash, he considered his options. What was the Maine Warden Service doing here, and did they suspect him? He had waited too long to answer, and this would raise suspicions. His training took over. He smiled. "It's okay, officer. Just decided to stay inside the car and get warm." He shivered from the cold and, to his horror, realized that he'd slurred his words. The warden approached. There was still time to take him down, but it was too risky.

"Okay, sorry to bother you," said the warden. "Just want to check your license and registration. You can get them from your vehicle. Just keep your hands where I can see them, sir."

"Sure, sure," replied Jack. He reentered his vehicle and, through the open window, offered the papers to the warden, who took them and returned to his truck.

He waited, miffed to be harassed like this. But he was okay. His papers were in order. It seemed to take forever. Finally, the warden returned.

"I'm going to ask you to get out of your vehicle, Mr. Pierce," said the warden. "Please keep your hands where I can see them."

"Anything wrong, officer?" It took great concentration to keep his voice calm and steady because he was on edge. Better comply, he thought, or it will get worse. There can't be a problem.

"Sir. Just put your hands on the top of the truck where I can see them. Your license seems to be in order, sir, but the truck is registered to someone else, a Michael Levin. So, who is this Michael Levin?"

"It's his truck," Jack said, as calmly as possible. "He loaned it to me. You can call him, and he'll confirm it. His number is right on the registration."

"Where does he reside?"

"Oh, he's down in Portland."

"And what does he do there?"

"I believe that he's in the business of leasing out cars."

"Sir, is it all right with you if I inspect your vehicle?"

Bizarre. But better play along or he'll get suspicious. Keep my options open. He's got probable cause now. "Sure, go ahead."

"All right. Please stand over there while I make a brief inspection of the vehicle's interior." The warden pointed away from the vehicle and he complied. It didn't take long for the warden to find the weapon under the front seat. He held it up. "Got a permit for this, sir?"

"Certainly. In the glove compartment."

"All right. I'll look." The warden fished out the permit and inspected it with his flashlight.

The warden returned to his truck and, a few minutes later, reappeared. "Okay, here's the deal. Maine's new carry law makes it lawful to possess a concealed weapon with a non-resident permit, but you failed to inform me of your concealed weapon, and that's a misdemeanor." Okay, no big deal. The warden handed him the citation, which he signed.

"Okay, sir," said the warden. "Here's your copy. Don't forget to show up in court on that date."

"Yes, sir."

"You're free to go," said the warden. Jack watched the warden slowly recede in his rear-view mirror.

Chapter 27

Sam Morse had come to the resort to meet Dynamite for drinks and dinner. Driving into the parking lot, he'd seen the lone truck far from the other parked vehicles and noticed it was occupied. Something didn't look right. The driver sitting in the dark, no smoke from the car's exhaust, in the cold. Had the driver fallen asleep? Another suicide? The routine check now over, he entered the lodge and greeted Melanie and her friends. They were still discussing their climb.

"Where've you been?" asked Dynamite. "Thought you'd be here sooner."

"When I got here, spotted a parked car, someone sitting in it, motor off. Had to check it out. Sorry I'm late. Strange. Guy from Virginia with a loaner from Portland. Found a weapon in his car, but he had a permit."

"Wait a minute." Melanie suddenly looked pale and nauseous. "Virginia? Way up here? What did he look like?"

"Male, dark hair, maybe six feet tall, slim, muscular build."

"What was he doing here?"

"That's the odd thing. Didn't look like a climber. Wearing dress pants and shoes."

"Sam…" Eyes wide, face ashen, Melanie's hands went to her mouth as she tried to catch her breath.

"Mel, you're hyperventilating. Slow down and take it easy."

After she calmed down, he asked, "What is it?"

"I'm freaking out. Sam, I did everything possible to escape this guy when I left Portland, and I think it's him. Jack Pierce."

"Okay, maybe it's him. His Virginia license had his name as Jacob Pierce."

"Sam, he's tracked me down. To this place. He's here. At the mountain. He can do anything. Sam, I'm scared…"

They needed a place to talk. Jud Jenkins' newspaper office was just down the road at the edge of town. Jud was hunched over his computer when they arrived.

"Something's up," Jud said. "You've both got that look. Follow me." Two other reporters watched, thinking, no doubt, that Jud had another scoop. He led them to a small conference room in back with no windows, where they took seats around a table. Sam summed up what had happened for Jud's benefit.

"So, he follows you up here, so what?" Jud was playing devil's advocate. "Perhaps he likes you. Maybe he's in love with you. I can see why, but what makes you think he's dangerous?"

"Okay, nothing I can prove, but hear me out," Melanie said. "Two people on our ship disappeared in mysterious circumstances. First, the cook, Alberto. He disappeared the night before Jack came on board calling himself Sergey then. Jack just shows up when, surprise, surprise, we need a cook so we can get out of port ahead of the hurricane, and corporate is pushing us to get to sea. He just shows up at the perfect time, when no one is going to look too closely at his papers or credentials. Peter, the third mate, handled all the Coast Guard stuff, all the personnel stuff and papers. Peter comes to me and says his papers look forged. And just as the hurricane is starting to hit and it's getting dicey, Bobby Irish, the steward, disappears. He's just gone—and it's right after the steward claimed that Sergey was dangerous, hiding a handgun and maybe a bomb in his room, and people are asking about him, and we don't have time to look into it. But I don't think Jack killed the steward, because they couldn't find a handgun or a bomb, and I know the steward was washed overboard, so he couldn't have killed him. Anyway, Jack follows me to Maine, and I meet him, and Jack says he's a CIA agent, and he's trying to leave the CIA, and they're after him." She'd been gesticulating, almost yelling, and suddenly she stopped.

Jud looked up. He'd been taking notes. Melanie had his attention. He was no longer playing devil's advocate. He waited for her to continue. She was shaking her head, as if to say it was all too much, too unbelievable. But Jud knew she believed it.

"And guess what?" Melanie said. "When Jack contacts me back here in Maine, I mean, he tracks me down, knows where my parents live, for God's sake, and he calls me and says something to show that he's been watching me out there in the dark, and then we meet at a Dunkin' Donuts and there's this incredible thing. He says he's changed his appearance and now he's Jack Pierce again. And he says that I can't tell anyone because they're trying to find him. And they're watching me. He said all that. It's him."

"Okay," Sam said. "It's probably him. The description fits."

Melanie looked distraught. "Sam, I can't prove any of it."

"Look," Sam said, "he's gone for now. Let's get a drink and we can think about this."

They went to the Lost Bar & Grill and ordered drinks and dinner. They were waiting for their meals when Sam said, "I have an idea." They were all ears. "We need to smoke him out."

"And just how're you going to do that, old buddy?" asked Jud.

"We watch Melanie, and we wait until he makes his move. And then we've got him."

"Oh, great," said Jud. "You want her to be the bait?"

"I'll do it!" Melanie looked determined.

Jud wasn't so sure. "If everything Melanie says is right, then this guy is very dangerous, and I wonder if he's of sound mind."

"You need to talk with Paul Appleby," Melanie said. "The investigator. He works for John Edmonds, the lawyer in Portland."

"We know Edmonds," said Sam. "He defended Danny Tracy in that murder trial a couple years ago, the one where I was the arresting officer."

"Edmonds was going to look into Pierce's connection with the CIA, to see if it's true."

Sam said, "The feds will be interested, all right."

"If Pierce is claiming he's a CIA agent," said Jud, "surely, someone can find out."

"Yeah," said Sam. "But we need help."

"Jeez, Sam," said Jud, "you mean this isn't something the Maine Warden's Service deals with every day?"

"Cut it, Jud." But Sam was laughing. They both took a sip of bourbon. "I think the United States attorney might be interested if Jack Pierce is misrepresenting himself as a CIA agent, don't you?"

"So, who do you call?" asked Jud.

"I think I know someone," said Sam.

Next morning, Sam called Ben Murphy, one of several assistants in the U.S. attorney's office in Portland. Murphy had jumped ship from John Edmonds' firm, where trusts and estates had bored him, and he now spent his time in federal court prosecuting criminals. Sam had heard of Murphy, a rising star as a prosecutor, but figured Murphy would not know his name. So, Sam asked John Edwards for a favor, and Edmonds contacted Murphy to pave the way for Sam's phone call.

"We have only your friend's word for this, right?" Murphy asked.

"Right," replied Sam. "The word of a national hero. Look, this guy is dangerous. He's stalked her all the way to Greenville, and I stopped him a few days ago and found that he's carrying a weapon, which is all legit, so this is all we have on him."

"I'm interested," Murphy said. "Let me make a few phone calls. I can't promise anything, because the CIA has its own labyrinth of secret layers."

Murphy called Sam back. "Something's strange about this," he said. "It's all very hush-hush."

"What do you suggest?" asked Sam.

"Can we put a wire on her?"

"She's game for it," said Sam. "If we can get him in custody, maybe we can find out what he's all about. And protect her. She's a tough gal, survived a shipwreck, but this guy has her spooked."

"All right. You'd have to bring her to Bangor to see an FBI agent. Can you do that?

"I think so," Sam replied.

"Okay. I'll get an agent lined up to meet with you both."

***

Sam met with Melanie at Jud's office to give them both the good news. To his surprise, Dynamite advised against using Melanie as bait, and so did Jud. But Melanie was all for it.

"What makes you think he wants to talk with you?" Jud asked. "He may just want to rub you out."

"He's still not sure about me," she said. "He's been following me to see if I'll do anything to jeopardize him, and so far, I haven't. And he's infatuated with me. If I come on to him, he's mine."

"I just want to protect you," Jud said. "Can we do that, Sam?" Jud reached out and put his hand on Melanie's arm, but she shooed him away.

"Since we're playing the CIA misrepresentation card, it's federal law, and so it's the feds' ball game," Sam said. "She can back out if she's not comfortable with it."

***

In the federal building in Bangor, they met Agents Dave Cormier and Tony Brevard, both in dark suits and ties. Sam figured they wore shades outside, like stereotypical FBI agents. They went over the details. Melanie was eager to take the offensive. She had tried to disappear, to escape him. It hadn't worked. This way, she was in control.

***

The National Security Agency intercepts transmissions. An NSA clerk noted the reference to a known CIA agent, Jack Pierce, in a report by Warden Sam Morse regarding his encounter at Moose Mountain's parking lot. NSA passed it along to the CIA. The report now sat on the desk of Harry Field, who picked up his phone.

"He's in Greenville," was all he had to say, and he hung up.

Chapter 28

Back in Greenville, Melanie made it a point to remain alone. She'd wait for Jack to contact her. Under her bra, she wore a tiny wire and mike. Her every move was tracked by the FBI agents, who followed at a discreet distance, hearing her every breath. She'd taken a drive up to the mountain, where she started hiking up a ski trail covered with a new dusting of powdery snow. The fall foliage was alive with umber, vermillion, and gold. She was still in shape, breathing easily as she climbed up the steeper section of the trail under the empty chairs.

At times, she stopped, thinking she'd heard the crack of a dead branch, catching sight of the wave-like movement of evergreen branches in the breeze. "Hey," she whispered into the hidden mike, "still there?" She heard the quick breathy response: "Roger." And she replied, "All clear." It seemed so silly that she stopped checking in—the FBI agents knew she was here, and they were somewhere on the trail below her, too far away to save her if Jack really wanted to take her out. She was betting her life that he didn't want to. He'd had every opportunity; he must want something else. Was he infatuated with her? A stalker? He didn't seem the type—too manly, physically strong, not a wimp or a geek. And he'd said he loved her. Really? Maybe he was testing her, evaluating her for some reason he would reveal to her.

The plan had lots of holes.

***

She felt exposed out in the clear, a moving target for anyone hiding behind a pine tree, taking clear aim. She reminded herself this was her choice. She was the bait—a bad metaphor, like a dead fish. She talked silently to herself—I can do this. I'm a mariner. I'm a survivor. But so is he.

A shadow moved on her periphery.

He came out of the woods onto the trail a hundred feet higher up, where she was headed. She quashed the startle instinct and steeled herself against the urge to flee. This is it. Then she said, brightly, "Oh, my God, Jack! What are you doing here?" No response. He just stood there. Time froze. She had to say something. "What brings you up here?" She made it sound like a warm welcome, just a beautiful fall day out hiking.

"We have to talk." She heard his familiar voice, but she was blinded by the sun melting on the mountaintop before it slid down the other side and plunged them into shade. It was a good sign, the word "talk." She could do that. As he neared, his blurred image began to take shape, as if he were emerging from a desert mirage. She made out the ripped shirt, mud-streaked jeans, and long, unkempt hair. God, as thin as a man on a hunger strike. And fresh— his face streaked with sweat and striped with alder slashes, but not even breathing hard. He must be in great shape. He can outrun me, and he's stronger. Under a fretted brow, his dark eyes charted the terrain like a paratrooper on point. A small bulge under the shirt— no doubt a weapon—raised the stakes, already stacked heavily in his favor.

"Yes, let's talk. I'd like that." She imagined the agents sitting in their warm car in the parking lot in their suits, ties, and dress shoes. Idiots. They were going to listen and wait. It was all up to her. *Fair enough. I asked for this.* She took the lead based on pure instinct. "Jack, I know you like me, and I like you, too. How can I help you?

Here, sit with me." She gestured to the rock next to her and sat down on it, her boots swinging out. His unsmiling gaze sought her out, and she could see his mind considering his options, evaluating her—friend or enemy? Would he dare to trust? He stood before her on the downhill side, so that he looked directly into her eyes. He searched her face with such hunger and sorrow that she could melt. Finally—it seemed like her world hung in the balance—he exhaled, and with his escaping breath came a release from all the intensity in him. He seemed to collapse onto the rock. He sat beside her, and she felt that it was a relief to him, that he must have carried the cares of the world for God knows how long. She didn't know why he'd come here, and maybe she'd find out, but not now, because all she needed now was to get him to go with her, to trust her. She wanted to reach out to him to relieve his pain, because they'd both been through so much and no one else in the whole world could know what it was like. But she knew she must be very careful with him because he was dangerous, a trained killer. She put her hand on his knee and felt a tremor run through his body.

"I know. I know," she said. "The ship sinks, and we're tossed into the sea. And no one else in the whole world has gone through what we have."

He turned to face her. She could see that he was in agony. "What…what can we do? So much has happened," he cried out. They'll never understand."

Who was he talking about? She had to try to seize the moment. God, this better be right. "Jack, there's a way. Yes, there's a way for you to do the right thing. You say you are CIA, right?"

"Yes," he said. And she knew she had to pin him down, to get it on tape.

"Are you sure?"

"Yes, I'm CIA." There it was.

"Okay, then, they will help you. So, I'll help you to go back to the CIA. Where is it, Langley, Virginia?"

"Yes." And she could see he was thinking about this, his way out.

"Who do you report to?"

"Harry," he said. "Harry Field."

"I know some people who can help you. They'll help you get to Harry Field safely. And he's not going to abandon you." She didn't know this. How could she? If Jack was not CIA, they would prosecute him. But if he was, why wouldn't they take him back?

"Are they here?" Jack, now alarmed, jerked his head around, combing the area for the enemy.

"No! No! Jack!" she yelled in a panic. "They're not here to hurt you. They want to help you."

The two FBI agents burst from the nearby woods, weapons zeroed in on the target at close range. "FBI! Drop to the ground! Raise your hands over your head!" The agents had been listening. When they heard Melanie speak to their target, they'd slipped into the woods off the trail, a classic military double envelopment, one on either side. Jack Pierce was surrounded. Surprise was the best tactic. In a flash, he knew. Melanie had betrayed him.

They cuffed him, led him down the mountain to the car, and pushed him into the back seat with a hand on his head. Melanie was in shock. This was not supposed to happen. She tried to tell him this, but the agents shut her up—they wouldn't let her talk with him. They read him his rights. Melanie said nothing and stared straight ahead, avoiding eye contact with Jack.

She twisted around to see him. "It's going to be okay, Jack, believe me." Then a window rose to shut off the front from the back seat, and she could no longer hear him. She wouldn't shut up. She spoke to the driver, Agent Cormier. "He's a national hero, and you're treating him like a common criminal."

Cormier stared stolidly ahead, silent at the wheel. "Just following orders, ma'am."

She didn't quit. "We're both survivors from *El Barco*. And he's asking for your help to get him back to CIA headquarters at Langley, Virginia. Do you think you can help us with that?"

"Ma'am," said Cormier, "You can ask my supervisor or the U.S. attorney."

"I'll do that," she said, and sat back in her seat, fuming.

***

She called Dynamite. Melanie explained to her that they were in Bangor and they were both okay. "You won't believe it, Dy. Jack is in custody. Seems it's true: he's CIA, just like he said. The agents called the guy at Langley, the one Jack mentioned—name's Harry something—and Harry exists at Langley. The FBI guys seemed disappointed, perhaps wanting to nail Jack for impersonating a federal agent. They're going to take him down to Langley so he can turn himself in. I don't understand everything. I mean, they're saying Jack's the real deal. I'm so happy for him. Maybe they can give him the help he needs."

"Mel, you were spectacular. This could have ended badly. Nice going. And you know what? You may have saved him. I'm proud of you, girl. We all are."

"Dynamite?"

"What is it?"

"I'm heading back to Greenville. I should be there at about five."

"Meet you at the Lost Woods Bar."

"You got it."

***

The trees were bare, the sun was down, and there were few cars and trucks on the road. The hills were descending into darkness as Melanie pulled into a parking space in front of the Lost Woods Bar

& Grill in Greenville. It was so quiet outside, and the noise from inside felt like a welcome, and she was feeling safe. *God, they're a rowdy bunch in there.* Melanie pushed open the door, and Dynamite greeted her. Soon they found themselves surrounded by a host of faces, all smiling, and they burst into song: "For she's a jolly good fellow…" Melanie thought, how nice, they love Dynamite, and when she saw Dynamite leave to find Sam, they all kept cheering for her. *Wow. They love me. I'm home.* There were hugs all around. Jud gave her a bear hug and it felt good. Still, among all these friends, there was an emptiness in her.

She remembered her battle against the hurricane and how alone she'd felt, and yet she'd never felt so alive or felt such a will to live. For what? A depressing thought. No one to share it with. Jud had joined the merrymakers. Melanie took a seat at the bar alongside guys who were drinking to forget their lonely lives. She ordered a bourbon on the rocks and held the glass up to the light, swirling the golden-brown liquid over the ice. She raised the glass to her lips ever so slowly as her eyes met those of a total stranger on the other side of the bar. She watched him take a pull on his beer. She took a big swallow of the bourbon and felt the warmth spread in her gut. She'd never felt so alone.

Chapter 29

As soon as he heard they'd picked up Jack Pierce, Harry Field dialed the number. "Where are you?"

"Just got to Greenville," came the raspy voice of the Watchman. "He's mine. Found his motel room."

"You're too late. He's coming back to us. Mission canceled." He heard a loud noise, as if the Watchman had slammed his fist against the wall, just as the receiver went dead.

***

When he arrived at Langley, they put him in a small interrogation room. Jack expected the worst—no drinks and red carpet here. He'd been trained to suffer abuse, even torture, and he steeled himself for whatever they'd do to him. For over an hour, he sat alone. When Harry Field entered and sat at the table opposite him, Harry's frown and abrupt manner said it all—no warm welcome. Harry silently read his file, and several minutes passed before he looked up.

"Hello, Jack. I'm glad you're back."

Jack said nothing.

"You've led us on quite a chase since you disappeared in Paris months ago. And then you called me. And, as you may have surmised, we sent an agent, Alan Black, to find and follow you. Soon as you called, we knew you were in Maine, so we sent him up there.

He was a little green, Black was. Nice pun, eh? So, we instructed him not to harm you, just to watch. But he disappeared, so it seems you dispatched him."

He watched Harry lift a cigarette pack from his shirt pocket, flip open a lighter and pull his thumb over it to ignite a flame, then lean forward, touching the flame to the end of the cigarette. Harry inhaled deeply until the tip glowed red, then clicked the lighter closed. Sitting back, he exhaled. Jack watched him through the smoke, unsmiling. Jack was familiar with CIA interrogation tactics. Harry wouldn't offer him a smoke or a drink. Harry looked bored. "I'm just giving you a quick summary of what we know, Jack, but a few things we don't know, and you're going to tell us everything, or it's going to be very unpleasant for you, you understand?"

"How will you know if what I tell you is the truth?"

"Ah, the truth. What is truth? A famous line from the gospel, eh? Well, we have information from sources inside the Ukraine government, and we'd just like to confirm that information."

"And if I don't tell you the truth?"

"Well, that would be a big mistake on your part. You see, the information we already have is enough to interest the United States attorney here in Virginia in charging you with treason, sedition, and murder, and he'd probably seek the death penalty and make a name for himself. But we'd rather not make all this public."

Touché. So, they know. What don't they know? "So, if I cooperate and just tell you what happened, what do I get in return?"

"Well, there's no *if*, you see, because you will tell us, whether you want to or not. And we want to be sure you tell us everything, so Dr. Treslow is ready to give you a shot of truth serum. He's a trained hypnotist and just loves to use his skills, so he'll get you talking, and it will all come out." Harry looked smug.

"Harry, you don't need to do all that because I'll tell you everything. And you know that truth serum and hypnosis are unreliable. You can confirm with your inside agents if what I tell you is true or not. Does that work for you?"

"Yes. I appreciate that, Jack. Forgive me for sounding a bit coercive. You know that I've always liked working with you, and I'm sure we can resume our old relationship. In fact, what I'm going to recommend to my boss is that, once we get through this information-gathering business, then we explore your next role here. I think we can find something a little less stressful for you to do while still using your trade skills. Does that sound like something you would like?"

"Of course," Jack said. He was rather pleased with this turn of events, but he wouldn't count on it happening.

He told Harry everything that had happened in Paris and then on his mission on *El Barco*, and why the explosion didn't happen because the ship went down in the hurricane. But he made no mention of the girl, Melanie. He'd never tell them about her. Harry listened intently, but he was not taking notes. When Harry finally stood, he invited Jack to follow him to Dr. Treslow's office.

"Hello, Jack," said Dr. Treslow. Dressed in a white coat, Dr. Treslow stood in front of a white wall—everything was white, even his hair. Harry explained that he had to leave. "Dr. Treslow will do another quick debrief and some re-training—that is, if you don't disagree."

"No," he said, "that will be fine." Harry left the room, and Jack waited, his thoughts turning to Melanie as they always did when he needed to focus his mind on screening out anything bad.

"Shall we begin?"

"Yes, doctor. Where would you like to start?"

"I'd like to start by giving you an injection of sodium pentothal. It's standard procedure, Jack, as you know. It will relax you. Have you ever had it?"

He had, and he'd prepared himself for this.

The injection made him giddy, and he chuckled to himself as he lay on a couch. In the distance, a voice told him to follow a moving object and repeat certain words. He knew all about hypnosis and how to deal with it. He wanted to think of Melanie and the smell of her hair, but he must hide his thoughts of her.

Soon the voice triggered thoughts, and the thoughts became words. He thought of his mother and how he used to cry for her, and she never came, so he stopped crying. He couldn't even visualize her face, but a vision began to form.

***

Looking down at a wooden casket being lowered into a deep hole, he knows it's her, his dead mother. He stands at attention, his father's orders, and his legs ache but he doesn't dare move. In front of him, his father stands unmoving, his unshaven face blotched with tears. His father peers down into the black hole and begins to wail. And it feels like revenge to him. And he hears his own voice saying, "I hate you," and he means his father, of course, but also his mother, for leaving him. Why?

Ma!

He could picture her, those deep blue eyes staring into his. Why, Ma? Don't leave me!

I have to go, she's saying through her tears.

Don't go.

I have to, baby, but I'll come for you when I can, I promise.

So, he did love her, and he'd cried for her, not because he hated her, but because he loved her so much. He could still feel her touch, those lovely hands on his face, her smiling eyes. He knew why she'd left the major, the brute. But why didn't you come back for me? How had she died? The major never told me...

***

"Jack?" The voice cut through his vision.

"Yes."

"You can relax now."

"Okay."

"Jack, what happened to you in Paris?"

***

Paris. In a warehouse overlooking a crowded square. Cigarette smoke in his eyes, then a shot, a jolt to his right shoulder, and the acrid smell of cigarette smoke and gunpowder. In his sights, a head explodes…

***

His thoughts turned into words. The words kept spilling out, because the serum made him feel so wonderful and he wanted to tell everything. "I completed our joint mission to assassinate the mayor, and then they gave me a second mission, to bomb the ship."

"What do you mean?"

"I took the money, and I became a double agent."

"How?"

"They told me to board a container ship, and it was easy to do."

"How did you do it?"

"I was in a bar, and there was this cook from the container ship due to sail for San Juan. He talked too much. I could learn how to cook. I followed him and gave him a ride out of town so he couldn't get back to his ship."

"You killed him?"

"No, no. I had the papers and a shipping card. Medved, the Ukrainian general—he was acting for the oligarchs—he gave them to me, and they told me how to arm the bomb."

"So, what did you do?"

"I became the cook."

"But you didn't do it."

"No. I couldn't do it. I couldn't blow up the ship."

"Why not?"

"Because of Hurricane Hilda. That's all. There's no other reason."

***

Dr. Treslow made a note: "says he couldn't do it. Reason unclear." Treslow looked puzzled. "Jack, we need to go back to something you said. You said you did two missions, one to bomb the ship and you couldn't do it. And the other was to assassinate the mayor?"

"Yes."

"We know about the Mayor of Sebastopol, but we need to confirm that you did that."

"Yes, I did."

"Wait there a minute. You will remain under hypnosis; do you understand?"

"Yes."

Slowly, he became aware of his surroundings—the serum must have worn off. He was alone in the room. Where had Dr. Treslow gone? The door opened, and the psychiatrist returned with Harry. Jack sat up.

"Jack," said Harry, "you've done well. Could you repeat for me what you told Dr. Treslow about your mission in Paris?"

"Yes, certainly." Once he told the story to Harry, Harry asked Dr. Treslow to leave them alone. Harry then smiled at Jack.

"You should know, Jack, you did the United States government a great service. We were able to blame the Ukrainians for the assassination of the Russian's mayor. So, thank you."

Jack tried not to betray his surprise. "You're welcome."

"Jack, I'm sorry to surprise you with the hypnosis and truth serum. We had to make sure. Standard stuff. Doc Treslow has some retraining for you. Basically, it will help you to forget your assignments, stuff you'd probably just as soon put past you. Make you more mentally healthy, you know. This is still experimental, but it's just a few simple exercises. Doc can explain it to you, and then we can move on and find you some meaningful work. You won't be in the field, but we can use your tradecraft and experience to train other agents. That sound good to you?"

***

There would be more sessions. He was allowed to make phone calls and send letters—he figured they monitored them all—so he made the call to Melanie and listened to her voice message. He felt disappointed that she didn't answer, but he was thrilled to hear her recorded voice. The phone quivered in his shaky hand. He held the mouthpiece away so that she wouldn't hear him cough and clear his throat. When he returned it to his mouth, he said it just as he'd rehearsed it:

"Melanie." He paused. "This is Jack. I'm doing well. Please call me. I'd love to speak with you." A bead of sweat formed on his brow. He gave his call-back number and promptly hung up. She might not call back, but he would persist.

Chapter 30

She decided to drive down to Portland. It was late when she arrived at her home on Munjoy Hill. Her mailbox was full, and more mail spilled onto the floor inside. After weeding through bills and junk mail, she came across a letter posted from Washington, D.C. She thought she recognized the handwriting. She ripped the envelope open and pulled out a one-page handwritten letter. As she read it, a sense of alarm rose within her.

Dear Melanie:

I don't know how to begin to thank you. I have been in treatment for over a month now. For so long, I was lost. I must have scared you when I pursued you. I have always loved you. I know it was thanks to you that I was brought here. So, you saved me. Thank you for that.

I would like to see you when I leave here. I am not sure when that will be. I will not leave here until I am completely well again. I promise that I will not see you unless you want to see me. I hope you do.

Sincerely,

Jack

She sank into a plush living room chair, the letter open on her lap. Memories from her time at sea came rushing back like the tide. She felt powerless as foamy waters sucked at her ankles, sweeping her up, entangling her in seaweed and ropes of olive-green kelp, dragging her down to the dark depths. Jack Pierce. She remembered where she'd seen his handwriting—Peter had shown her his papers and told her they looked forged. Maybe she should have listened to Peter. To think that she'd fallen for Jack, seduced him. And she'd overcome all that. Took charge and tricked him, to save him. *Why do I always try to save people? Is he still fixated on me?* She thought she was safe from him. How could she trust him? Here he was again. Well, she'd had the gumption to deal with him before, and she could do it again. She would not let him haunt her like this. Besides, Jack was locked up in the bowels of Langley. But they would let him out sometime. What then? He wanted to see her. Should she reply to his letter? Better not to encourage him. Let him forget her. Better to get on with her life. Still, she had to give him some sort of reply to let him know she no longer wished to see him.

She slept fitfully, rose early, showered, and dressed. Strolling on the hill overlooking the Casco Bay islands, she saw there were no longer boats at mooring and the trees had shed their leaves—the bleak time before the first snowflake. She felt the need to talk with someone with no connection to her maritime life. On her cell phone, she dialed the number of a friend from school days, Beth Myers. To her surprise, Beth answered.

They met at one of the many coffee houses that had sprung up in Portland. After hugs, they sat before a blazing fireplace. Melanie felt herself drifting away from the conversation as Beth rambled on about her customer service job at IDEXX Labs, lauding the pay, the benefits, the endless perks. Her friend's mundane life and lifestyle seemed stultifying. Beth was safe and secure. But what had happened to her? Backstage during a high school musical, they'd shared their dreams in whispers—Melanie's to go to sea and Beth's to be a professional singer.

Melanie was relieved to leave the coffee house and walk among the tourists who had spilled from a Norwegian cruise ship hovering over Commercial Street. It was good to feel the cold air fill her lungs. She wandered from the waterfront up to Congress Square, where she stood in front of the Civil War statue, noting the few passersby and pigeons.

The nearly empty square mirrored darkening thoughts of her lost shipmates, leaving an empty ache in her gut. Nothing here for her but loss. Her mind turned to her new friends in Greenville— Dynamite, who seemed happy with her wild and rugged lifestyle. Jud, so out of place, yet so full of life. The scudding clouds lifted, and a smile crinkled Melanie's sunny face. She decided to return to Greenville.

But first, there were two things she had to do.

She walked up Congress Street and Munjoy Hill to her home, sat at her desk, and pulled out a sheet of her monogrammed stationery and a pen. She wrote:

Dear Jack,

Thank you for your letter. We were both fortunate to survive, and I confess I feel guilty every day that I am alive.

I wish you well in your recovery. I hope you will be able to move on with your life, as I am trying to do.

Best,

Melanie

She thought it over. Had she gone too far? Would he get the message? She decided to mail it and dropped it into the drive-by slot at the post office. Immediately, she wished she hadn't.

Chapter 31

Snow coated the ground on a cold December day. The days were getting short and the nights long, sprinkled with diamond-bright stars. Mainers had their neatly stacked wood piles, spent their evenings before their wood fires, and gave thanks for another magical summer and for the fact that they now had their state back because all the tourists had returned to where they came from. The drive up Route 1 past Bath, Wiscasset, and beyond to Camden was uneventful. Bare trees. Snow yet to come.

The coastal campus was just as she remembered it. Camden was the most incredible spot for a college campus, the academy from whence she had come. She was feeling how much she owed to her fellow academy grads, and all those who had perished. She was here to bear witness. She'd been reluctant to come but finally yielded to talk with a select group of midshipmen—just a small group, they'd told her.

How lucky she was to have been here. She parked outside the president's office and went inside. She was surprised that the only person there was a midshipman, who offered to escort her to the auditorium. She was thinking this made no sense because the auditorium was too large for the small group she'd agreed to meet with. Her escort opened the heavy outside door, then led her down the hall, where their steps echoed off the walls. They passed bookcases full of trophies and photos of famous graduates. Her guide stopped at the inner auditorium doors. "Are you ready for this, ma'am?"

What was she talking about?

When the auditorium doors swung open wide and the guide stepped aside, her hand shot up to her mouth. *Oh, my God!* She'd come prepared to share her experiences with a few midshipmen. And there, standing before her, was the entire student body.

The guide led Melanie up the stairs to the platform, where she shook the hands of the president and other officials, and the cascade of applause grew into a crescendo. Stunned, she stood and faced the ranks of uniformed midshipmen and almost fell over. Tears welled up inside her, and she felt overwhelmed.

The president led her to the center of the platform and gestured for her to stand before a microphone. She faced the audience. Chairs scraped as midshipmen took their seats. She'd never spoken to such a crowd. Looking back at the president, she mouthed the words: "No fair. You tricked me." But she was smiling. How could she not?

She took a deep breath and began.

"I'm so glad to be here, and so fortunate…" Her words echoed off the walls. *Sure I am.* She looked up to see all the eyes fixed on her and smiled briefly, a nervous smile. "I don't know why the good Lord favored me. And I tell you that what I most feel is a sharp sense of guilt. Because there were thirty-two other souls on board my ship…" She was determined not to choke up, but the sudden hush, the silence of the auditorium—no sound of scraping chairs now— almost got to her. "And, as you know, there were fellow graduates with me who perished. Captain David Downs was my hero. I miss him every day. He was my polestar, the captain of my ship, and I can tell you the instant I knew that he would go down with his ship and it was when he implored me to survive, so that I could be here to bear witness to him and the others. And so, I am here, God knows how."

It's true. Why am I here? What do they want to hear? She plunged ahead. "I love that you had your candlelight service here at

Camden. I wish I could have been here for that." She choked back a sob. "But I was not going to miss the service for my captain held at Rockland the other day. That's when I said goodbye to him, someone I admired…" She paused and struggled to regain her composure.

"We—our captain and crew—did everything possible to save our ship. Know this: there have been few such disasters in our maritime history. You can look forward to a good life at sea in the maritime service of our nation. And I wish you Godspeed because the nation needs you." There was more applause, but she sensed they wanted more. She was glad that she had prepared some remarks, and now she pulled out the paper and read from it.

"Mark Twain, the great American writer, said, 'Twenty years from now, you will be more disappointed by the things you didn't do than the things you did. So, throw off the bowlines. Sail away from safe harbor. Catch the wind in your sails. Explore. Dream. Discover.'"

She looked out on the faces, so earnest, so young. "I see great things for you. There will be toils and difficulties. Carry on. Get to know your shipmates. The world awaits you. I would love to talk with any of you who would like to chat. This is a special place, so enjoy your time here, and know that what awaits you is a world of adventure and excitement. And I implore you to embrace it. Thank you, and good luck."

They drowned her in applause, then broke into cheers. She stood there basking in the glow for what seemed like forever. She struggled to understand. *Why? Why me, out of all of them? I should have stayed with Captain Downs.*

After they settled down, there were many questions. "Were you afraid that you were going to die?" *How do you answer that? Tell them the truth; they can handle it.*

"Yes. And you will face that, too; it's part of the risk of going to sea. But the sooner you face it, the sooner you can get to work to solve the problem and save yourself and your crew. I just wish I could have saved mine."

"Do you think the settlement was fair to the victims' families?"

The question triggered thoughts and feelings she'd buried, and they came rushing to the surface. She felt anger at Pegasus for blaming her captain for the ship's loss—the company officials were blaming him for his decision to leave port, for his decision to take the course that led them to sail into the hurricane, and more. They knew better—the ship would not have sunk had she not been unseaworthy. And she felt regret—she had failed to help Mary with their son Jamie. And most of all, she had not stayed with the ship.

She could say nothing about the settlement. The terms included a confidentiality clause that required the families to keep it secret. She had to say something, and she chose her words carefully.

"The settlement is confidential. I very much doubt it was fair. But I'm glad the families got something."

"Will you go to sea again?" asked a midshipman.

Tough question. Same one I keep asking myself.

"To be honest, I'm not sure. There's a lot going on in my life now, and I need some time."

"What did you like the best being at sea?" asked another midshipman.

She did not hesitate. "There's nothing like it. You are responsible for your crew and cargo, and you are in control of this monster of a ship with incredible tools at your disposal, and you are out there on the high seas under sun, moon, and stars with the most beautiful sights and sounds, and you sometimes pinch yourself to feel there are times when you, alone, control all this and when you can do what you've been taught to do. You have a high purpose and it's what you're called to do."

Driving back to Portland, she was still in the glow of all those bright eyes and smiling young faces, but it seemed so unmerited, that she was unworthy of it. That kind of adulation, she realized, must be earned, and she knew that she had not earned it. She started to breathe hard, trying to catch her breath. Must be hyperventilating again. A sharp pain in her side almost doubled her over, and she had to pull over to the side of the road. *Relax*. Her breathing slowed, and the pain subsided.

When she pulled back onto the road, her thoughts returned, and that's when it came to her that she'd sold them a lie—she told the midshipmen to face the risks at sea to save their crew. But the truth was that the hurricane had scared her to death. And didn't she abandon her mates? Surely, she hadn't saved them. Captain Downs was the good captain who went down with his ship. Not her. She saved herself. If she'd been honest, she'd have told them that nothing had prepared her for this disaster at sea, a disaster from which she could not recover and which continued to haunt her.

She had spent most of her adult life preparing for and going to sea. Now, on solid land, she felt lost, more at sea than ever before. She was not ready to go back to sea—it still scared her. Unsure what to do with her life, she felt lost and unmoored. She'd lost her way and was desperate to see Dr. Deering.

<h1 style="text-align:center">Chapter 32</h1>

She sat in the same chair facing Dr. Deering and the picture window onto the harbor, and she told Dr. Deering about her appearance at the academy. "All that adulation, it made me feel, well, so unworthy."

"Yes, of course. None of us is worthy of that kind of pedestal. You're no more worthy than any other member of your crew. But you did survive, and they did not. How does that make you feel?"

"It makes me feel guilty."

"What, because you're a woman? Women learned to get over that a long time ago. But you're a strong woman, Melanie, so we both know it's more than that, don't we?"

"What do you mean?"

"What can you tell me about what happened to your little brother, Charlie?"

In the silence that followed, Melanie thought about this. Is this why she was feeling guilty? Was it all about Charlie? Other thoughts came, unbidden…

***

She sits on her bed covered with a quilt, the one with reds and pinks, the one she loves. In her room, she's put her pictures on the wall with Scotch tape. There's a teddy bear beside her on the pillow. She's finished drawing her mom and dad and herself and Charlie, and now she needs more colors for the rainbow. There's got to be a rainbow. She reaches for a new color in her favorite box of colored crayons, and little Charlie is scribbling beside her. Oh, no. "Charlie, Charlie." She takes his hand, the one with the red crayon. "Do it on the paper, here, like this." He giggles, and she laughs, he's so funny…

She's outside with Charlie in the sunshine, and they're walking on grass wet with dew, and she wants to take his hand, but he wriggles away and starts to run from her, so she runs after him toward the pond, which is all black. Why does everything look black? And then she knows. She knows what's coming…

***

She did not want these memories to intrude, could not share these terrible thoughts, could not put them into words. She had to hold something, to get a grip. She picked up her purse to find something, anything. Perhaps she should leave. No, that was silly. She could trust this woman who would tell no one, no matter how awful it was. And then she could not help herself, and the words began to pour out of her.

"We were at our grandparents' farm, playing in the field by the pond, and Charlie fell in over his head. I…couldn't… Oh, my God!" She reached for a tissue as she struggled for the words that she had never said for the many years she'd hidden them, submerged under a façade of bravado.

"Your parents never spoke of it?"

"No. Not after that day. We all buried it with him."

"You know it was not your fault, don't you?"

"No! No! It was! I froze. I should have saved him!" Her eyes wide with the shock of this realization, Melanie's hands reached to cover her open mouth.

"You were a little girl. What? Five? Six?"

141

"Yes. I know, but I still feel—"

"Tell me what you remember of him, of growing up with him."

Dr. Deering waited patiently, and so she began to talk about Charlie, and when she had exhausted her memories, Dr. Deering asked her, "Can you picture him now? Your little brother, Charlie? Just as he was then?"

"Oh yes, I see him. Often."

"Can you see yourself as you were then? That little girl?"

Melanie's eyes glistened with tears as she searched her memory. "No. I can't," she said, distraught.

Dr. Deering swiveled her chair around and reached for something behind her desk. She turned and handed the object to Melanie. It was a stuffed bear, tattered and worn, both eyes gone.

"A bear?"

"Yes. Melanie, I want you to take this little stuffed bear and hold it in both your hands."

Melanie held it. She felt this was silly, even comical. It was soft and cuddly, the kind of bear a young child would take to bed at night, and it brought back memories of the Winnie the Pooh she'd always slept with, keeping it close, until she'd grown older, and her parents decided she no longer needed it.

"Now I want you to close your eyes."

She did.

"Now let's just be quiet so that little Melanie can be with us. Okay?"

Once again, it seemed silly, and she almost refused. Melanie heard the clock ticking and sounds from the harbor. As she grasped the bear to her breast, she felt a peace descend on her. And then there were sounds from her house—her grandma's lilting voice calling, "Melanie! Charlie!" And they were running in the field through the tall grass on a hot summer day.

"I see her—I mean me," she whispered. "I'm at the pond with Charlie, and I can hear our grandmother calling us."

"Melanie," said the gentle voice of Dr. Deering. "I want you to talk to her. Tell her it's okay. That it's not her fault."

***

Melanie is there in the field with the wind in her face, the sweet smell of mown hay, and the sound of the cicadas like a whining telephone line. The tall grass brushes her legs and she and Charlie reach the pond and run out onto the pier, the cool water below.

***

"What do you see?" Dr. Deering's gentle voice was like a balm she could not resist, even as she was also there in the field with Charlie.

And then she was no longer the little girl in the field, but she could see her there, crying, and her heart broke for her. Squeezing the stuffed bear tight, she whispered, "It's okay. It's not your fault. It's not your fault."

When she opened her eyes, it was like a lifetime had passed, and everything there was the same, but somehow different—the same desk, the same picture window on the harbor, and before them, Dr. Deering, with a quizzical look. "What did she tell you?"

Without hesitation, Melanie told her: "She said, 'I know. But thanks, anyway.' And then she gave me this very pretty smile, tossed her head, and ran off, waving at me."

For a long moment, Dr. Deering remained silent, letting it sink in. "Well," she said, "What a blessing for you. Accept the blessing, Melanie. And cherish it. And let it make you free from the past, so you can embrace your future."

They talked some more. Melanie was curious about the underwater dreams, especially the one she'd had before her ship sailed, the one that still haunted her. "What does it mean?" she asked.

"Melanie, your dreams were about drowning, and that makes sense, doesn't it? Your brother drowned, and in your dream, you see yourself as Charlie, underwater, struggling for air, because you blamed yourself. In your dream, you want it to be you, not Charlie. You were just a little girl. And you've carried that burden all your life, until now. And this last sea voyage? You feared you'd drown at sea. But you didn't. And sometimes you wish you had. Survivor's guilt is very common. But Melanie, you were meant to survive. It's not a punishment. And you're meant to find yourself. And you will. Just give it time."

"Will I still have the dreams?"

"I don't know for sure, but I don't think so. That little girl has released you from them. But if you do, let me know. I will work with you, and in time they'll go away, I'm almost certain."

Melanie felt the relief wash over her.

"But listen," Dr. Deering said. "Understand that you represent your fellow shipmates. You happen to have survived. So, you're the lucky one. Whatever. But they celebrate you because they're grieving the loss of all the others. Can you understand that? Can you welcome that, or allow that?"

Melanie nodded, beginning to understand.

"So that's your job, to represent them all. So, just know that, when they cheer you, you're allowing them to cheer all of those who are lost. And you can feel honored for them all. Just take their cheers and pass them along to your fellow shipmates, and join in it, and give thanks for it and them. Can you do that?"

Maybe, just maybe, she could. If she could avoid testifying. "There's something else."

"What is it?"

"I was served with a subpoena." She handed the paperwork to Dr. Deering, who perused it thoughtfully.

"It's a hearing before the Coast Guard Board of Inquiry in Jacksonville. They want you to testify."

"Yes." Melanie's hands twitched as she sat waiting to hear some way out.

"I see," said Dr. Deering.

"I can't do it."

"Melanie, you should not have to face this now. You need time to heal. But you're going to get better, and then you'll be able to do this. When you're ready. And when you're ready, it's something you should do. And they'll want your story. But not now."

"But this subpoena says I must appear in Jacksonville next week. So can you give me a medical excuse in writing?"

"Yes, of course. Do you have a lawyer?"

"Not yet. I know the lawyer in Portland who represents Mary Downs, the captain's wife, and he's already involved in that hearing, but I don't know if he can represent me, too. I plan to call him and find out."

"Well, if he can't represent you, perhaps he can refer you to someone who can."

"Right."

"I can give you a written statement saying you're not able to appear at this time due to the stress it would cause you. Your lawyer will have to figure out the procedure to save you from having to appear."

"Thank you so much."

She left Dr. Deering's office. Maybe there was a way out.

Chapter 33

She drove back to Portland in the dark. The winter solstice neared. Christmas lights in town cheered her. There were two more letters from Jack. She decided to ignore them. She called the lawyer's office, and he said it would be a conflict of interest to represent her, so she'd have to find her own lawyer. Edmonds recommended one, who filed a motion to postpone her appearance. How long could she stave it off? For now, Dr. Deering's affidavit would do the trick.

Melanie felt relieved. But what now? There was nothing for her in Portland. She could drive one and a half hours to North Norway to be with her parents on Christmas, or she could drive north three hours to Greenville. She dialed the number. Her mother was delighted to hear from her.

"I'm really sorry, Mom."

"It must be someone special."

"Really, Mom. There's no one special."

"Well, I hope he's nice." *God, how do they know?*

"Okay," she said, "maybe there's someone. But it's too early to tell. I need to go there to find out. You forgive me?"

"Of course, honey. Just call us when you get there."

"Sure. Tell Dad I love him, and I'll see you both soon."

***

Snow. Flakes streaming into the headlights, obscuring her view. She stopped from time to time to wipe away the snow and ice. No traffic on I-95 north of Bangor. One set of tracks through the deepening snow led into a blur of whiteness—no road markers, no streetlights. Just total concentration.

It was exhausting, and doubts besieged her—a mistake to make this trip at night in winter. Coffee kept her going, but the Christmas music on NPR lulled her; she almost nodded off, then jerked awake before sliding off the side of the road. She eased off the highway at the Newport exit and stopped for gas, a bathroom break, and more coffee.

North on Route 15, she felt lost. If she went off the road into a snowbank, no one would find her till spring. There were a few lone pickup trucks, and she followed their tracks to Greenville. And her friends. Like Jud, so likable, but he didn't exactly sweep her off her feet. Was it too much to ask for? What if he had to choose between her and his job? What if they were not all friends—Dynamite, Sam, and Jud? Useless questions. Her mind wandered to Jack, who had always loved her, and no doubt still did. All those letters. Flattering, but scary. The letter she'd just read lay on the passenger seat.

Dear Melanie,

I want you to know that I am doing well here at Langley. I'm working with my instructors and a therapist. They're helping me to get past the things I've had to do, both in the Marines and here at the CIA. They tell me that I am a patriot, that I followed orders and did what I was trained to do. Even though everything in me cried out against it. Even though I sometimes still weep over those things I had to do. They're helping to cleanse my mind and my thoughts, and I no longer have bad dreams.

I am thankful for what you did to get me back here safely. That took courage, and maybe even love. I think of you every day and it is my salvation.

Jack

How unsettling. Why did she turn him in? Was it love? Not really. She'd acted out of fear and her desire to be free from him. But his letter touched her heart. Was it guilt? Or love? She must write to him. But what to say?

After Monson, she felt she could make it. Thank God for four-wheel drive. Then the sign: Entering Greenville. And another moose sign warning her to reduce speed. She slowed, knowing they came out of nowhere with their long legs. Every year, tourists ignored the warning and were crushed under a ton of moose meat. Down the hill into the town of Greenville, a left onto the main street, and she parked in front of the Lost Woods Bar & Grille. The clock read 1:35 a.m. She wondered if anyone was still there. The door was unlocked.

"Well, hello there. What brings you back from the dead?" June White was cleaning up.

"Oh, my God, June. You have no idea how glad I am to see you."

"Come over here," June said, hanging a closed sign on the front door. They sat at a table, and Melanie told her everything she could.

Chapter 34

Rising early, Melanie dressed for warmth, with multiple layers, after noting the outdoor thermometer—minus 15 degrees Fahrenheit. Was that possible? Maybe it was stuck. Outside, the cold smacked her, bored into her bones. Her car wouldn't start. She called Jud.

"I need a boost."

"Dead battery, eh? You didn't plug it in last night, did you?"

"Plug it in? I've never heard of this. Are we in the Arctic or something?

"Hey, I'm just saying…"

"Stop laughing. You're enjoying yourself a bit too much."

"Take a look around. Everyone does it here. You're just another spoiled flatlander."

Jud bought her a block heater with an electric cord she could plug into an outside outlet. Of course, he used the opportunity to present it to her at a gathering of locals at the Greenville Inn around a lighted Christmas tree. There was much frivolity. "Come on, show us you know how to use it," someone called out, to which another quipped, "Where's the battery located, in the bow or the stern?" And there were a few off-color jokes, "You better get Jud to come up and show you. I'll bet he can plug it in." Somehow, it felt special, like she belonged, but she was embarrassed—she and Jud had remained close friends, but they were just that, friends without benefits. She knew he wanted more. *What's stopping me? We're never alone. It's not as if we're dating. Why does everyone treat us as if we're a couple?*

Before long, Jud left for the office; he had a deadline. There was always a deadline.

***

It was a charmed winter, and there was always something to do. Who would have believed it? Mornings at minus 20 degrees. Mornings when she was glad that she'd plugged in her car's radiator. Days skiing with the north wind coming off Moosehead Lake, when she and Jud stayed out there on the trails—a matter of pride not to come in till the drinking hour, when the band played, and they quaffed beer and somehow drove home on roads that felt like ski slopes. And there were the huskies…

It was exhilarating, flying over snow-covered ice behind a team of sled dogs. Wrapped in fur covering all but slits for her eyes, she bumped along in the sled's sole seat, gripping the sides with her muscles tense and tiring. It was better than standing up on a ship's bridge, protected from the elements. Down on the ice and snow, the biting wind smacked you in the face. Behind her, Dynamite drove her team of five Alaskan huskies, two pairs behind their leader directed by nothing but voice commands. And the huskies responded as one to "mush," "gee," or "haw," lunging across the lake, emitting white puffs, eating the air, and lapping up snow.

"They look fresh and happy," she told Dynamite as they were leaving the dogs in their outdoor kennel.

"You know," Dynamite said, "if I let them, they would run all day."

The huskies inspired Melanie. They were so engaged, committed to the team with all their willpower and strength, following orders, nothing held back, giving their all for their teammates. Clearly, any would die for the others. Why was she holding back?

She knew Jud was interested. And yet she held back, refusing to commit. Melanie wondered if she was ready for a relationship. She remembered her last visit with Dr. Deering. "Find yourself first," Dr. Deering had said. She was trying.

Chapter 35

Dynamite had driven Melanie to the Greenville Inn, where she had time to freshen up. She'd lost all feeling in her frozen toes, and in the hot shower, it slowly returned. Her toes screamed as if they were on fire. She tried jumping up and down. The pain disappeared, a distant memory, the way pregnant women are said to forget the agony of childbirth. She took care descending the curved, carved-oak stairway in her black dress and flats. When she looked up, there to greet her at the bottom of the stairs was Jud. She rushed to him and threw her arms around him.

"Well, well." He held her at arm's length, looking her all over. "What do we have here? Something different about you. I hear you've been out on the lake mushing while your star local journalist was reporting all the news that's unfit to print."

Melanie threw her head back in abandoned laughter. "Oh Jud, it was a glorious day out there with the huskies, and I learned so much from them."

"Come on, beautiful, let's hit the bar with the locals, and you can tell me more."

They joined the group standing around the piano and sang the old songs that everyone knew, and there was a feeling of camaraderie there, if only for the evening. Jud harmonized with his strong bass voice, and Melanie's soprano soared. She felt transported by the song, an old spiritual. And, suddenly—she hadn't noticed—they all stopped to focus on her voice as it carried out to the adjacent dining room. Everyone was listening to her. Singing solo in public was something she'd never done. Never had the courage or confidence. And now it felt right. She let it out and finished in a high vibrato. When she ended the song, there was a slight silence, and then everyone clapped, and she felt Jud's beaming smile. She'd never felt so adored. Don't lose this, a voice in her head warned her. Remember the huskies.

She rose, and so did Jud, and nobody noticed when they left the group. He walked her over to the stairway and put his arm around her waist. She was already feeling the glow from the booze and the Christmas cheer, and his touch sparked a fire within that she was not going to resist. Not this time. She turned to look into his eyes and could see the desire. She grabbed his hand. "Come on. You look like a lost puppy, and I'm taking you home." She led him up the stairs and down the hall, fumbled for the key from her purse, then unlocked the door and flung it open. She wrapped her legs around him, locking her ankles behind his back as he carried her to the bed.

God, she lay there thinking afterward, it had been a while. Sex. Amazing how she could live without it for so long. She wanted to laugh out loud, but didn't wish to wake him from his deep sleep. Propped on one elbow, she watched his hairy chest rise and fall like a contented walrus. Such a nice guy. She'd taken him to her bed in the heat of desire. Now, she felt satisfied, and yet, an enormous emptiness hollowed out her insides. *What have I done?*

Outside the frosted window, a few stars shone through the town lights, and she thought it was nothing like being out at sea at night. Her father once told her God sprinkled stars like diamond dust to create the Milky Way. Out at sea on a calm night, the sea itself reflected the whole Milky Way. Alone on the bridge, she'd felt enveloped by diamond dust in the starry sky above and on the surface of the waters below. The vastness of the ocean and its endless variations in light and color evoked in her a sense of wonder and purpose—always going somewhere with a purpose. Not land-locked, hemmed in, going nowhere…like now. She thought of Dynamite and Sam and Jud. Interesting. She realized she always thought of them as a package.

Chapter 36

The letters kept coming, one a month. She regretted writing to the man who used to be Sergey. It was bizarre. Who else has an alias, for God's sake? Clearly, it was a mistake. It looked like Jack was still infatuated with her. His last letter mentioned coming to Maine. *What do I tell Jud*? Jud had mentioned living together, and she'd told him they should wait. Maybe she was ready to say yes. Jack could screw everything up. She decided to write to him one more time. She wrote, "Dearest Jack," then stopped. No. Can't say that. She wrote:

Dear Jack:

I am glad that you are doing well now, but I hope you realize that I do not wish to have a relationship with you. Please do not come to Maine to see me.

Thank you,

Melanie.

At the last minute, she decided not to send it. Melanie worried the letter sounded too harsh and might tip him over the edge.

***

Winter would end soon. It was time to face the future. One morning, Melanie and Jud met for coffee at the Lost Woods Bar & Grille.

"Jud, I've got to do something," she said. "I've been living off my savings and you and your friends, and my savings are almost exhausted. It's time for me to get a job or something or go live with my parents. Ugh." She looked defeated.

"Okay," he said. "Is this news fit to print?"

"Jud, can you be serious for once?"

"You don't have to do this, you know."

"No, but I should. I can't escape it forever." Six months seemed like a year.

"Sure, when you're ready. I don't think you are, not yet. What are you thinking?"

"That's the thing. I have no idea what to do. I can't take a job at a desk all day. I'd die. I've talked with the career planners at the academy, and they say there are good jobs out there, maybe in the energy business. I've been at sea my whole working life, but my shrink says I'm not ready to get back on a ship."

"What do you think?"

"I don't know. What do you think?"

"I think you can do whatever you set your mind to. So, what will you do?"

"I'm going back to Portland, and I'll see what develops."

"I'll come with you. I could write freelance. But you know you could move in with me right here in Greenville. You like it here. And I'm kind of wedded to my work at the paper. You have friends here."

It was true. She did, and she could. He was being so generous. As always. She felt grateful. How many women had that? So charming. How could she resist this kind man?

"Will you marry me, Melanie Ricker?" His timing was right. Tears came to her eyes, tears of relief, a way out.

"Yes, Jud, I will. But there's something we need to talk about."

"What's that?" he asked.

"Jack Pierce," she said.

***

"Here's to you both," Dynamite said, raising her glass to Melanie and Jud.

Sam and Jud stood at the bar for another round. Sam was off duty. "About time, you dolt," Sam said. "What took you so long?"

Jud frowned. "I know. I know. You know what?" Jud lowered his voice to a whisper. "She wants to meet with him."

Sam looked confused. "Who?"

"The spook guy. You know, the guy she caught and got sent back to Langley."

"What? That's nuts."

"Right. I told her no way, but she's insisting. Have Dynamite talk to her, will you?"

Soon as she heard, Dynamite called Melanie. "What's this I hear? You want to meet with Jack?"

"Yeah. Jud told you?"

"He told Sam. What's going on, Mel?"

"Can I trust you, Dy? I mean, you can't tell Sam, 'cause then Jud will know, and I don't want to hurt him."

"Of course."

"It's complicated. I've never talked about it with Jud, or anyone. It was so long ago." She paused to collect her thoughts. "When I was in high school, well, that summer before high school, that's when I met Jack. He was the first boy who'd really paid any attention to me. I was all messed up. You know, middle school—everyone wants to forget it. Anyway, Jack really saved me."

"What do you mean?"

"Dy, have you ever been taunted by other girls? Well, I was.

And you would not have recognized me back then."

"Jeez. I'm sorry. I didn't know, but Mel, that was years ago, and you've got over all that, and—"

"Not completely. I had dreams—nightmares—about drowning after my little brother Charlie drowned when I was six—"

"My God, that's awful."

"That's the thing, the dreams. They stopped after I met Jack."

"They did?"

"Yes, they did. And that's not all. He's the one who got me to run and it's how I became this...this athlete...and my life, everything changed, all because of Jack."

"So, he helped you, so what? I don't mean to be crass, but Mel, you're engaged, and I don't see why—"

"I know. I know. But Dy, we stayed in touch. We've been swapping emails and letters."

"What, you and Jack Pierce?"

"Yes."

"How long?"

"For years."

"Is this still going on?"

"Yeah, 'fraid so. I know, it's crazy. I couldn't tell him it was over. I just couldn't. So, you see, I need to see him again to be sure about..."

"You're not sure about Jud?" So, what are you saying? That you love this Pierce guy? From way back then? Can you wait a minute? Someone's at the door..."

Melanie waited. Did she love Jack? And then Dynamite was back. "It was nothing, sorry."

"Dy, I don't know how to tell you this. It is not just guilt. I mean, I understand that's not a good reason to love someone. But I loved Jack, despite all his problems, and then we met again on the ship—"

"So, he was the CIA spy on the loose, and you felt threatened by him, and you got him to turn himself in.”

"Yes. He did that for me.”

"And you want to see if you love Jud or this former assassin?”

"Yes. I need to do this, Dy.”

"What are you going to tell Jud?”

"I'm telling him I need to tell Jack I'm engaged to Jud and help him get over me.”

"Wow. Mel, you're really throwing the dice here, do you know that?”

"Jud's going to be okay with it, or at least he's weakening. I'll appeal to his manhood, as protector, you know?”

"What about 'No' does this guy not understand?”

"I know. I know. But you see, I think Jack misunderstood. It was my fault. I shouldn't have sent him that first letter, and then I should have sent him the second one, and—”

"Right,” said Dynamite, jumping on this. "You clearly told him 'No,' and he didn't get it? Come on.”

"Just do this for me, Dy. Okay?”

What Melanie couldn't say was that she needed to see Jack for another reason—to make sure she was making the right choice. Reluctantly, they agreed to go with her. Melanie called and left a message that she would meet with him when he got out. There were messages back and forth with the staff at Langley. She had a date, time, and place.

Chapter 37

Harry Field laughed to think how he'd pulled it off. It was unprecedented. The agency had never retired an agent who'd been licensed to kill. Harry had not threatened to disclose Pierce's assassinations, most of them sanctioned, some not. It was enough to leave the suggestion hanging. He recalled the director's reaction. "Harry, you son of a bitch." The Director of Covert Operations was beside himself. "You're trying to put me over a barrel, and I won't have it, damn it! You know full well that any leak and the Justice Department would be all over us."

"Well, sir, I understand that. What I'm saying is, we can control this."

"How do you know that? He's done some very bad things."

"Yes, we know he's done some very bad things, and we are responsible for them all. We made him what he is."

"He went off the reservation. We talked about this. And when that happens, we have to…"

"I know, I know, yes, sir, he went rogue, but if any of this comes to light, we're the ones who take the hit."

"So, what are you getting to?"

"What I'm getting to is, we keep him on a tether, and we put him on our payroll to train our agents, and if that's leaked, who cares? What it gives us is some control, some insurance. I mean, even if someone leaks who he is, the fallout is nothing compared to the complete disaster of someone leaking what he's done. And who knows about that? You, me, Doc Treslow, and Jack Pierce."

"What does Treslow say?"

"Doc Treslow assures me that all his misdeeds have been repressed in his mind, so he's not going to be able to tell."

"Is that possible?" asked Robinson.

"Yes, it's a new technique. Very interesting. You give someone two lists and tell them to concentrate on one of them and not the other, and the other begins to recede from short-term memory, and eventually, the mind simply fails to recall it. Of course, it's not gone altogether. We've tested it, and it works."

"Fascinating," said Robinson. "Good work."

"Thank you, sir."

***

He'd been told this was to be his last session. He didn't expect to see Harry with Doc Treslow.

"Thought we'd celebrate your accomplishment," said Harry. "We just came from seeing Robinson, and he's blessed the plan. Congratulations."

"Thanks. What's next?"

"Report for your first training session this coming Monday morning. We'll start you slow. You'll meet with a handful of new agents. Just talk with them about your experiences. We'll give you feedback and help you learn how to improve."

***

He recalled Treslow's words: "You're a new man, Jack, so enjoy your new life. I don't think you'll have any memory of past misdeeds." Treslow had called them "daring escapades for home and country" and "rogue actions." He'd said his memory had been "scrubbed clean," and he'd no longer recall them.

Jack knew this was nonsense. He still remembered most everything. And yet, he felt different. He no longer felt like a spy because he'd followed orders—well, mostly—and he'd done it for his country. Maybe there was something to what Doc Treslow had told him. *Now you can fit in.* Maybe it was true. They said he'd been programmed to fit in, to act more normal. He'd always been a risk taker, so he'd thrown the dice in going through deprogramming. It had been his only option to avoid prosecution for crimes he'd committed. Treason and murder were high on the list. He knew the CIA would have found out—they had too many sources inside the Ukrainian government. By choosing to come in, he could play ball with them and restore his good name. And it had all worked out— they said he and they would forget about his misdeeds. Well, he hoped he could forget. And they'd told him, "You're a patriot, Jack, and you've served your country well." He believed this. He was excited to serve in his new capacity as a desk agent. Right after this weekend. When he would see Melanie.

***

On a cold spring Saturday, Jack Pierce stepped out of CIA headquarters, clean-shaven, hair cropped short, dressed in a white shirt and blue blazer. In the mirror before leaving, he'd liked his new look—Melanie would approve.

The black Suburban SUV pulled up to the entrance, a suit stepped out to open the back door for Jack Pierce, who entered the vehicle and sat in the back seat. As the SUV pulled away, he kept his eyes forward, not from fear of the proverbial pillar of salt or any nostalgia for his past life, but rather for the promise of what lay ahead.

The Suburban rolled to a stop under the awning of a fancy hotel in downtown D.C. A uniformed doorman ushered him from the vehicle as he watched the last vestige of his past life, the bulletproof Suburban, drive away and disappear into traffic. He pushed through the revolving doors into a festive lobby scene—the noise, the smell of energy and of deals in the works. It seemed like a new world opening in front of him, a world full of glitter and hope. He wondered if it would happen or if it was all a fanciful dream.

"Jack!" A woman's voice, strong, familiar. His eyes searched the lobby and spotted her. Melanie approached him, looking cheery and somehow different. She wore an elegant navy-blue dress and strapped sandals. Her blond hair was stylishly coiffed. He waited for her to do whatever people do in this situation—he would let her take the lead. He would play defense and adjust to her moves. He took her proffered hand to shake it, and when she turned her face and presented her cheek, he obliged with a polite peck. She always took his breath away, even now. He held her back to look her over, and her breezy air made him dizzy and lamb-happy. It struck him that she'd called him by his real name, and this was pleasing, too.

"These are my friends," she said with her fetching smile.

It's the smile he remembered all through his sessions, the smile that had kept him going. As Melanie turned her head, he followed her gaze reluctantly to take in this other man and woman. *Why are they here?*

"I don't think you've met them," Melanie was saying. "They're from Greenville." The other woman stepped forward to meet him.

"Dynamite MacKenzie," said Melanie. "And Jud Jenkins." Jack glanced at this other woman called Dynamite but focused his full attention on the man standing next to her. Jack did what he always did—in an instant, he sized up the man, this man called Jud. Short, chubby, thirty-something, unshaven, curly dark hair, chinos, white shirt open at the neck, and a gaudy gold chain hanging there. His first thought—this man is no threat. Jack quickly dismissed him. He turned to size up the woman called Dynamite. Tall and slim, she moved like an athlete, then stood next to Melanie, hands on hips. In an instant, he knew she was a force. He'd been mistaken to focus on

Jud first. But Melanie was talking, and she was asking him something. He tried to focus and clear his mind.

"They were nice to come with me to see you," Melanie was saying. "So, Jack, what are you doing now?"

His mind struggled for the right note. "I'm… I'm…" He realized his voice must sound wooden. He made a quick adjustment and cleared his throat. How much should he tell them? "I'm still with the agency, as I said—"

"You said you'll be teaching others. That sounds great."

Now that he was focused on Melanie, something about her seemed off—there was something about her face and the way she seemed to want him to pay attention to the others, when he just wanted her. He was trying to take in the situation, to adjust—something he and Doc Treslow had worked on. She didn't look him in the eye, and it threw him. What would Doc Treslow say? Jack sensed something in the air—something she was saying that he didn't want to hear. He got up the courage to ask her, "So, what about you?"

"Jack," said Melanie, "Jud and I are engaged to marry…"

He couldn't help the slight twitch in the facial muscles in his right cheek below his right eye. He'd seen it in the mirror. Doc Treslow had said it was due to stress. Maybe they wouldn't notice it.

But she'd seen it. He knew this. She must be thinking this was a mistake. He could tell she wanted to get out of there. And a rage began to build inside him.

"Jack, are you okay? They said you were okay now."

He turned on his heel, busted through the turnstile door, and, once outside, kept walking, and as he did, he reviewed his assessment. One, I love her—she's worth the battle. Two, this Jud is unworthy of her. Therefore, three, she really loves me—there must be some other reason. Four, this Dynamite is a formidable opponent, but she can't protect Melanie. Conclusion, the battle is not over. It has just begun.

***

They retreated to the hotel bar to talk about it.

"Well," said Dynamite, "I guess you accomplished your mission. Now, he knows. No question about it."

"That," Jud said, "was a scary dude."

Melanie was thinking, what did I expect him to do? Sweep me off my feet and declare his undying love? She was still disturbed by Jack's abrupt departure. He was clearly upset. What would he do next? He was so unpredictable. Well, maybe she had accomplished her goal. Now she could forget about Jack. It was looking like she'd made the right choice.

Chapter 38

Back in his apartment, he looked at his haggard image in the mirror. *Who is this man?*

Sometimes he no longer knew who he was, but he knew one thing—he wanted Melanie. "It's not your fault," he said to himself. "And it's not your fault, Melanie." He thought about Melanie. How could she have fallen for this Jud? Jud was a mistake. Melanie would understand her mistake. He would convince her.

"It's your fault," he said, his voice now steady and cold as ice. He meant the agency and their retraining—he'd been injected with truth serum and gone through hypnosis, sleep deprivation, and isolation, and it had wrung out of him any vestige of his earlier self. He recalled Doc Treslow's voice: "It's the price you must pay, Jack, to become human again." At the end, they assured him, "You are no longer a danger to society, and we think you will be able to repress, and eventually unable to recall, your assignments. It will make you a better person." Okay, he thought, I no longer wish to take another's life. He had forgiven his father but still grieved his mother. "It was a fair deal," he finally told the mirror. "But only if I can have her." Because Melanie had saved him. Because of her, he'd survived the program.

***

He knew how to disappear. It took time and planning. The government has too many tools to find you. He withdrew cash in small amounts from the sizable bank account they set up for his new life as a CIA advisor. He showed up at Langley every workday to train the new agents; he loved the irony. His plan? Use his tradecraft to disappear at the right time. He convinced his new superiors of his need to be armed—after all, he'd made enemies. He took the time to get a concealed weapons permit. He would keep his name for now—he'd change it later. And he would make good use of it at the right time. As he began to withdraw from social media, his profile and personal stamp diminished daily.

He looked at himself in the mirror. "You're ready," he said to himself. Days and weeks of deception, going to work at Langley as if he wanted to fit in, to do this job, training other agents. No more. He drove his car to a back lot in a rough section of the city and abandoned it with no trace left behind. Just like his apartment—not a trace. He wore shoddy clothes, work boots, glasses, a money belt, and a baseball cap. He'd blackened his hair. In his backpack, a loaded handgun with his carry permit, extra bullets, and cash. He walked to a nearby bus stop and boarded the next local bus to the Greyhound station, where he bought a one-way ticket to Portland, Maine.

***

Harry Field knew right where Jack Pierce was, thanks to that chip he'd had implanted, the one Jack would never find. Harry was not worried. He knew all about Jack's obsession with Melanie. Doc Treslow had figured that out. Harry knew something else about Jack Pierce—he got that from Doc Treslow, too—Jack might look dangerous, but he was not. Harry was proud of how they'd taken the urge to kill right out of him. Harry felt he owed Jack for his service. It's like all those stars on the wall at Langley—former agents who had sacrificed their lives for the nation. Jack Pierce had done that.

Jack Pierce had paid the price. Harry said to himself, we owe Jack Pierce big-time, and I'm going to protect him. So, let him go to Maine. Let him find this girl, Melanie. And I'll be there for him, he thought. Harry was sticking out his neck here. Robinson would never agree, the cold-hearted bastard. To Robinson, all their agents were dispensable. So, fuck him.

PART 4

Mount Katahdin

<h1 align="center">Chapter 39</h1>

Their packs were heavy as they hiked the popular Roaring Brook Trail, arriving at Chimney Pond after 10 a.m., the cutoff time for those who wished to climb to the peak.

Dynamite had put the small group together—a young couple from Quebec, Charles and Isabelle Clermont, an older man from Boston, Ken Strong, and Melanie. The rigors of winter in the Maine North Woods had restored Melanie's stamina and spirit. Excited by the challenge, she relished a day away from the drudgery of wedding preparations.

They would spend the night in the camp that Dynamite had reserved; they would take on the peak in the morning, weather permitting. The Baxter State Park ranger had to give them the okay to continue. Even with permission to make the final climb up to the peak, climbers risked sudden and unexpected violent storms and whiteouts.

They were halfway up the mountain, where Chimney Pond forms a basin just below the tree line. It was a rare day of clear visibility. "It may seem like summer down here, but up there..." Dynamite gestured toward the distant peak, and the heads of the small knot of hikers swiveled in unison. "Up there, it can turn into a wintry day."

As the quarter moon rose over the rim, the massif of Mount Katahdin hovered over them, outlined by moonlight, and it looked fearsome. After sunset, they sat around a bonfire and felt the warmth of food in their bellies. Dynamite brought out a small Indian drum and began to thump on it in four beats, the first beat stronger. And they felt the charm of it. The sound reverberated across the pond and bounced back from the dark mountainside. Dynamite began to speak, her breath white in the cold night, telling them the old Penobscot Indian story to the sound of the drum—BOOM, boom, boom, boom…

"The Penobscots lived up here before any white man, and they passed their stories down through the ages." Dynamite paused to let it sink in, and they could all picture the time when only the Indians came here. As they listened to her distinctive Maine accent, harsh to their ears but charming too, softened by her beauty, they sat mesmerized, silent, their faces glowing in the firelight. And they looked knowingly at each other. For this is why they'd come here, even without knowing why. They were caught up in the spell of the moment, and the drum—BOOM, boom, boom, boom…

"The Penobscot Indians believed that Katahdin—and it's the Penobscots who gave it that name—that Katahdin was ruled by their thunder god, Pamola, who has the body of a man and the wings of an eagle. They believed that anyone who climbs to the summit will be killed or devoured by Pamola. And so, they dared not climb beyond the tree line to where Pamola lives."

The drum became more insistent, and as her voice hushed, they strained to hear.

"When the Penobscot braves led a climbing party like this one, they would not go up beyond the tree line, because if they did, they might not return because Pamola would be angry." She paused, and the drum went silent. They could hear splashing in the lake, maybe trout or a moose. Dynamite continued, "But there was an old sachem of the tribe who decided to challenge Pamola, and he went up the mountain, and he dared to climb up above the tree line. Look! Right over there. See that?"

They looked, and they could see the rocks and, in their imagination, where a trail might pass between them.

"Right up there, he found a cave. It was very cold, and he covered the entrance with water, which froze and sealed the mouth of the cave. And late that night, Pamola came down, and he was angry, so he banged on the ice that covered the cave." She pounded the drum—BOOM, and they jumped.

"And he jumped at the sound of Pamola pounding on the cave entrance. And he could not sleep because he knew he'd done a very foolish thing. He decided that if he lived, he would tell the tribe never to challenge Pamola. And when the sun came up, Pamola returned to the top of the mountain where he lived. And so, the sachem came back down the mountain and told everyone, "Never tempt the mountain spirits, because if you do…" She struck the side of the drum with the stick. BAM! And they all jumped again. And then they laughed.

"Others say, if you challenge the mountain, you never conquer it. It's only because Pamola has allowed you to go up."

***

Melanie listened to the night sounds, the distant roaring brook, and the cry of a loon. She remembered a time not so long ago when lonesomeness had come to her like a dog worries a bone. Now, she could laugh about it. Love. She'd thought she'd loved Cliff. A mistake. She loved David, her captain, but it was more like admiration for a mentor. Just as she had loved all her crewmates. She had loved Jack once and now was saddened to think of what had happened to him. And now there was Jud. At first, she'd resisted for reasons that now seemed silly and immature. Her parents wouldn't like him. He wasn't handsome. A parade of objections—wedded to his work as a journalist, bit of a groupie, a follower, totally connected with Sam and Dynamite. But time and circumstance conspired to help him win her, or so it seemed.

"You awake?" Dynamite asked. She was raised up on one elbow, her image backlit by a window full of moonglow. In parallel zero-degree sleeping bags laid out on the floor of the tiny camp, they spoke in an intimate hush. "Is this hard for you?" Dynamite whispered. "I mean being here, this climb in the middle of nowhere?"

"No. No. Out here, it's a lot like being at sea, the freedom, the risk, the physical challenge."

"But you chose to be here. You didn't choose to get hit by a hurricane."

"Well, in a way, I chose both. I mean, I was the one who charted our course, to run the risk, not take the safe way out. I tried to convince our captain to take the safer route, but, hey." She had never told anyone. Why was it she felt she could talk to this woman?

"You blame yourself?" There it was. Make a choice. Go ahead if you dare expose yourself. Take a chance.

"I suppose I am. I do. My parents always said I tend to take on others' problems."

"Wise parents. Ought to listen to them."

"Hah. Touché."

"Ever think about why God chose to save you?" At first, Melanie was shocked at the question. How dare she? But once again, she made the choice to take the chance.

"I haven't thought much about God. Guess I should. I mean, I used to be a churchgoer, but I felt like I was going through the motions."

"That's the thing about religion—no sitting on the sidelines—you're either in or you're out. That sound radical?"

"Yes, but I've always known that I would at some point. I mean, I knew I would have to make that decision. Maybe God saved me so I could."

"Smart gal. I was like you. Worse. I was a wicked sinner."

"What happened?"

"I met a guy."

"Sam? I like him. You're lucky."

"Yup. I sure am. But what about you?"

"That's the thing. I was feeling very alone until I came here, and now, thanks to you and Jud…" Melanie realized that just talking about it, naming it, was like taking out your dirty laundry, and when you did, you could come clean and begin to feel better. What had been a gray pillow over her head was now thrown out into the open air. Survival was the easy part, at least for her, because she'd done nothing more than follow her training, and the rest was luck. Or maybe she was now, for the first time, willing to consider God's will. So that would mean there was a purpose to her life. She remembered it was what Sam had suggested back at the Lost Woods Bar & Grill. And she remembered when she'd made the decision to see Jud again and see what would happen. She would be more open to what God might have in mind for her life after the storm. If He, or She, existed. She laughed softly to herself. All this because Pamola gave his blessing to their climb to the peak. Silly Indian story.

***

Dynamite MacKenzie knew she was blessed. From a tiny village called Allagash near the Canadian border, she'd followed her dad into the Maine woods as a logger, then joined the Maine Loggers' Association to fight the paper companies and landowners. When no one was protesting the clearcutting, she'd formed her eco-terrorist band, inspired by writers like Wallace Stegner and Edward Abby. She didn't know Melanie well enough to tell her about Hannah White and how she died. Dynamite gave thanks to Sam and the Good Lord for saving her. And for being here now in Baxter State Park, a vast wilderness—thanks to Maine's Governor Baxter, "forever wild."

Dynamite's last thought before falling asleep: tomorrow is a big day.

Chapter 40

Jack sat in his pickup truck in the Roaring Brook parking lot and turned up the heat. It was near the summer solstice, but the sun still lay behind the dark mass of Katahdin and hadn't begun to warm the cold spring air. He used his powers of concentration to slow his heart rate and focus on his mission. He strapped on his sidearm and slipped on a light windbreaker to conceal it. Melanie and her fellow hikers would be up soon, but it would take them an hour or two before they broke camp. They'd have breakfast before starting their ascent.

Thanks to the helpful clerk at the Greenville Inn, he knew who they were, what they looked like, and where they were going. Intelligence on the ground was essential to any operation. True, the clerk knew his description, but they'd never find him.

Once he had Melanie with him, he could implement his plan. Together, they could disappear. He would create a new identity for them both.

From his position in the parking lot, it was an easy climb of three miles to Chimney Pond. His legs and ankles were weak from lack of exercise, but he was hardened to pain. He looked at the map. Once he reached Chimney Pond, he would hike the shorter, steeper Cathedral Trail. They would take the Saddle Trail because it was an easier climb to the tableland. This would give him an advantage because the Saddle Trail was longer, more than two miles from Chimney Pond to the peak. And they'd be slowed by the old man with white hair. Maybe Jack could stay hidden on the Cathedral Trail—the park ranger said huge boulders lined the trail. Perhaps he'd beat them to the cutoff, where the two trails joined together up on the tableland before reaching the peak. Up on the tundra, he'd follow the markers—the ranger called them cairns—until he reached the Knife Edge. They would surely cross it. There, they'd be exposed on the treacherous edge. He could easily spot her there. With sheer drop-offs on both sides, it was a mile-long tightrope with no escape. He'd catch Melanie on the Knife Edge. He just needed time with her, and then she'd agree to come with him.

Maybe it was an abundance of confidence, or maybe his trade-craft was slipping. He left his backpack with extra clothing, food, and water in the car.

Chapter 41

Melanie brought up the rear of Dynamite's small group. "See all those huge boulders rising up like a church cathedral?" she heard Dynamite say, and she looked to where Dynamite was pointing to the Cathedral Trail as they passed it.

"Looks impossible," said Isabelle. "You'd have to use your hands to pull yourself up and over all those boulders." They were happy to climb the less challenging Saddle Trail. There was the usual chatter at the start, everyone fresh and eager for their climb to the summit.

"Good thing we had a hearty breakfast."

"Yeah, nuts and raisins, my favorite."

"Delicious."

"Okay," said Dynamite. "Be sure to stay together on the trail. Melanie, you take the lead."

Melanie moved up front while Dynamite brought up the rear.

Melanie's breathing remained steady, and her legs felt strong, her renewed confidence an elixir. She needed the physical challenge, the hard work that gave her the high experienced by marathon runners and top athletes. She sat on a large rock, waiting for them to catch up. Several layers insulated her body from the chill. In her backpack were first aid supplies, more nuts and berries, a windbreaker, a poncho, and her flashlight. She sipped water from a thermos—there was no water above the tree line. Her frustration mounted as Dynamite cajoled and encouraged the laggards. Isabelle was slow and steady. Ken was out of breath—he stopped to rest once more. Ahead of them, Melanie threw her arms up, then pointed up the mountain—a signal she wished to go on alone.

Dynamite gave her a thumbs up. "Wait for us at the peak!" she yelled.

Up above the tree line, the lichen-covered rocks appeared strewn about from the time of creation, and there was little other vegetation. A mist appeared out of nothing. Melanie looked back down the trail, and all was lost in the mist as it cast its white mantle over her world, only to dissolve and float away to reveal rocks and sky and then swallow her once again, fogged in without a view. It was like smoke from a campfire, enveloping and blinding, then wafting away. As she climbed the trail, its worn path marked by small piles of stones, her boots slipped on the wet rocks. She learned to tread lightly in short, quick strides. In moments when the mist cleared, she glanced down below to see a smattering of small ponds, like a smashed mirror, its slivers scattered over the land.

In less than an hour, Melanie reached the intersection where the Cathedral Trail joined the Saddle Trail. She decided to stop and wait for them there. She sat cross-legged on the ground with her backpack beside her. Two hikers appeared out of the mist—a tall, thin man with a beard and ponytail and a woman with blond hair in pigtails, coming up Cathedral and looking as fit as Swiss mountaineers out for a Sunday walk. They moved fast with long, loping strides. Melanie smiled.

"Nice day for a climb," she said.

"Every day's a good day for a climb," the man replied, smiling.

To Melanie, all hikers were part of the club. Some elite hikers would be on their last mile of the Appalachian Trail, about to celebrate their long journey from Georgia. She watched them slip out of sight into the mist. She was entombed in silence once again. Her penalty for forging ahead: this seemingly endless lone vigil atop Maine's highest mountain, which was swaddled in white.

And yet Melanie was elated to be here, regaining her physical strength, finding herself and her footing. She pulled out a map of Katahdin and noted the alternative trails back down. Abol Trail was closed due to slides. The Hunt Trail offered a longer and more gradual trek down but then required a long walk back to their SUV. Dynamite had said she planned to take the Dudley Trail down the mountain from the Knife Edge back to Chimney Pond, and thence via the same Roaring Brook Trail they had climbed the day before.

***

Dynamite had allowed her party to be split, and she now regretted it. Isabelle and Ken were in no shape to continue the climb. There were no other hikers in sight. She'd have to leave her exhausted charges to find Melanie. It would take no more than an hour or two to reach Melanie and return to her laggards with time to get them down the mountain before dark.

***

Sure-footed and fleet, driven with purpose, he climbed swiftly alongside the roaring brook that drowned out all sounds under a deep forest canopy. When he reached the tree line, the view opened to what lay before him. Immense cathedral rocks rose into the mist like an altar.

Jack struggled to pull himself up and over boulders on an almost vertical trail, boulder after immense boulder. It sapped his energy. Stupid. Overconfident and foolish, he had headed up the mountain with nothing—no water, no food, no extra clothes. Now, parched and weak, he felt punched in the gut. Would this trail never end? His exertion caused him to sweat, and when he stopped to rest, the cold air chilled him, and the sweat froze on his back. His one thought: keep moving, find Melanie, and put an end to the pain.

Thirst drove him on. Where would she be now? Dehydration causes confusion, and he was not immune to this. His hands blistered from the rocks, feet and ankles shrieking, he reached the tableland, where he stopped, panting, to see what lay around him.

He could barely make out the trail ahead. There in the mist, he saw a form, maybe a person sitting on the ground.

Chapter 42

Melanie peered into the mist back down Saddle for any sign of Dynamite and the rest of the group. When she turned her gaze to the Cathedral Trail, another hiker appeared out of the mist like a ghost. A lone male hiker, his short black hair wet. He wore no backpack and carried nothing as he stumbled toward the trail intersection where Melanie waited. He looked exhausted, about to fall.

As the lone hiker drew closer, she noticed steam rising from his body and quick white puffs of breath from his crooked mouth. Now alarmed, she stood. Maybe he was in distress. "Can I help you?" she called to him. His eyes were pinpricks of ink, and his hands reached out to her as if he knew her. Her mind searched through its deep recesses and snatched pieces of memory, patching these pieces into an image from the past.

"Oh, my God! Jack? What are you doing here?" She reached out to help him as he slumped onto the rocky ground. His voice, distant, almost a squeak, uttered the words, "It's you." An accusation? Or an expression of relief at finding her? As she hovered over him, he pulled himself up to a sitting position on the small, hard rocks.

"Water," he said, his voice like a croak, weak and scratchy.

She handed him her water bottle and held it up for him to drink, giving him a little at a time until the water dripped down his chin and he slumped back onto the bare ground, resting his eyes on her. That look, the one she recalled from the ship. The same look she'd first seen in his eyes when they'd met on East End Beach back when they were teenagers. Once again, she felt her heart melt. How incredible. How could he still do that to her?

But now there was something else—a hint of danger.

Her mind raced to find answers. *God, he must have followed me here.* She remembered the scene in D.C., ending when he stormed out of the hotel. *What are my options?* Alone on a mountaintop with the man she'd once feared, the man she'd once run from and then confronted. Got him help. Thought he was cured. Healed by the same people at the CIA who'd ruined him. Was he healed? Why was he here now? It was all too bizarre.

Silence surrounded her. Sunk in her own confused thoughts and bathed in the hazy afternoon light, she had so many questions but no answers. Should she leave him here and seek help? Dynamite and her group were somewhere down there on the Saddle Trail. *What if he's still dangerous?* Her instincts told her to protect Dynamite. "Jack!" No response. "Jack!" His eyes opened, and a smile began to form on his lips as he stared at her.

"Jack, say something." Nothing. Melanie shrugged her shoulders. "So here we are. What next?"

"Melanie, I found you." His voice was raspy, surprisingly strong.

"Why? Why are you here, Jack?" She could see that he was unable to say more, but he didn't seem to understand how ridiculous this was. Without her prodding, he sat up, and without asking, he took some nuts and berries from her backpack.

"You're welcome," she said with sarcasm.

"Thanks," he said, without humor.

She marveled at his speedy recovery. He stood, eyes now clear, as he scanned the tableland. He seemed to be assessing, analyzing, fearful of something, though she knew not what. There were no other hikers in view. His gaze returned to rest on her, and he seemed to relax.

Perhaps it was time to see if they could get down off this mountain; otherwise, she knew it would be a long wait for a rescue party. As if he could read her mind, he said, "Let's go."

"Which way?" she asked. Just play along. Play for time.

"Come," he said, pointing to the other way down, away from the Saddle Trail, away from Dynamite and her group. Well, she thought, that's safer all around, until I know more, what you're up to. "Okay," she said. She let him lead. They headed toward the Knife Edge.

Their small steps crunched the crushed rocks that lay between the occasional cairns marking the trail. All around them, mist lay over the tableland. Her eyes searched for other hikers, but she saw no one.

Chapter 43

The man called Boris lost Pierce's trail in Portland. A man of his description had checked out of the fleabag hotel in downtown Portland after paying cash. It didn't take agent Boris Mikhailovich Berezovsky long—neighbors said Melanie had gone to Greenville. He was sure Pierce had followed her trail. In Greenville, a twenty-dollar bill to the desk clerk at the Indian Hill Motel revealed that one guest had paid cash and left in a black Ford pickup. The license plate was not listed. He must have stolen the car or paid cash for it.

Boris found the car—Greenville was a small town—and attached a tracking device under the frame. When the image on his hand-held computer began to move, Boris followed it to Mount Katahdin, where he found the car in the Roaring Brook parking lot. For Boris, this was personal—he'd known Alexei Korovchenko, Sebastopol's new mayor, now deceased, from their early days in Putin's GRU, the successor to the Soviets' KGB. Boris had infiltrated the Ukrainian government, and so Boris learned who had assassinated his friend—Sergey Robichek, a.k.a. Jack Pierce. Now, he had his man.

The Roaring Brook Trail was well travelled by hikers. Boris had no way to track his target, but he had time on his side. And he was well armed—a sniper rifle with a scope, broken down to fit in his backpack. He began to climb, leaping from rock to rock. It was already late morning. No park ranger was going to stop him.

***

Melanie gave him water when he demanded it. Jack's occasional coughing fits turned his pale face red. She stopped from time to time and he egged her on, gaining strength, until he was outpacing her, insisting she take the lead, pushing her to move faster.

She thought that Dynamite would stop to wait for her at the top of Cathedral Trail. Melanie took her cell phone from her pack and saw there was no signal. Maybe Dynamite would realize something was wrong and she'd call for help. Melanie would have to be ready for anything and react to events. What did Jack want from her? What did he intend to do with her? Or to her? They'd survived the hurricane and then she'd saved him, got him to turn himself in at Langley. She'd come back to this wilderness to find herself. And here he was again after that terrible meeting in D.C. when he walked away from her. But he was here now, claiming he was in love with her. Was she in love with him? Maybe she could play along and gain time. She had nothing to lose by talking, and she might learn something valuable. She turned to face him, and he almost bumped into her. "Jack, Jack, listen to me. I still don't know why you're here."

"Mel, I came a long way for you. Come with me. I've changed. I'm better now."

"Where? Where are we going? Why do you want me to come with you? Do I get a choice here?"

He looked into her eyes. "You don't want that guy Jud. I love you. Don't you love me?"

"I don't know, Jack. I'm engaged to Jud, and maybe I still have feelings for you, but I need more time. You have to give me more time. Can you do that?"

"Do you remember when we made love?"

"Yes, Jack, it was nice, but then you went to Langley because you needed help for all your issues." She could see him thinking about it, perhaps remembering his time at Langley, and she searched his face as he seemed to withdraw into another time and place. *Do I still love him?*

***

The mist surrounded them. Jack stood on a rocky path. He suddenly felt cold and wet. He remembered why he was here—the girl, the girl whose image remained with him through all the months of pain, throughout his treatment. Well, he'd fooled Doc Treslow in his white coat and his white room. He'd learned how to concentrate his mind on her, making Doc Treslow think he was under hypnosis. So he could leave. So he could find her here on this mountain. He'd survived the drugs, the hypnosis, and their endless questions. To be here with this woman who'd rejected him once. Not again. Not this time.

Chapter 44

Dynamite reached the tableland and followed the path marked by cairns. She came to a stop where the two trails intersected, perplexed that Melanie was not there—no sign of her. This was not like her. "Hello!" she called out. "Melanie!"

Silence. Not even an echo. Dynamite's voice was swallowed up by the darkening mist. She had to get the others back down to safety before dark. And Melanie? Able to take care of herself. No way to know if she was still walking along the tableland, heading for the Knife Edge, even now on her way back down to Chimney Pond. But this made no sense—they'd agreed to wait for each other here. Something happened to change that. Dynamite took out her cell phone. Any reception up here? Yes. She called Sam Morse and left a message.

"Sam, we have a problem. Up on top of Katahdin. Melanie's missing. Can't find her. I've got to take the rest of my group back down the mountain. Call me ASAP."

***

Sam Morse didn't get Dynamite's call right away—no reception. He was in his warden's truck, searching for a poacher in one of Maine's remote townships. An hour later, he got his messages. As soon as he heard the message from Dynamite, he called her.

"Where are you?"

"I'm okay," she said. "I'm on the Roaring Brook trail headed back down with my party, but I had to leave Melanie up there. I think she got tired of waiting for me at the top and decided to go on ahead. She's probably heading back down by now. But I'm worried. The rest of my group is tuckered out, and I need to take them back down now. I'll probably see her at the parking lot. Where are you?"

"I'm in Greenville. I'll get a chopper up there. See what I can see. Just get your crew down safe."

"Thanks, Sam. Love you. Bye."

***

"Impressive, eh?" Sam Morse said, speaking into his headset to Jud Jenkins, who sat in the copilot's seat. Jud nodded.

Katahdin dominated the vast wilderness from which it sprung up, crowned by peaks rising into a spine as sharp as a knife. As the chopper neared it, they could see the side sculpted into a bowl as if struck by a meteor. "It's got its own weather system," Sam said. "Might be tricky up on top."

Sam was a seasoned veteran, having survived his rookie year as a warden. He'd piloted helicopters in Afghanistan. When Dynamite had called about her friend in need up on Katahdin, Sam headed for the helipad in Greenville. Jud was along for the ride to cover the story for the *Greenville Times* and, of course, out of his concern for his fiancée. They belted up, lifted off the pad, and Sam wheeled the chopper northward over Moosehead Lake, then headed northeast over trackless forests lined with logging trails toward the unmistakable outline of Mount Katahdin.

Sam spoke into the intercom. "Looks like it's under cover on top, but you never know till you get there." He radioed to wardens on the ground to send available units to Katahdin. Two wardens near the site responded and agreed to head there.

"You think Melanie can handle herself?" asked Jud.

"I think Melanie has proven herself in action, so yeah, you bet. She's a tough cookie."

Sam brought his chopper up to the peak, where he hovered. It sent a signal to Melanie—we're here, and we're coming to help you. But the mountaintop was cloud-covered. "Can't land," he said. "Out of the question." Sam peeled off and swung down and around the mountaintop toward open sky. He could see the parking lot at the base of Roaring Brook Trail. He called Dynamite's number.

"I hear you, Sam. Any luck up there?"

"No. It's socked in. Where are you?"

"Almost at the parking lot. We're fine. Can you send some wardens up there on foot?"

"We have two wardens in the area headed there, but it's a big mountain, and we don't know how she will descend. And we've notified the park rangers. They'll have boots on the ground. I'm going to land at the Roaring Brook parking lot, where you should come out. Come find me. I can stop to see you for a minute, but I've got to get back to Greenville."

Chapter 45

The unmistakable flutter of chopper blades tore the air over-head. Melanie could see nothing, but she knew who was in pursuit—Sam. Maybe Dynamite had called him. She hoped so. Jack looked up into the void and ducked as if he were the hare, not the fox. "They're after us," he said.

"They're our friends, Jack. They want to help us. Do you understand?"

"We have to go."

Darkness had not yet fallen, but hikers were beginning their descent from Katahdin's peak.

"Are you strong enough?" Melanie asked him. "Here, eat this." She gave him what was left from her backpack, and he wolfed it down, then drank from her water bottle, now almost empty. They started walking and came to the turnoff for the Hunt Trail, an easier descent. "It's over five miles," she said, challenging him.

"They'll expect us to cross the Knife Edge," he said. She didn't want to risk the Knife Edge. She'd heard stories about those who had fallen to their death. "Let's do it," he said, indicating the Hunt Trail. He let her take the lead. They waved to the Swiss couple eating their lunch. Melanie wanted to give them a sign to alert them but could do nothing.

He's amazing, getting stronger. Get him talking. Search out his motives. "Jack, why are you here?" No response. "Why did you come after me?" Her voice louder, she was frustrated with his stony indifference. "It's all very flattering, but, my God, what am I to think? What do you want?" she asked. She would wait for his answer if it took a mile, whatever it took…

"You," he said. "I want you."

"But I told you, I'm engaged."

"You don't love him. He's not worthy of you, Mel. We both survived. And you got me through the therapy, all of it. And I'm here for you."

She almost fell into him when he turned to face her, his expression pained, hands upraised. "Melanie. You know I've always loved you. Back in high school, when we ran together, you loved me, too. Come on, admit it. And again, when we saw each other on the ship, the chemistry was still there. Yes, I did some bad things, and I wanted to find out what you knew so I could answer any questions you had. And then you saved me. Got me to turn myself in. We've been through so much together. Can't you give it a chance?"

She began to weaken. He'd stated his case, and it meant something because it was true. To a point. She said, "Why didn't you fight for me when I came to see you in D.C., huh? Why not then? Instead, you walked away. After I'd come down there to see if I still loved you?"

"Wow. Is that true?"

"Yes," she shouted into the void. "Yes."

"I didn't know, Mel. Honest. And I'm sorry."

They stood there, their breaths visible now in the chill, and looked out across the sweep of land that was endless forest.

"What did they do to you there?" she asked in a quiet voice.

"What? The deprogramming? It was hypnosis, drugs, lots of bad stuff."

"How could you go through all that?"

"I focused on you. I made them think I was under their spell, you see."

"I guess." She struggled to understand. "So why did you follow me here? Up a frigging mountain?"

"I'm trying to tell you. I'm not used to feeling like this. And look, I'm such a mess. They've messed me up… I'm in trouble with them. It's not because of you. Well, maybe it is because of you. I know I'm not making much sense."

"Jack, you've been through a lot. I'm sorry." She reached out to touch his arm, and he didn't pull away.

"Thanks. I think I know why I'm attracted to you. Because you're so good. You're a good person. And you're beautiful, too, but, I mean, I see your goodness, and I haven't had much of that in my life."

She felt for him. But was it love? Not if she was under duress. Not if he was giving her no choice. "Jack, we had something once. When we were just kids. And I felt it when we made love on the ship. And you did, too." Had she gone too far? She had to play for time.

"Yes," he said.

They sat on the ground and talked, and she tried to understand him. They had turned him into a spy and an assassin. It was incredible, what he'd been through. No family. No one to love him. And he'd sought her out to save himself, saw her goodness as a beacon. But this was crazy—was he kidnapping her or not?

"What's that around your neck?" he asked.

Her fingers went to the locket. "It's a very old photo of my little brother Charlie and me. I carry it everywhere. It keeps me calm."

"Can I see it?"

She'd never shown anyone. She opened the locket and showed him the black-and-white photo, crinkled and yellowed from age.

"It's beautiful. Here, let me show you something." He reached into his pocket, removed his wallet, and opened it to show her a photo, creased, and Melanie could see her own image, younger but the same blue eyes, golden hair, and shy smile. God, she looked so young and happy. When she was with Jack.

"It's me," she said, surprised.

"Yes."

"When did you take it?"

"That summer on the beach." He looked away, overcome with emotion. "Well, you must remember."

She looked at him in a new light. All these years, he'd carried her photo. "Yes, of course I remember. I never told you I was sorry. I wasn't ready. Do you understand?"

"Of course. But when I lost you, I lost everything that mattered to me in the world."

What to say? She imagined him as a teenager, left alone, and she felt sympathy for him once again, but only to a point, because she knew his dark side. She wanted to ask him about Alberto, the cook, but didn't dare. She'd heard his explanation, but it still weighed on her.

"I know you had to do some bad things, Jack. Do you think you can put that all behind you? I mean, did they help you to do that at Langley?" She was hoping, but had serious doubts.

"Yes, they did, and I think I can. I know I've done things… things I was trained to do. But it wasn't me. And the retraining was helpful, and I am changing my life."

Jack pulled her to her feet and urged her down the trail. The Swiss hikers greeted them as they passed the sign indicating the way to the Knife Edge. Here, the Hunt Trail descended from the tableland to where the trees began…

Chapter 46

The man called Boris, dressed in black and silhouetted against the misty sky, passed by two hikers sitting on a rock, a blond woman with pigtails and a tall man with a ponytail—they pointed to where the two other hikers, a man and a woman, had just taken the Hunt Trail. "You'll catch them soon," they said, their voices bright and cheery.

Boris began his descent from the tableland onto the Hunt Trail. He spotted them, still above tree level. Boris did not bother to set up his rifle. With a rapid and determined pace, he set off in haste down the mountain trail, unstrapping the knife from its hiding place in the shoulder holster under his windbreaker. As he began to close the distance to his target, they remained there, unmoving. They were making it easy.

***

They'd almost reached the tree line at the edge of the forest when Jack noticed the hiker approaching, head hooded, wearing all black. Strange how the hiker's eyes seemed fixed upon him—hikers always focused upon the rocky trail for their footing. Why are his eyes locked on me? From training or instinct, he sensed something was wrong—the man in black moved with stealth, like he was trained to do this, sliding over the rocks and staying low to the ground. Hikers didn't do this. The man approached them on the narrow path and appeared to wrap his arms around his waist like a Western gunslinger about to draw pistols. Instinctively, Jack stepped to the trail's edge in front of Melanie and pushed her off the trail to shield her.

He noticed everything in a flash before he could understand what it meant, and it gave him time, a heartbeat, to turn away from the knife thrust to his chest.

The knife, gleaming in the sun. Jack, on his heels…a miss. The knife slitting his shirt into tatters, flaying in the wind. Off balance, the attacker stumbles…falling…recovering, but not in time—Jack's right hand chops down onto the exposed neck. A sharp thwack! Stuns him. A guttural oath escapes his lips—maybe Russian. The knife clatters onto the rocks and the attacker falls to his knees.

It was a close thing. Jack thwarted his attacker in stellar defense, but a battle can change in a heartbeat. Before he could close in on him, the attacker sprang to his feet in one motion and wheeled around to face Jack, ready to fend off another blow. His attacker was fast and nimble. He was fresh and strong, and Jack was not. Jack thought, *strike back now or you're done for*. Before he could draw his handgun, his attacker charged forward and thrust his head into Jack's gut. Reeling backward, Jack tripped on the rocks behind him and fell on his back onto hard rocks. Pain shot up his spine. The attacker fell upon him. Jack's eyes searched for Melanie but couldn't find her. He opened his mouth to scream, to tell her to run, to get out, to save herself, but no sound escaped him, because the last blow from his attacker's head had taken the wind out of him. Jack used his last gasp of depleted energy to kick the man off him and to roll him onto the ground. He hoped to pin him, but the man smiled at this futile effort as he raised his arm to strike, knife in hand—how did he find it? Or did he have another? The attacker began to swing his arm in an arc, dagger pointed at Jack's chest. His last vision…blurred, dark, ominous…

Chapter 47

Light. A dim, hazy yellow light behind his eyelids seeped into his consciousness as if he were waking from a wondrous dream. Is it real or imaginary? There, in front of his eyes, a face took form—hair fell around her face, tears streamed down her cheeks. And he wished to stay in this moment forever. Pain pulled him back to reality. He tried to speak, and all that came out was a muted sound. "Wha…?"

She whispered, "Don't try. Just stay there and rest."

Tears came to his eyes. "What happened?"

"I hit him with a big rock. I don't think I killed him. But he's out cold."

He tried to sit up but fell back. His training kicked in, and he swiveled his head around, surveying the mountaintop. "Others? Were there others?" he said, frantic to fend off any unseen attackers.

"No, I don't think so. He was alone."

Jack stumbled to his feet and gathered his wits, despite the sharp pains shooting down his back and legs. He knelt to feel his attacker's pulse—still alive. At any moment, he could regain consciousness. Jack searched the backpack, and his hands grasped the rifle and scope. He patted down his attacker's clothing—no identification. But Jack had seen his photo and had heard of him—Boris something—the resemblance was striking. Raising his eyes to scan the mountaintop once more, he could see no one. Melanie was right—a lone assassin—it's how the Soviet KGB had worked, and how he'd worked—alone, so he could slip away. This Russian GRU agent? Black ops and licensed to kill. Like Jack. Maybe there were others.

"What now? What's going on, Jack?" Melanie shook all over. "Who is this guy? Why did he attack you?"

"I'm the target. This guy's a hired killer."

"Who's after you…or us?"

"He's a Russian agent. Boris something. I've read about him."

In a flash, he decided. It's what the Russians would expect him to do. He drew his Glock and pointed it at his attacker's temple. He slowly increased his finger pressure…then hesitated and released the trigger. He returned the Glock to its holster and heard it click, indicating he'd secured it. His eyes scanned the area, searching the nearby rocks until they fell upon the same rock Melanie had used. Swiftly, Jack raised the rock and struck the attacker's head, maybe not hard enough to kill him. The man called Boris would remain unconscious long enough for them to escape down the mountain. Having neutralized his attacker, he searched for clues to avoid the next threat.

Jack turned to see her standing at his side, watching him. "You saved me, Melanie. You did it. You were amazing."

***

Melanie, stunned by the sudden attack, stood wide-eyed, hands over her mouth. She struggled to comprehend what had happened. She heard Jack mumbling something about a cell phone, some way his attacker could communicate with his handlers, apparently trying to find it on his body.

She needed the distraction, time to figure it all out. Time to make a decision, soon—that was now clear. Before they reached the parking lot, where they would find Dynamite and maybe Sam and

Jud.

And what about Jud? Had she rushed too soon into this engagement? Did she love him? Was he just one of her Greenville friends? A safe choice. Not strong and daring like Jack, who'd defied everyone, death itself, to have her. Who'd just killed this other agent, or maybe not; perhaps he was just unconscious. But Jack was right about the threat. Jack was a lesser threat, but still a threat. *How can I love a man who is so violent?*

She had to decide. She would get away from him. And she could not tell him. Because she sensed that Jack would not let her go. She had no idea how to do this.

Melanie reached out to him. "Well, he can't hurt us now," she said, trying to reassure him that she was still on his side.

"No," he said. She thought, he's killed before, and it is nothing to him.

"Listen, Jack. We've got to get down the mountain and get to the base camp. We'll find the ranger there, and we'll tell him what happened. And get out of here."

"No. We tell them nothing. They'll have no clue." He was busy throwing rocks. Why? Trying to get rid of fingerprints? Searching for the ejected shell? When he drew the sidearm, he'd pulled the top mechanism back to make sure it was loaded, and that was when she saw the bullet eject before he slammed another round into the chamber. "We're not heading down the Hunt Trail," he said. "We're going to retrace our steps."

"What do you mean?" She couldn't disguise the concern in her voice. Jack had walked away from her. What is he doing? It looked like he was talking with someone, maybe on a cell phone. Who? Maybe his CIA handler?

When Jack returned to her side, he said, "We're going back up to the top of the mountain. They'll never know we were here. Then we'll go over the Knife Edge and down to the Roaring Brook trail, and back to the parking lot where my car is. It's our best chance to get away. Then we're in the clear." He grabbed his attacker's back-pack. "I'll toss this off the Knife Edge."

She was not about to disagree with him, and she could see that his plan made sense—the two hikers they passed at the trailhead had seen them going down the Hunt Trail. The Russians would surely find out where they were on Katahdin. Now, they'd surely send another agent. She figured that she and Jack were still in great danger.

***

Jack had called Harry on his cell phone—it's why he'd distanced himself from Melanie. All Jack said was, "Harry, a Russian GRU agent just tried to kill me. I got him. They know where I am. The GRU must know I killed their man in Sebastopol. What's our plan?"

"Call you right back," Harry said. "Get down to the parking lot ASAP. You with anyone?"

"Yeah. Melanie. The other survivor. The girl I love."

"Figured that," said Harry. "I'll come up with something."

***

Harry would try to hatch a plan. But there wasn't much time. Harry was counting on an old friend from his college days at Holy Cross—Clyde Brody. Harry had followed Brody's career, and Brody had done well—he was now a captain with the Maine Warden's Service. Would he answer the call?

"Brody here," came the answer. Thank God.

"Hey Brody, it's your old pal Harry Field…"

"How's the CIA treating you?"

"No time to chat. We've got an agent who just dispatched a Russian agent on top of Mount Katahdin, and we have a problem.

Can you contact your warden, guy named Sam Morse?"

"Hell, yeah, I trained him. Good man. Follows orders. What's the plan?"

"I'll let you know," said Brody. "No time to spare, buddy. Just let me know when you've contacted Sam Morse, and I'll call my agent."

Chapter 48

The peak stretched out before her in the distance, narrowing to a thin blade slicing into the azure sky. To Melanie, it looked impossible to cross. Directly in front of her, the Knife Edge was no more than a thin strip of boulders extending in a crooked line into the distance, maybe a mile or half a mile long, creased by a paper-thin path worn out of the rock by hikers; on either side, deep, dark crevasses fell off into nothingness. A false step threatened to snap bones. But she was able to climb over the boulders and walk the path, which was barely wide enough. She tried to ignore the emptiness on either side. She realized it was an optical illusion from a distance, seemingly too narrow to pass over. But as you neared the Knife Edge, you could see that it widened just enough to allow another hiker to pass by from the opposite direction. The few hikers who passed them kept their eyes riveted to the trail and offered only a casual greeting. Rockslides on either side threatened to carry an errant hiker down hundreds of feet of glacial debris to certain death.

She turned, stretching her neck, to see Jack heave the attacker's backpack over the rim. She tried to quicken her pace to steal an advance on him, but he was surprisingly agile and quick, and she could not lengthen her lead. It became a tiring slog. Melanie stopped and sat on a rock to rest. He sat beside her.

"Where will we go?" she asked. "You must have something in mind."

"I have a plan."

"Can't you tell me?"

"You don't want to know. I won't put you in harm's way."

"It's got something to do with how you were treated at Langley, right?"

He seemed to ponder what to tell her. "Look, Melanie. They did some very bad things. I've learned how not to go over the line—not anymore—that's all in the past."

"Okay, but are we in harm's way, as you call it?"

"These are very dangerous people. You've just seen an example of that. They're not going to go away. So—"

"So, when we get down off this mountain, I'm going to see some people I know, and they're going to want some answers. So, what do I tell them?"

He smiled. "Little as possible."

She decided to risk asking, to take one last chance to find common ground. "Jack, I know you are very brave, and you've risked everything to find me. But I need to know. Do I have a choice? Or are you just going to force me to come with you? Because if you are…"

They gazed at distant dots of water, faraway lakes and streams. He looked into her eyes, and there was a warmth there that she had not seen before. "You know," he said, "that I can't live without you, right?"

"So, if I don't choose you, then what?"

"Well, we'll see, won't we?"

So, she would not know. Everything was in play, and it was all up to her. Was he capable of understanding what he was doing? Was he kidnapping her? He'd crossed state lines—a federal felony. He could get prison for life. Perhaps he hoped she would succumb to that syndrome where you fall in love with your captor. Maybe she had. But she was still scared. She'd read of women who'd been captured as young girls and reached womanhood before escaping. Stockholm Syndrome. She recalled being amazed at how long they'd submitted and how fragile had become their will to fight. She wondered how far she'd be willing to go to gain her freedom and at what cost. To herself. To her friends. To her fiancé.

They passed Chimney Peak and were about to head down the Dudley Trail to Chimney Pond. They could run into Dynamite there, exposing her to danger, yet Melanie craved to see her.

Jack gently grabbed her arm. "Down this way," he said, pointing off to the right, to another trail that ran almost parallel to Chimney Pond Trail. She hesitated, resisting this decision, her whole body leaning the other way.

"They won't expect us to go this way," he said, smiling, as if she would welcome this news.

She knew they'd end up at the same place, the Roaring Brook parking lot. It would only postpone a possible confrontation. But he was right—the park rangers, even if warned by Dynamite, would search the other trail, not this one.

Out on the exposed face of the ridge, the wind had gained force. Behind them, the clouds swallowed the mountain. At times, Melanie felt the gusts almost sweep her off the ridge, and she struggled to keep her footing. She was about to fall when Jack grabbed hold of her windbreaker and pulled her to him. She felt a surge of pleasure at the physical contact. She realized she'd felt not a hint of fear, even as she gazed out over the lip, out to empty space. Surprising. Maybe she didn't care anymore. Was it a death wish? She told herself to get a grip and steel herself. Maybe it was time to fight for her independence, and her life.

Out on the exposed ridge, any separation from Jack seemed out of the question. Then they were off the ridge and into the scrub pines, where they scrambled over huge boulders. Her leg muscles screamed with every step.

Chapter 49

Dynamite reached Chimney Pond. As the remnants of her weary group rested, she spoke with the bespectacled young park ranger wearing a Smokey Bear hat. "She's got long blond hair, wearing a khaki shirt and shorts and a dark green windbreaker. In her thirties. Slim. In good shape. Maybe five-foot-four. She's alone."

The ranger checked his log and shook his head. "Nope, no one with that description," he said in a clipped Maine accent. "We record names of all the hikers comin' through here. And we check 'em off when they come back down. Could have missed her, I suppose."

"Can't you send a team to the top to search for her?" she asked. The rangers were used to these requests—they took them seriously. Two rangers headed up, one on Saddle Trail, one on Dudley—few day hikers were fit enough to descend Cathedral. The plan was to meet at Baxter Peak, the highest point on the Knife Edge. If Melanie was above tree line, they'd find her.

Dynamite tried to check in with Sam Morse but had to leave a voice message. "Hi, Sam. My group's tired. We're about to head down Chimney Pond Trail. Hope to see you at Roaring Brook lot in a couple hours. Might be getting dark then. I tried to find Melanie at the top, but she must have gone ahead and is probably past us on the way down to the parking lot. We'll meet up there. You'll probably see her before I do. Bye." She couldn't camouflage the concern in her voice.

***

Melanie combed through possible clues to leave behind. How to leave a message? An outhouse at the parking lot at the base of Chimney Pond Trail? Jack would have to let her go inside alone. Maybe a message on toilet paper? Nothing to write with. Roaring Brook Campground? Maybe a store there. Would he let her go inside? Not likely. Maybe he'd let her get something they needed. But what? The Baxter State Park exit? Usually a ranger there. How to signal her distress? Run for it? He was armed, but with a crowd… Get rid of the gun? How?

Nothing was obvious. Every option looked too risky. Time was short. She had to do something. They halted and she sat on a large rock, where she massaged her sore calf muscles. "I can't go on, Jack," she said, her voice reflecting her state of exhaustion, or at least she hoped so. It was part ruse and part true—surprising how this mountain exhausted you.

***

Jack stretched his arms, then his legs—his strength had never failed him, and it wouldn't fail him now. His mind cleared. He was so close to a new and better life. He'd survived years of hell in a world run by secret and powerful forces, doing their bidding. Memories flooded back of his childhood, when he'd been lost in a haze of drugs and depression. He owed his survival to Melanie—all through his years in the Marines and later as an assassin, thinking about her had kept him sane. He'd survived CIA deprogramming by focusing on the memory of her. Now, against all odds, he'd found her here. He'd had to fight everyone and everything to get her. And he could feel her coming closer to him.

***

"Take a short break," he said. "Then we go. We're almost there." Melanie could see no expression on his bronzed face, no sweat on his brow. He seemed to welcome the rest. So did she. But it was all too short. It seemed like seconds, and then he urged her to stand. She refused. Without hesitation, he reached down and hoisted her onto his shoulders like a sack of flour. She towered over the rocky trail. If he stumbled, she would pitch headfirst onto the rocks. She marveled at his agility and power. He lifted her off his neck and lowered her onto his back, and she looped her arms around his neck. She had no choice but to cling to him, her legs pinned to his sides, his arms wrapped securely around her legs. It was almost sexual, riding piggyback, glued to him, feeling every ripple of his body, his every move. Her right leg brushed against something hard—it must be the gun. Could she reach for it under his open shirt? She tried to remember her small arms training—years ago, mostly forgotten. Slowly, she pulled her right arm off his neck.

"Hey," Jack grunted. "Hold on."

She'd expected that. Melanie returned her right arm to its hold around his neck. "Sorry," she said. "Got an itch. Darned bug bites. Just need to scratch."

From time to time, she released one arm's hold, pretending to scratch her back or her leg, alternating, first the left arm, then the right, not too often, getting him used to it, always returning her arm to secure her hold around his neck. His bulging muscles were taut as sailors' knots. As she reached to scratch her right leg, she could feel where his shirt lay open outside his jeans. After several tries, she lightly touched the outline of the pistol on his right hip.

She held her breath as she slipped her right hand under his open shirt. There—the holster, maybe plastic. Was there a clip or catch to prevent a quick release? She recalled on the mountain top how he drew it, quick as lightning, then slipped it back into the plastic holder on his hip. Maybe a Glock. She'd fired one years ago. She struggled to remember—where was the safety? Out of the distant past, the raspy voice of the leathery instructor came to her. "Thing about Glocks," he said, "no safety." The instructor had slammed in the clip, then pulled it back. "Racking the slide," he called it. She'd been surprised when it slammed forward. Melanie wasn't sure of anything, and she'd have to chance it. But the instant she withdrew the gun, he would feel the loss of weight and he'd drop her in an instant. Or dash her into a tree or boulder. She'd have no time to fire. She felt a sudden sense of hopelessness. It was too risky. Unless…

She bided her time. He had to let her down sometime.

He seemed tireless. Minutes passed. Her head bounced against his powerful neck and the motion, like a rolling sea, lulling her mind. Exhausted, she stopped fighting the rocking motion, letting her head fall on him, letting go, letting her head stay cradled on his neck. She fought against the notion that it felt good to be close to him, because there was too high a price…

Melanie was jerked awake. She must have dozed off. The motions had stopped, and she heard him whisper, "We're here." Dazed, she looked up, and she remembered it all. She fought to overcome the panic.

"What? Where are we?"

"Shhhh," he whispered. "Quiet. See there?"

Through the darkening gloom of the enveloping forest, framed by the outline of Jack's head and shoulders, there was a glow—the Roaring Brook parking lot. She saw the beam of headlights: cars. There were still cars there. And a white van. Perhaps Dynamite was there.

"Okay, down you go," he whispered.

It was almost instantaneous, just as she'd planned it. A daring plan, hatched from necessity. As she felt herself sliding down off his back, her right hand reached under his shirt. She flipped up the flap and grabbed for the pistol butt, desperate to lock her fingers on it. The gun slid up and out without a sound, and she wrapped her right hand around the butt, then covered it with her left hand, her fingers gripping the metal. She tensed as she pulled back the mechanism—more resistance than she'd expected—then let it slam forward, a round in the chamber. There was an audible snap.

When Jack released her body onto the soft ground, his eyes still scanning the parking lot for potential danger, his body already leaning forward, ready to move down the trail as if to search for what lay ahead, he heard the telltale, unmistakable metallic sound. It registered on reflexes honed from living on the edge, from a life of survival, nerves on constant high alert.

Melanie focused on her target, and he became a blur. Everything happened in slow motion. She forced her eyes to rest on the sight so that she could not even see his slack-jawed face when his right hand reached for the holster and came up empty, and puzzle solved, instinct becoming deadly intent.

He was on her in an instant, and she slammed her left knee into his crotch, just as her right index finger found the trigger.

Chapter 50

Sam Morse had a bad feeling when he left Greenville in his warden's truck headed for Mount Katahdin, a good two hours north toward the Golden Road, the east-west dirt highway for logging trucks carrying downed trees to the Great North Paper mill in Millinocket. He'd called Jud Jenkins on his cell phone. "Be there. Pick you up in ten. Fill you in later." Outside the newsroom, Jud was waiting.

With Jud now alongside him, Sam explained, "Doesn't sound good. Dy called me earlier and left a message. She hadn't heard from Melanie. Left her above the tree line. Seems they split and failed to connect. Dy was headed down the mountain with the rest of her group. Sent rangers up. She sounded concerned. Oh, and I got a call from the Greenville Inn. Seems the clerk was grilled by some guy who was a bit too interested in where the group was headed, and she admits she told him everything, even described Melanie. Then got cold feet and called me."

"Did she describe him?" asked Jud, who was nervously finger-ing the gold chain hanging from his neck.

"Tall, dark, and dangerous-looking was what she said. Right after they left early this morning, he showed up. Said he was a good friend and was supposed to meet them at the mountain. She gave him directions."

"Why'd she wait so long to call you?"

"Hell, I don't know. Been eating at her all day, she said. She apologized."

"Great. You think it could be this Jack Pierce dude?"

"What I'm thinking."

"Shit."

Sam drove fast and hit the blue lights when necessary. They whizzed past the small store at Kokadjo and onto a rough dirt road, then bounced along until they hit the Golden Road. The light was beginning to fade when they stopped briefly at the ranger's gate leading into Baxter State Park. As the truck skidded to a stop at the Roaring Brook parking lot, they spied Dynamite pacing in front of her tour bus.

Sam and Jud approached Dynamite. Sam was delighted to see her. Suddenly, the unmistakable report of a gunshot echoed off the hills, halting them in their tracks. Sam dropped into a crouch, hand on his weapon. "Get down, Dynamite!" he yelled. Sam warily approached the trailhead. Acting on instinct, he slipped his nine-millimeter Sig-Sauer out of its holster, waiting for some clue as to what, or who, lay up the trail. Jud stood with Dynamite behind the tour van, where the rest of her group huddled on the floor, eyes peering out the windows.

***

Melanie sat on the forest floor, hands clasped around her knees, lost in a trance. The Glock was gone. She'd fired it once into the air. Nothing was going to stop Jack. He'd turned at the telltale sound of the cocking of the pistol and looked into her eyes. And there was that all-knowing smirk—it told her that he knew she couldn't do it. He took the gun from her. She let him take it. She remembered thinking, now he'll kill me. Instead, bent over in pain, she watched him recover and then walk away from her. She feared what he would do, but she could do nothing to stop him. It was out of her hands. He was in control.

She lost track of time. As the shock wore off, she became aware of the sounds of the woods, and logical thoughts returned. She'd made her choice back there on the trail. And when she grabbed his gun, she saw that look of recognition—he knew it. Jack now knew that she didn't choose him. Now all time would be known to them both as before and after, like a great divide. She gazed into the woods, silent as a tomb that cared nothing for her. Doubts, second thoughts, and conflicting emotions intruded. Did I make the right choice? What matters to me? Who matters? Anyone? And what did I choose? Jud? Or freedom? The only thing clear was that she'd rejected Jack Pierce. She was surprised to feel remorse. And loss. Because she knew he loved her, said he couldn't live without her. And they shared something special—the only survivors. She had rejected the only other soul who could share that unique loss. And she wept for her loss. And soon her tears become tears of joy. For she had survived once again.

Sounds from the parking lot broke her reverie. They were like sounds from another world. When she stood, she almost fell, her legs weak and wobbly. Through the opening in the forest canopy, she saw Sam approach, and when he spotted her, he holstered his weapon and waited for her to come to him. Behind him, Dynamite stood by the van. And with her, Jud. And what struck Melanie was the certainty that Jud would never understand her heart, and she could never reveal this to him. Slowly, she walked out of the woods. And then they were all there, Sam, Dynamite, and Jud, their arms all around Melanie.

"Oh, Jud."

"It's okay, Mel," he said. Tears ran down her cheeks.

"Where is he?" she asked.

"Who?" asked Jud. "What happened?"

"Jud, he was kidnapping me."

"Melanie," Sam said. "Listen." He grasped her shoulder, needing to know. "Melanie, we heard a shot. Did he shoot at you?"

"It was me, Sam. I got his gun, and I fired the shot. I couldn't shoot him. I just tried to scare him. And then…" She looked dazed. "He just looked at me and calmly took the gun out of my hand."

Sam looked confused. "Where is he?"

"He walked into the woods and disappeared." She looked up at Sam. "You didn't see him?"

"No." Sam's eyes canvassed the area. "You mean you didn't shoot him? He just walked away?"

"Yes, he just smiled at me and…"

"Melanie," said Sam, "I've got to leave you here to check the area. Just stay in the van, okay?"

"Okay."

Sam disappeared into the woods. Dynamite led Melanie to the van. On board, Jud tried to comfort Melanie as she continued to talk, repeating herself, still in shock.

***

Dynamite looked worried. Half-listening to Melanie, she watched eagerly for Sam to reappear. To Dynamite, it was her fault—if she'd kept her group together, none of this would have happened. Thank God Melanie had found the courage to act, to escape from Pierce. If not, Dynamite didn't wish to think what could have happened to Melanie. Darkness was falling, and Dynamite needed to drive her group back to Greenville.

***

Sam Morse could find no bullet casing, but it was already dark, and they would have to comb the area later with lights. He headed back to the parking lot. On his cell phone, he called headquarters in Greenville. "We've got a situation here at Baxter. Somebody fired a gun. No body. No injuries. There's a missing suspect, said to be armed. I'm standing on the Chimney Pond Trail near the Roaring Brook parking lot. Looks like the suspect has disappeared. Name is Sergey Robichek, also known as Jack Pierce. Thought to be driving a Ford pickup with Maine plates."

"Ten-four. Stand by," came the reply. Sam waited, shifting his weight, itching to get out of the forest and back to Dynamite, needing to talk with Melanie about all this to make sense of it all. After a long pause, the dispatcher was back. "Okay, Sam. You still there?" "Yeah," he replied. "You're to remain there until further instructions. Interview witnesses. Protect the crime scene. Okay?" It was normal procedure.

Sam headed back to the van. Curious faces peered out at him from the van's windows. Sam boarded the van, glanced at Dynamite, then faced the others—it was hushed as a church in there. In his periphery, there was movement from the woods near the parking lot.

Sam turned to see a man approaching. Dark clothing. Slim. Fast. Headed right for the van. Sam tensed, sensing trouble.

Who is this guy? The man neared the van, then stopped.

"Melanie!" the man yelled.

Melanie's face, still as a stone, pressed against the window.

"What's he want?" said Sam.

"He wants me. Let me go." Melanie was in Jud's grip—he was protecting her, not letting her out of the van.

Sam measured his options. "Okay," he said to no one in particular, "that's enough." He exited the van and approached the man, holding out his I.D. "Sir, Maine Warden Service. I'm asking you to get away from that van."

The man looked familiar to Sam. The man stood his ground.

"Got a right to be here," he said, his voice steely and sure. "I've come for her." Louder, he yelled, "Melanie, come out here."

Melanie somehow detached herself from Jud, and she stepped from the van. "Sam, it's okay. I'm going to see him. I know him. It's

Jack. His name is Jack Pierce."

Sam was on alert—the stalker, the guy he'd stopped at the mountain, the guy who tried to kidnap Melanie. Armed. One dangerous son-of-a-bitch.

"Sir, raise your hands," Sam commanded, drawing his weapon. "You're under arrest for criminal threatening." But the man kept coming, oblivious to Sam's commands, and Sam, knowing what was coming, his laser eyes zeroed in on the man…as the man reached down with his right hand to draw his sidearm…

"No!" Melanie yelled.

"Don't!" Sam yelled. "Don't or I'll shoot!"

It happened too fast. As if in slow motion, Jack drew his weapon and began to raise it. Sam fired. Jack dropped. Melanie fell on Jack and her screams became sobs. Jud and Dynamite pulled her off him. Sam felt Jack's neck for a pulse. "Still alive. Let's get him out of here fast," he said to the two EMTs who appeared with the emergency vehicle. They got him onto a stretcher and into the vehicle. "We'll get him on a Medevac chopper to Millinocket," one of the EMTs told Sam. "They'll fly him to Eastern Maine Medical in Bangor. He might make it."

Chapter 51

Sam had herded the group back into the van.

"Okay, here's the thing," he told them. "You've got to stay in the van until we get an investigator here to sort things out. I'm sure it will be quick. They'll need to talk briefly with each of you, and then I'm sure you can all get back home. I'm sorry for the delay. If anyone needs to use the john over there, tell me now. But you're not to discuss what happened with anyone. Is that clear?" Sam was looking right at Melanie. He hoped she got the message—shut up and say nothing.

In the van, stunned silence. "How long we got to wait here?" asked someone.

"I honestly don't know," Sam replied. "I'll be back shortly. No one gets off this van, you got it?" He left them, found the yellow tape and a flashlight in his truck, and returned to the scene. He strung the yellow tape all around the immediate area. No one would be coming through there this late, but he followed protocol—protect the crime scene; leave everything just as it is. Sam had finished when he saw headlights sweep the parking lot. Using his flashlight to illuminate his footsteps, Sam approached the car. He saw the familiar figure of Trooper Albert Locke of the Maine State Police, all six-foot-four of him, step out of the blue cruiser.

Locke, a welcome sight—the wide-brimmed hat and creased blue uniform, black boots, and, dangling from his belt, a sidearm, billy club, and handcuffs. Sam had worked with him before and trusted him. Al Locke would leave no doubt as to who was in charge.

Sam briefed Trooper Locke as they crossed the lot to the van. They ducked under the tape.

" 'Let's see what we can find,' said Locke. They observed the depression where Pierce had lain on the ground. "Where's the gun?" asked Locke. Sam explained how he'd dropped it, together with the clip and ejected round, into the evidence bag.

"There wasn't much blood. The EMTs cleaned up the scene real good."

"His Glock, right?"

"Yeah, must have been," Sam said. "Girl on the van named Melanie, she told me they were at the base of the trail, almost at the parking lot, when she was able to grab his gun. She fired a shot into the air—a warning shot, she called it. And she just let him take the gun from her. So, I knew he was armed when he drew on me…"

"Holster must still be on him," said Locke. "Must fit on his belt, is my guess. You say she fired it, but he didn't?"

"Al, he was drawing on me and I warned him not to, and, sonofabitch, I can see the gun in his hand, and he just keeps raising it, as if he was going to fire at me. It was like slow motion."

"Maybe it's a suicide by cop—that is, if he doesn't make it. Did he have any reason for that?"

"We'll have to talk with the girl, Melanie. She and this guy have a history—"

"Did they all see it?" He was looking over at the occupants of the van.

"Yeah. Ringside seat," said Sam.

"You say he was calling for the girl to come out?"

"Yeah, like a challenge. Sounded like a threat, so I gave him a clear order to leave the scene and he kept coming, and then this Melanie identified him as the guy who'd been stalking her, so I ordered him to raise his hands, said he was under arrest, and he kept coming."

"Okay. Got it." Locke was looking at the evidence bag. "No safety on these things. And she said she fired one round and missed him?" Sam nodded. "And you ejected one round from the chamber?" Another nod.

"Al, I know the girl, Melanie Ricker." Sam didn't expect Locke's steely stare. Locke had a way of making Sam feel uncomfortable, wanting to tell all. "And I know who this guy is."

"I don't get it," said Locke, frowning.

"Melanie. The girl he was after. She shared a lot of her background with Dynamite and me. She and this guy were on *El Barco de Oro*."

"The what?"

"The container ship that sank in the hurricane last fall. He and Melanie were the only two survivors. And then he stalked her, followed her to Maine, and followed her up here to Greenville. She's a friend of Dynamite's. I helped Melanie get this guy to turn himself in at Langley."

"Langley? What do you mean? This guy's CIA?"

"Yeah. Think so."

"What else you not telling me?"

"Hey, Al, I'm leveling with you here." Sam felt trapped. He'd have to give it all up. "I set up a meeting so Melanie could get help from the U.S. Attorney's Office. Got her to wear a wire. How we got the guy to turn himself in at Langley back then. So, she's been through this before with him. We all thought he was done with her…till he shows up here again."

"Okay, okay," Locke said. "I'm not sure I understand this. I'll need to talk with her. Get her story. You know they'll do an internal investigation because you shot him, you understand?" Sam nodded. "Probably means you should stay out of this, but I want you in there because you've got the background, okay?"

"Sure. Let's do it," Sam said.

Locke's cell phone rang, and he took the call. He hung up, shaking his head. "We got another body over on the Hunt Trail. Rangers were making the nightly sweep and found him."

"No shit," replied Sam. "Think it's a coincidence?"

"Mighty strange. No I.D. on him. Let's talk to those witnesses."

They brought them, one by one, from the van over to the ranger station. Inside, there was a small office with a desk and chairs.

When it was her turn, Melanie slumped into the chair across from Sam and looked up to face Trooper Locke. She looked haggard, but her eyes still showed the determination to get through this.

"Look," Locke said, "everyone's exhausted. We can go over the whole story later. Right now, I just want you to tell me in your own words what happened just before this Jack Pierce, or whatever his name is, was shot. And I'm going to ask you to sign a statement before we leave here. Okay?"

"Yes," she said quietly.

***

Melanie was thinking many things, but she knew that only one thing mattered right now—the need to get Sam off the hook. She waited for them to begin. She shuddered as she drew in her breath, then released it, and tried to focus, to keep out all the other thoughts and feelings.

"Okay," said Trooper Locke. "What happened?"

"I was his captive. He was stalking me, followed me to Maine. After I got him to turn himself in at Langley—"

"Ms. Ricker," said Trooper Locke, "we'll want you to tell the whole story later, but for now, can you just get to what happened when you were in the van after you'd come back down the mountain and you saw this kidnapper, this Jack Pierce, again?"

"Yes, sorry. I just wanted to say that Jack Pierce—that's his real name, but he had another name on board *El Barco*, Sergey—he'd kidnapped me up on the mountain, and he had a handgun, a Glock, I think. So, Sam had no choice." She took them step-by-step through what she saw.

"Ms. Ricker, they found a body up on the Hunt Trail. You know anything about that?"

"Yes. It was this guy who attacked Jack Pierce."

"Ms. Ricker, what happened to this other guy?"

"He attacked Jack with a knife, but we foiled him, we—"

"What do you mean, 'we foiled him'?"

"I mean, he was going to stab Sergey, I mean Jack, with his knife, so I hit him over the head with a rock."

"*You* did?"

"Yes."

"And then what happened?"

"Well, it all happened so fast. Jack came to, and he searched the guy—his clothes and his backpack and everything."

"They didn't find any backpack or I.D."

"Right, because Jack threw it all over the rim. The attacker had a rifle in his backpack with a scope. We were scared he'd come to and come find us and kill us. Jack is CIA. He said this guy was a Russian agent. I think Jack hit him again."

"You think?"

"I mean I know he did."

***

Trooper Locke had heard enough to know there were red flags. "Okay," he said. "Just a minute." Locke stood up and started for the door. "Sam, come with me." Sam followed Locke outside the ranger station, where Locke stopped and, in a hushed voice, said, "Sam, I've got to call my boss, the colonel. This shit is serious. We've got ourselves into a hell of a situation here. We're talking CIA and national security, and God knows how many federal laws we could be about to violate here. And if the press gets hold of this… I've got to get some advice from the top. I'm guessing they'll want to call the FBI in on this, and meanwhile, we don't want anyone mentioning the CIA. You got it?"

"Right. Make the call."

Locke called Augusta and got Colonel Ridge of the Maine State Police on the line. "The colonel will call the FBI," he told Sam. "He instructed me to get brief statements from the witnesses limited to the shooting incident and then to return them to Greenville to await further questioning. Meanwhile, they are to keep everything quiet."

The other witnesses were brief. They all told the same story as Melanie about the shooting. Locke was about to leave. "Sam?"

"Yeah?"

"You seem to know this Melanie pretty well?"

"Yeah."

"You can't be talking with her about this. She could be a suspect. She's admitted she hit the dead guy over the head with a rock. We may have to give her the Miranda warning."

"Yeah. I know."

Chapter 52

Melanie rode in the van, stewing in silence about Jud, who got a ride with Sam, leaving her in the van with Dynamite, who was saying nothing. Dynamite was up front, driving the van and her hikers back to Greenville. Her mood as dark as the blackness outside, she sat in the rear, watching the headlights pierce the darkness ahead. The other hikers had fallen asleep to the van's rocking motions. Melanie stared out the window into the dark and imagined Jack fighting for his life, all because of her. She marveled that he wanted her that much, couldn't live without her. She shivered from the chill of the night air, feeling alone and abandoned. *Turn on the damn heater, Dy.*

Melanie was scared. The trooper's focus on the death of the Russian agent—what did that mean? Was she a suspect? Had she said too much? And then the trooper and Sam just walked away. They would question her again in the morning. Would they accuse her of murder? The only one who could clear her was Jack, and she'd got him shot—might as well have pulled the trigger. Surprising how it affected her. Now that she was safe from him, she was suffused with a deep sense of loss. She feared he would die and said a prayer for him.

Melanie made her way up the aisle and stood just behind Dynamite, whose vision was focused on the cone of highway lit by the van's headlights.

"We need to talk," Melanie whispered into Dynamite's ear.

"We can't." Dynamite's eyes remained riveted to the road. "Sam said—"

"I know," said Melanie, "but I'm in trouble, Dy, and Sam can't help me."

"Listen, Melanie, I need to stay clear of this. When you get back, talk with Jud. I'm not telling you this, you understand?" There was nothing Melanie could say. Her closest friend could do nothing.

"Right. Got it." Melanie returned to her seat. Sleep would not come.

When the van arrived in Greenville, the hikers were sent home and told to report the next morning at the wardens' headquarters.

When Melanie arrived, exhausted, at the Greenville Inn, she called Jud.

"Hi. It's me."

"Melanie. God, are you okay? I'm worried about you."

"Jud, I've got to talk to someone, and maybe I need to tell you the whole story. Can you pick me up? I'm too tired to drive."

"Be there right away."

He drove her to his office. Outside, the big lake lay black and silent. He led her inside. The office was empty at this late hour. She told him everything. Like a good reporter, Jud listened, taking notes but saying nothing, until she finished her story. Then he stood and paced. She thought, he's thinking of a way out. He will think of something. When he turned to face her, she saw in his face not reason but anger.

"You helped him!" Jud said.

The accusation, unexpected, stunned her. "Well, yes," she said, taken aback. "He was almost helpless, dehydrated, and ready to faint. I mean, anyone would—"

"Melanie, you're not just anyone, for God's sake, you're the person he was stalking! Again! After you got the FBI to arrest him!"

"What are you saying?" she asked, reeling from his assault. Why was he accusing her? Wasn't she the victim here? Was everyone against her now?

"And then he forced you down the mountain, and he's attacked by this hit man, and you save his life? You maybe kill this other agent? What the hell, Melanie! What are people going to say?"

Her mind spun furiously, and she could not see, for the life of her, where he was coming from. What was his problem? He was being so unfair. *He has no idea what I've been through.*

"Is that all you're worried about? What people are going to say? Are you jealous? Is that it? Jealous because he loves me?" She turned her back on him to hide her tears of remorse.

"Do you love him? You sobbed all over him. That was certainly embarrassing."

How self-centered, she thought. *Sam shot Jack and I was in shock, and he's embarrassed?* "Well, I'm so sorry I embarrassed you," she said, her voice cold, sarcastic. "And, no, I don't love him," she lied.

She turned her head away to hide the tears of resentment, and when she turned to face him, they were tears of denial, even though her heart knew this was false. Because the only feelings left in her were exhaustion and outrage at this man.

She figured Jud was already thinking about the scoop, his next story. They stood apart, brooding in silence, the air between them thick with accusations and misunderstanding. She felt humiliated by her own petty life here with this man who cared more about his job than her. That ring on her finger? She wanted to toss it in his face. She'd fought for her life, for God's sake! And now this? Did Jud even love her? She could give a shit.

It was Jud who brought her back to reality. "Well, if he dies, they're going to charge you with his murder. That's what I think."

"So, what do we do?"

"We've got to publish it," he said.

"What?"

"The whole story. Your story. Now. Before they interrogate you again."

Yes, that fits, she thought. It's what Jud really wants, to write the story and publish it. But she could see that he was right—she needed to clear herself and Sam. Dr. Deering had said she needed to tell her story when she was ready. She was ready now.

***

Jud dropped her off at the Greenville Inn and returned to his newspaper office. He worked late to get the story into the next morning's edition.

Under the byline *Reporter Jud Jenkins*, the headline read, "Melanie Ricker Survives Mount Katahdin Ordeal. Ricker Kidnapped. Attacker Shot." Readers would know by morning that the matter was under investigation. But the word was out. Sergey Robichek, the other survivor of the *El Barco* disaster, had stalked Melanie, she'd escaped, and Maine Game Warden Sam Morse had shot him to save Melanie and others. Melanie and Sam would be heroes. And everyone would know that Sergey was a CIA agent whose real name was Jack Pierce and that Jack Pierce had killed a Russian agent on Katahdin before threatening Melanie.

The story hit the national news outlets like Reuters, and the press hounded Jud and Melanie for comments. But they would say nothing. Jud was reading another Reuters report—Jack Pierce had died on the flight to the hospital.

Chapter 53

Harry Field was sitting at his desk when he got a call from Special Operations Director Daniel Robinson, who sounded panicked.

"Jack Pierce's dead, Harry," Robinson said, "and this story in the Greenville, Maine, paper is trouble. They think Jack Pierce is CIA and that he's the other survivor from *El Barco*, and they'll be asking why one of our agents killed a Russian agent and then kidnapped and threatened their hometown heroine, Melanie, and got himself shot. So, what was our agent doing on *El Barco* in the first place? Hell, I don't even know. This is a shit show, Harry!"

"Send it over," Harry said. "Let me take a look, and I'll call you back."

"Shit," he said, after reading it. Major snafu. Got to call in the big guns. He dialed Robinson.

"Sir," Harry said, "Let me call Harold Isaacson."

"Who's he?" asked Robinson.

"He's a fixer," said Harry.

***

Harold Isaacson, special counsel for the Senate Select Committee on Intelligence, was a powerful man. One call to the U.S. attorney general triggered a late-night meeting at the Senate Office Building. Isaacson chaired the meeting and laid out the agenda. All agreed: squelch this story fast. It was the classic cover-up.

Around 4 a.m., Isaacson climbed aboard a chopper at the Langley heliport and flew to Ronald Reagan Washington National Airport, then boarded a Gulfstream 550 for a night flight to Maine. Once aloft, he made a call to the home of Maine's attorney general, Janet Dimillo, who did not oppose his plan. Next, he called the FBI special-agent-in-charge in Bangor, Maine, who dispatched two agents in black Chevrolet Suburban SUVs to the small airfield in Greenville, where Isaacson was about to land. Less than an hour later, the SUVs crossed the tarmac and stopped next to the jet. Isaacson deplaned and took a back seat in one SUV, which headed for the Greenville Inn, where Isaacson waited for the agent, who arrived in time to bang on Melanie's door just before 6 a.m. The other SUV headed for the home of Jud Jenkins.

Melanie, awakened from a deep sleep, opened the door in her nightgown, hair askew.

A short while later, Melanie and Jud sat facing Isaacson and the two black-suited FBI agents in the *Greenville Times* office. "It's a good thing you haven't said anything more," said Harold Isaacson, addressing them both.

The agents had given Melanie scant time to dress, then spirited her to Jud's office, where she sat in silence next to Jud, wondering what she'd gotten herself and Jud into. How could they have arrived overnight from D.C.? Amazing to get such attention so fast.

"We're going to want you both to issue a retraction," said Isaacson. "Otherwise, you're both facing federal charges for violating national secrecy laws. And as for you, Ms. Ricker, the Maine attorney general is about to indict you for murdering a man up on the mountain." The words echoed in Melanie's mind as she imagined her dirt-smeared face behind steel bars.

"Sounds like we need a lawyer," said Jud. "You can't hold us here without charging us."

"Oh, you can be sure we can and will charge you. As we speak,

Justice is preparing charges. And, yes, you can lawyer up, but you may want to think twice about that."

"Why is that?" asked Jud.

Melanie was amazed—how could he be so brazen? She was in no position to say a word.

"Because this story is going to be buried, and if you cooperate, there'll be no charges, federal or state. You get me, Ms. Ricker? You go free and clear, you agree to appear before the Senate Select Committee on Intelligence, and you sign a confidentiality agreement. That's the deal. Take it now, or we'll see you in court in an orange jumpsuit. I'll give you one phone call to your lawyer right now if you wish."

"No," she said. "I mean, no phone call. I'll take the deal. And so will he."

"I will?" said Jud, sounding indignant. "The hell I will!"

She froze him with a stare. "Yes, Jud, you will."

***

Jud published the retraction in the next day's paper. The article quoted Melanie—she'd been mistaken about the attacker's identity. The District Attorney's Office had agreed to conclude its investigation into the two deaths at Katahdin with no charges. The medical examiner cited heart failure as the unidentified second victim's cause of death.

Melanie thanked Jud for his help. But it remained something for them both to deal with. Melanie decided to speak with Dynamite about it.

They agreed to meet for coffee at the Lost Woods Bar & Grille. When Melanie entered, June White welcomed her.

"You just grab a seat over by the picture window and don't mind me." June busied herself sweeping up from the night before. It was okay with Melanie if June eavesdropped. June was like family.

When Dynamite came in, she took a seat at the table with Melanie. June served them both coffees. "Quite a story in today's paper," June said. "You know, Dy, this girl's the toast of the town. Our local hero."

"Hell, yeah," said Dynamite with gusto.

"Well, I think Jud is a bit miffed at me," Melanie said.

"Oh, he'll get over it, girl," said June. "Men always do." They all laughed. Melanie felt better. Dynamite agreed to talk with Jud and smooth things out. "Jud can't hold a grudge. Everything will be fine," she assured Melanie.

***

When Melanie returned to the Greenville Inn, she decided to do some research on her laptop. She was encouraged by the search results. The ship had a funny name—the *Bruarfoss*, owned by an Icelandic company called *Einskip*. Melanie had proven herself on a mountain top. She had her sea legs back. Maybe it was time. Time to be true to herself, and to her calling. Time to cast aside doubt and fear. There would be a price to pay. But isn't there always? She removed the ring from her finger.

Chapter 54

It was standing room only.

In plain civilian get-up—a black dress, minimal makeup, her blond hair down over her shoulders—Melanie Ricker stood to take the oath. She brushed aside a strand of hair that fell over her face, then sat alone before a microphone and faced the members of the United States Coast Guard Marine Board of Inquiry investigating the sinking of *El Barco de Oro*. Also at the head table: an official of the National Transportation Safety Board.

She surveyed the scene around her. At side tables sat recording secretaries and lawyers ready to record or pounce. Three of the lawyers had identified themselves as representing Pegasus Shipping. She was relieved that John Edmonds was there representing Mary Downs. In the presence of the impressive array of uniforms and suits—all men—Melanie felt small as a bug in the headlights.

Close behind her sat men and women who must be, Melanie realized, the victims' families—hushed, respectful, and expectant, all eyes on her. She wanted to tell them, "I'm so sorry." Around the room were ranks of media, all focused on her with steely, inquiring eyes. The national news media had picked up the story, published weeks ago by the *Greenville Times* under the byline of Jud Jenkins, about the other survivor with the mysterious name, Sergey, who vanished after his miraculous rescue; then, after months in hiding, he had died on the way to the hospital after being shot in self-defense by a Maine warden.

Melanie was ready. Dr. Deering had told her, "It's time for you to tell your story, and I don't need to see you anymore." The board was eager to hear testimony from the only witness with personal, first-hand knowledge of the disaster.

The bar was overflowing at the Lost Woods Bar & Grille in Greenville, and all TV sets featured Melanie. Those in the crowd held their breath, waiting to hear from this young woman they all knew and liked.

Cameras whirred as she cleared her throat and began.

"Gentlemen, thank you for allowing me to appear before you today." Melanie paused to get a sense of what she must sound like, a self-assessment or check. She would be okay. "I have a brief statement I would like to read before I answer questions." She took a deep breath.

"I know that your purpose here is to try to assess responsibility for this tragedy that took the lives of my fellow mariners. But we all know that nothing…" The word "nothing" hung in the air like an empty void. She didn't mean to pause, and she told herself to focus, not to let emotion overtake her, because that would be her undoing. Okay. "Nothing can bring them back." Another pause. "And we all grieve their loss deeply. It has haunted me ever since." She turned to look straight at Mary Downs. Tears streamed down Mary's cheeks as she nodded in thanks. Melanie, now under control, once again faced the board.

"I am here to praise those who perished for their courage under harrowing conditions." She was hitting her stride—now she could do this. "We all know when we go to sea, we will face peril. I can assure you that Captain Downs was a brave and competent master, one of the best, and that he accounted himself well right to the end. He would not leave the ship, even when I begged him to. At the last, he was urging us to put on life jackets and throw out life rafts. To the end, he fought to save his ship, his officers, and his crew."

She knew the board had heard the voices on the voyage data recorder, or black box, recovered from the bottom of the sea. They'd heard her voice. How awful to listen to the voices of the dead.

"Our captain, David Downs, relied on me, and I feel like I failed him. Of course, we all felt pressure to leave port knowing that a tropical storm was headed toward our path, but it was Captain Downs who told me you're often safer at sea in a hurricane. It is for you to determine whether our ship was unseaworthy and should have been taken out of service before it sailed into a category-four hurricane. I hope that you will find ways to improve the safety of our merchant vessels for all mariners."

There was a brief silence. The commanding officer called for an adjournment. Melanie walked straight to Mary Downs in the front row. They embraced. "Thank you," Mary said. Melanie approached the counsel table and the Pegasus lawyer, the one who had deposed her. As she neared him, his face seemed caught in the unaccustomed expression of surprise and confusion, and he stood awkwardly to receive her greeting, but Melanie brushed by his outstretched hand. She smiled and greeted John Edmonds. The cameras whirred. She had made her point for all to see.

When they resumed the hearing, board members praised her heroism and thanked her for coming. The members' leading questions allowed her the opportunity to demonstrate why *El Barco* was unseaworthy. When the chair yielded to counsel for the parties in interest, there were none, until the lawyer for Pegasus Shipping stood. Tall, in a dark blue suit and red tie, hair longish over his ears—a hint of gel to it—he raised himself up to full height, adjusted his spectacles, and paused to arrange the papers before him. Everything seemed orchestrated for a star performance before the television cameras. Melanie steeled herself. She shifted her weight, reached one hand to brush back her hair, and felt faint. Unwanted memories of her deposition flashed into her mind like a black-and-white cameo, how she'd cowered as the bastard had savaged her. She knew his opening questions were for show—he sounded friendly and caring—and she knew what was coming.

And then he smiled and said, "Thank you, Ms. Ricker. No further questions," and sat down. She couldn't believe it. All these months, she'd feared this moment. She wanted to laugh.

When the hearing ended, there were drinks on the house at the Lost Woods Bar & Grille in Greenville.

***

Melanie walked into the sun outside the hearing room, and it felt like a small shaft of sunlight had slain her personal darkness. Just like Dr. Deering had promised her. Now that she remembered Dr. Deering's promise, she could no longer put aside what had come with the promise—an assignment. Melanie had put off this assignment for far too long. "You've never talked with your parents about Charlie," Dr. Deering had told her. "It's something you must do."

Maybe now she could.

Chapter 55

Melanie's father drove the Ford F-150 pickup truck. Melanie sat in the front seat between her parents. Her dad shifted to a lower gear as they climbed the steep hill. It was August—high summer.

Melanie recalled how, back in her late teens, she'd run up this hill. At the top, she'd be panting for air, and she'd turn to assess the hill she climbed, then cast her eyes across the valley to the apple tree farm, its treetops carpeted with white blossoms in early June. Now the late summer heat had produced clouds, and peals of thunder could be heard across the valley.

Easing off the gas, her dad turned onto the dirt road, and they circled up through manicured woods until the woods opened onto a mown field around a neat one-story house with a perfectly stacked woodpile and a stunning view of Norway Lake.

Her dad pulled the truck over and stopped just past the field of dwarf apple trees next to the house. An iron gate surrounded the small, perfectly groomed cemetery. The few headstones bore names—some unknown, some covered by lichen-green scabs healing forgotten wounds, some marked with small American flags and dates from before the Revolution…and one with carvings still frightfully fresh and stark as a stab to the heart.

In silence, they stood before the headstone that read, "Charles Ricker, March 10, 1992–August 14, 1997," under the carved image of a winged angel.

Melanie said a brief prayer as they held hands.

Back at the farm, they talked over tea, and the parrot perched in its cage and listened. Melanie gazed out the picture window, staring at the pond. Her parents sat at a small table, the parrot behind them.

"You never talked about him," she said, facing them. "Why? Why did we have to act like it never happened?"

"We wanted to protect you, Mel," said her dad. He'd aged some; now silver-haired, he still carried a thin, wiry frame, still handsome—your typical Mainer, a man of a few pithy words, always thoughtful and caring.

"It was for your own good," said her mother, her lips pursed. Her ever-cheerful mother was now strangely quiet and morose, her beauty more fragile.

As Melanie listened, she felt the anger rise inside her. Protect her from the truth?

"My own good! My own good!" she protested, wishing to spare them from what must be torment, but she had to do it, for them, for herself. "It's haunted me every day of my life, Mom. It wasn't good for me. I wanted to know. How could you just hold it all inside? Didn't you realize what it did to me?"

"Did to me," mocked the parrot, interrupting the silence.

Melanie winced from the pain she was causing, realizing she was making it all about her needs, oblivious to her parents' feelings, but she needed an answer, even though there could be no good answer.

"I didn't even know where he was buried," Melanie said, "until you told me years later."

"Yes, of course," they said.

"And you still couldn't talk about it?"

Her mom took Melanie's hand. "I suppose it was because it became too difficult to talk about, and it was easier not to…you know, not to bring it up."

"Easier? There was nothing easy about this wall of silence, Mom. Do you know I had to see a shrink, for God's sake—I had this dream, it was almost every night, and I was always down in the depths, underwater, drowning. I've been drowning ever since."

They let the silence take over—what was there to say?

"You were both still tots," her dad said. "Charlie was five, and you were six, and I can remember it all as if it were today."

"Yes," her mom said, looking down at her shoes.

Melanie got her a glass of water and sat next to her mom.

They'd left Charlie and her with their grandparents at the farm while they went off to some local event, a writer discussing her new novel, and then came the call from the Norway police, saying nothing, just come home, and they did, and the medics were there, and they couldn't even see Charlie, and it was awful.

"But you, Mel," her dad said, "it was like nothing happened. You were chatty, about everything and nothing, until we put you to bed. And then we buried him up on the hill."

She had no memory of it. Just Charlie going off the pier into the water and never coming up. "It must have been awful for you," she said.

"Yes," said her mom. "Can you forgive us?"

"Of course I can." How could she not? She hugged them. In the end, she realized, we all have our secrets. All her life, Melanie had kept hers hidden, until now.

"Do you still have the dreams?" her mom asked.

"No, not anymore."

Chapter 56

On a cloudless summer day, the wedding took place at the Greenville Inn against the backdrop of Moosehead Lake's deep, sunlit waters. The bride's father gave her away. The best man, Sam Morse, pretended to fumble for the ring and come up empty; he got a few nervous laughs until, with mock surprise, he produced it to relieved applause. Sam had reason to feel celebratory—he'd been cleared of wrongdoing in the death of Jack Pierce.

When the justice of the peace proclaimed the couple man and wife, Jud Jenkins lifted the veil for all to see his bride's radiant face. Quite beautiful, Maid of Honor Dynamite MacKenzie remarked to Sam. "Just not the one we all expected." Not the one who'd left Greenville for greener pastures and blue-green seas. It was a local girl whom everyone liked. Jud was looking happy and well pleased.

***

Melanie rose before dawn and strolled out to the park overlooking the Casco Bay Islands to wait for the first pink hues on the horizon. She stayed until the bright orange sun peeked over Peak's Island and bathed her in light, then drove down Commercial Street. Becky's Diner opened early. She took a seat at the counter alongside fishermen in woolen sweaters, overalls, and rubber boots. In thick Maine accents, they tossed wisecracks at young waitresses, who slapped down plates laden with eggs, bacon, and pancakes along with their own saucy remarks. Melanie ordered coffee, eggs over easy, bacon, and toast. The tourists had begun to show up when she paid the check and left the diner, catching the eye of several male tourists.

It was a short drive to the gate. She parked alongside stacks of containers bathed in baby blue and marked with the letters "EIN-SKIP." Across the gangplank, she boarded the ship, remarking how bright, ship-shape, and small she looked.

The *Bruarfoss*, one of Iceland's new fleet of container ships, lay moored on the Portland waterfront, taking on containers filled with blueberries, French fries, lobster, and more. After stowing her gear, Melanie went on deck and addressed the captain. "Melanie Ricker, Second Mate, reporting for duty, sir."

With a broad smile, he grasped her hand. "Welcome on board, Melanie," he said in a hearty voice. "Good to have you with us." He introduced her to the other officers. She had memorized the list and now tried to match names to faces, but it was all a blur. She'd have time to get to know them.

They sailed out of the harbor past the high-rise fronting Fort Allen Park on Munjoy Hill. Melanie watched her home recede above the ship's wake as they slipped past Cushing Island on the port side and historic Portland Head Light to their starboard, where a gaggle of tourists snapped photos.

She raised the binoculars to her eyes, pointing at the lighthouse. She adjusted the lens to focus and panned across the crowd. One man stood out. Young and handsome, he was waving at the passing ship. It seemed to Melanie that he was looking right at her, smiling at her. There was something about him. *Peter? Her lost third mate?* She remembered he'd once told her how, growing up in Portland, he had pulled his lobster traps right off Portland Head Light. She lowered the binoculars and smiled. No. Can't be him. Maybe it was a sign—this would be a good sail. "Thank you, Peter," she whispered.

Leaving land behind, the *Bruarfoss*, cruising at more than ten knots, plowed into heavy rolls coming out of the east. Melanie's shoulders, adorned with her second mate's epaulets, rose and fell on sure and steady sea legs. She turned to her captain. "Good to feel alive again, sir."

"Yes," said the captain. "I feel it, too. Take the conn, will you?"

"Me, sir?" she asked, feeling unworthy as the new rookie.

"It's a tradition for our new officers. You have the honors."

"Why, thank you, sir." They all clapped her on the back. Melanie took her place on the navigation bridge as the watch operating officer or WOO.

"Does the WOO have an order for the engine room?" asked the captain.

"Yes, Captain, I've got her," Melanie said. The order is full ahead, sir." Melanie gripped the engine room telegraph handle with her right hand and moved it forward to the "full ahead" position. The telegraph bell sounded. A pleasant sound, melodious and harmonic, not unlike bells from childhood—perhaps a merry-go-round? No, a bicycle bell. She remembered the feeling of freedom as her father released his hand and she sailed ahead on her bike for the first time, free from everything. She recalled how she had screamed with delight to be on her own, just for a moment, with the wind in her hair, her right thumb finding the bell and ringing it loud and clear. That same feeling of freedom came upon her now, and when the bell stopped ringing, she felt the power. Because the engine control room had responded to her command by moving the engine room to the corresponding "full ahead" position, thus transmitting almost instant power to the propeller. She felt the ship gather speed. She was sailing her new ship out into the broad reach of the Atlantic on a northeasterly course toward distant Iceland.

<h1 style="text-align:center">Chapter 57</h1>

Returning from Iceland under sunny skies and a following sea, the *Bruarfoss* docked in Portland Harbor. Melanie walked down the gangway and crossed the parking lot to her Volvo SUV. Driving along Commercial Street, she noticed many out-of-state license plates, made frequent stops for pedestrians, turned up India Street, climbed Munjoy Hill, and took a left onto Morning Street. There was room to park in front of her house—two stories, now remodeled with a new roof. Inside the front door, she picked up the mail from the floor near the mail slot, opened the inner door, and, out of habit, turned on the light switch.

"Hello."

Melanie jumped at the unexpected sound of a man's voice coming from the living room. "Who the hell?" She couldn't see him and walked toward the voice, her cell phone out, ready to call the cops.

When she saw him, the letters floated to the floor. She sagged, caught herself, and staggered toward him. "You… How? I don't understand. What happened?" She felt suddenly flushed and panicky, her world upside down.

"I can explain everything," Jack said, looking very much alive. "You might want to sit down."

She sat. And stared at him. Speechless. Trying to make sense of it. She'd thought him dead, gone from her life, and she had mourned him. And here he was, very much alive, dressed casually and wearing a big smile. He regarded her with spectacled eyes over hands shaped like a tent. He seemed to be enjoying this moment, looking pleased with himself, and it pissed her off.

"Bit of a shock, eh? I'm sure I gave you a terrible scare. Sorry to put you through that. Or maybe you were relieved that I was gone."

"Oh, my God, no," she said, embarrassed. She'd almost killed him with his own gun. What was going on? She was hopelessly confused and befuddled.

"But you were shot. I saw it. And they took you away in an ambulance and said you'd died on the way to the hospital." She sounded offended by the truth. In a way, she was.

"Melanie, remember how I told you I had a plan? A plan to disappear? They staged it to look like I was shot."

"Staged it? How? So, Sam didn't shoot you?"

"He fired a blank. Didn't you think it strange that an emergency vehicle just happened to show up just like that?"

Of course. She'd thought nothing of it then. "But why?"

"I told you I was CIA. They staged it because the Russian GRU is after me."

"You mean they're still after you?"

"You got it."

"But why?"

"They must think I'm valuable, or a threat, or both. I'm number one on their kill list. By the way, I'm trusting you to keep our secret."

"Oh, God, yes. I won't tell anyone. But how do you—"

"What? Keep it secret? Well, it's not the federal witness protection program, but let's just say it's a new identity and the bad guys think the old me is dead."

"So, who were you up on that mountain? I mean, I thought you were kidnapping me. Was that all staged, too?"

"We figured you'd either join me or fight me. Either way, it would work. If you'd agreed to come with me, we would have had you join in the deception."

"But you made me decide against you. My God, you were play-ing me. And I almost shot you. Do you understand what you put me through? Thinking I'd somehow caused your death?" She was angry. How dare they? How dare he?

"Did you really decide against me, Melanie? You chose your freedom, and I don't blame you for that, but you were saying you didn't want me, right?"

Did she? "Not what you were on Katahdin. Not if you were this raving lunatic forcing me to run away with you, a kidnapper, for God's sake." What was he now?

"But now you know I'm not. So how do you decide now, Mel? Now that you're free. Your choice. If you still don't want me, I'll leave, and you'll never see me again."

She needed time. To think. About him. About herself. And what she really wanted. She had a choice once again. There was that. And there were still more questions. "Who else was in on this? Sam, right? Dynamite, too? Jud?"

"Just Sam. He told Dynamite later, so she knows now. Jud? No. Never. You left him, right?"

"Yes. Can I talk with Sam and Dynamite about this?"

"Sure. Knock yourself out."

"How do I find you?"

"You can't. I'll find you." And he was gone.

Melanie left the house and took the walking trail and soon found herself at East End Beach, a touch of fall in the air, whitecaps on the harbor, and the sky the color of smoke; a northeast wind snapped the flags out straight. Perfect sailing day. A few boats out there were heeled over. She opened her cell phone and dialed the number.

Dynamite answered: "Hey, how's the famous mariner?"

"I saw him. He was here."

There was a long pause, as if Dynamite was unsure what to say.

"Okay. I knew he'd come see you. So, you're wondering what he really is, right?"

"How'd you know? You were always for Jud, as I recall. How is he, by the way?"

"Just between us? Happy as always. That's who he is. It was never about you. You know that, right?"

"I just didn't want to see it. Jud loves his job, he loves Sam, and he loves you, in that order. I could never win that contest."

"It's not a contest, Mel."

"Yes, it is. Anyway, I value your opinion. You were in the dark, like me, right? I mean about Jack Pierce. I thought I knew who he was, from back in our early days, but then people can change, right? He goes away and they make him a killer, and how do you come back from that?"

"Well, I didn't know him back when, like you did, and what I saw was a man in love. Okay, it was more than that. Obsessed. With you, my friend. Very understandable. I'd say you know him better than anyone. So go with your gut."

"What does Sam think?"

"Sam follows orders. Government tells him to stage a shooting, he does it."

"What do you mean? Who told him to do this?"

"His boss, Captain Clyde Brody. Seems Brody is a buddy of Pierce's boss at Langley, so Sam gets a phone call and he's told he can't tell a living soul, not even the Maine State Police. Except he's got to tell the Medivac team, right? They're all sworn to secrecy, National Secrets Act and all. And he tells me because he had to."

"What do you mean he had to?"

"Because I figured it out."

"How the hell did you do that, Dy?"

"Thought I knew Jack Pierce—a kidnapper like that, he'd never kill himself for anyone. So, I asked Sam if he really shot him, and Sam went bananas with me. You're the only other person who knows. Because that was part of the deal."

"What deal?"

"Jack Pierce and this Harry at CIA—Pierce tells Harry he gets to tell you, or it's no deal. By the way," Dynamite added, "Sam is Jud's pal, so he's a little hurt. But he'll forgive you, or I'll beat him up."

Melanie couldn't help it—she laughed. "Sam must have some thoughts, I mean, about Jack being an assassin for the CIA. Like Sam is paid to kill if he must, right? And you still love him. So, it doesn't define him, right?"

"Good point. But if Sam killed a felon, let's say he'd really shot and killed Jack, he'd be having bad dreams all his life. I wonder if Jack does."

"I don't know. And I don't know if he'd tell me the truth."

"Mel, whatever he does, does it matter? I mean if you love him?"

"Wow. That's profound, girl. I sort of knew I was lost to him."

In the end, it came down to that—did she love him?

She did. Had all along. She finally admitted it to herself. Melanie couldn't see herself sailing out there on the wide ocean, alone, without his love.

Maybe it was time to see if it was real. Or not.

There was nothing she could do. She couldn't call him or write him. She would have to be patient.

"I'll find you," he'd said.

EPILOGUE

Harry knocked and abruptly pushed his ample self into Jack Pierce's office.

"You're wanted," Harry said. "Something's happened."

"What's up?" asked Jack, without moving his eyes from the morning's briefing, a fat document that lay open on his desk.

"They don't tell me these things, but if I were you, I'd hotfoot it down there.

They called it "The Room," located in the bowels of Langley. The sign stenciled on the door's frosted glass window read "Special Activities Center." Jack had never been inside The Room before. His hand quivered as it touched the doorknob, and he gathered his breath, then opened the door.

As he entered, all eyes turned to him. Then, the momentary hush ended, and the loud chatter resumed. The Room was filled—some he knew, some he didn't. This Special Activities Center handled all Black Operations outside the U.S., typically covert or clandestine insertions of CIA paramilitary teams, like Delta Force, in sensitive spots around the world. By law, these activities were completely secret, unknown to the public, and generally unknown to Congress, sometimes even the President. Everyone in The Room knew that Russia had invaded Ukrainian territory in a massive thrust of armed forces into its interior, and this highly anticipated event had recently hit the national news. Few in the CIA had doubted Putin's intent.

Jack found a seat at the table, welcomed by a few nods from those he knew. Since his return to D.C. more than five years ago from an extended absence, he'd specialized in Ukrainian American relations. His knowledge of all things Ukrainian was now deep and included extensive contacts within the government and armed forces. No longer an agent in the field, he'd become a desk jockey. Jack recognized, even welcomed, the advantages of his new lifestyle. And yet he itched to return to the field in some role, perhaps as an agent or in operations.

Jack's musing on his new life ended suddenly—he was being addressed by a three-star general.

"Jack, we've called you in because we're assembling a black ops team to go into Ukraine to assist the Ukrainian Army in holding off and, eventually, driving back the Russian forces. You're here because of a personal request from General Medved. Seems he likes you. Can't live without you. You'll have a fully equipped team with intel support. Are you up to this?"

"Yes, sir."

"You'll be fully briefed and ready to depart in three days. All right. That's all. You'll no doubt want to take a day off to get your life in order, so report back tomorrow morning at zero eight hundred hours."

"Yes, sir."

As he rode the Metrorail home to the D.C. suburbs, his mind reeled with questions and doubts. Should have turned it down. Or asked for more time. What will my family say? How will they cope? Am I ready for this assignment?

He thought back to his deprogramming at the CIA—he'd tried to forget those assassinations, and they were mostly forgotten. But his training as an Army sniper remained. Can I still do it? With the same steel nerves and steady hands? And his teammates. Who are they? Won't they be better trained than me? Will they resent me because the general asked especially for me?

As the train neared his home, his mind eased. He could do this. He would discuss it with his wife. He couldn't wait to see the kids, his baby girl and little Charlie. There was still time to get out of it. When the train reached his destination, he found his car in the parking lot and drove home, as if by habit. They would be surprised to see him before noon.

As soon as he entered his home, she came to him, as if she knew something was wrong.

"Why so early?" she said.

Before he could put down his briefcase, she wrapped her arms around him, and it all came back to him—how they'd met when they were young, when she had the same beauty as now. Speechless, tears came to his eyes. "Mel," he said.

"What is it, darling?"

"I love you. Always have."

"I know," she said.

"We have to talk."

Jack had just begun to articulate his reasons for accepting the mission, and it wasn't going well. Melanie had listened patiently with an increasing sense of alarm. Suddenly, the house phone rang. She picked it up. "Yes? He's here. Just a second."

"It's for you, Jack."

"Who is it?"

"Harry." She handed him the phone.

"What's happening, Harry?"

"Mission's cancelled. Seems the President got wind of it, and he called his cabinet together in executive session, and it was unanimous–the United States has no interest in sending troops into Ukraine. Jack, we're looking at other options, like sending a few advisors, and you're high on the list. We can discuss it later, but you deserve a few days off."

Jack told Melanie, "Maybe it's time to get out."

Melanie was elated. It's what she'd wanted for a long time, but

now she had questions. Where would we go? They'd always wanted to find a quiet place on the Maine coast where Jack could write
about his experiences, a place where they could raise their children
in a safe and peaceful environment, and where Melanie could be
near the sea. The academy has been asking her to speak at special
events, and had mentioned finding other work, perhaps in their sailing program.

Jack had just the place in mind. "I've found a place for sale on
the Maine coast, in a town called Bernard, on Mount Desert Island,
near Bar Harbor. Are you free tomorrow to take a ride up to
Maine?"

"Oh, yes, Jack, that would perfect. I'll tell the kids."

After graduating from Bowdoin College "cum laude," Mason Pratt served as an intelligence officer and French linguist with the XVIII Airborne Corps and its 82nd Airborne Division. He then attended Harvard Law School, and practiced law for 47 years with Maine's largest law firm, Pierce Atwood.

He is a member of the Maine Writers' and Publishers' Alliance and the Southeastern Writers' Association. This is his second novel; his Maine North Woods murder mystery, *The Truth About Hannah White*, was published in 2015.

Mason lives with his wife on Sebago Lake in Standish, and owns a condo on Portland's Munjoy Hill.